Life and Death at the Dog Park

By Scott Sowers

Life and Death at the Dog Park, a novel by Scott Sowers

First Edition March 2015

This book is a work of fiction. Names, characters, places and incidents are either products of the author's imagination or are used fictitiously. Any resemblance to actual events, locales, or persons living or dead is entirely coincidental.

Library of Congress Control Number: 2014916126

ISBN: 0-9905251-1-2
ISBN-13: 978-0-9905251-1-0

DEDICATION

This book is dedicated to dogs everywhere and the humans who love them.

A Production of Big Gorilla Press 2014

ACKNOWLEDGMENTS

The "Novels in Progress" group remains the most potent motivator for my fiction writing. We gather once a month, more or less on the first Monday to review our manuscripts, critique, commiserate and kvetch. The group has teetered on non-existence, changed, evolved, and changed locations but without it, I would be much less-inspired and for that, I am grateful to Jerome Komisar, John Vartoukian, Darrell Delamaide, Jacci Duncan, Misty Ray and the other fine writers who have passed through our doors.

About the Author

Scott Sowers grew up in northeastern Ohio and began pitching stories to magazines while still in high school. After working his way through college he moved to Virginia Beach where he sold boats, tended bar and began writing features for the alternative press. He moved to Washington DC and began a successful freelance career as a television producer and print journalist. He now spends his days consulting, writing features, producing films and exercising his greatest passion – writing fiction

CHAPTER 1

The day that Mooky found the bone at the dog park began just like any other day. All the regulars were there, so everybody saw it happen. It was early summer, the sky was blue, and the smothering humidity that routinely hovers over Washington, D.C., like a damp blanket had yet to arrive. She came trotting out of the woods, ears down, tail wagging, in a subdued-yet-mischievous, black Lab fashion.

With a smattering of forensic training and some high school biology under her belt, Mooky's owner Vivien knew from yards away that the bone was a human femur. She immediately felt an electric snap in her brain.

"Is that what I think it is?" said Lenny, who happened to be standing next to her. Lenny was a gay psychotherapist who worked with AIDS patients and was Vivien's best friend at the dog park.

"Can't be," said Vivien. Her brain silently churned away, trying to deny what she was seeing—while at the same time hoping it was true.

"Oh dear," said Sasha.

Sasha was another regular in the group, the elderly ex-wife of a British diplomat. Her London accent had softened over the years, but an elegant trace was still there. "No. No. No," she said while turning away. She looked like she was going to be ill—which would have been the entirely proper thing to do at such a moment.

"Holy shit," said Walter. Walter, a consistently under-employed, chubby-schlubby, bad-haired writer, wiped a hand across his shiny forehead and squinted into the sun.

"Come here, Mooky, let's see what you got." Walter bent down to get on the same level as the dog and held his arms out as Mooky came closer. She was holding her head down, but her eyes looked up while her broom-like tail gently swooshed back and forth in long, steady strokes.

"Don't touch it!" screamed Vivien, surprised by the sudden volume of her own voice. "It's evidence." The dog's body tensed at the change in her tone, and Mooky stopped in her tracks.

"Evidence?" said Walter. "It's a deer bone, Viv."

"My ass," said Vivien, half under her breath. She'd spent three years on the Metro police force in Milwaukee, five with the Bureau of Alcohol, Tobacco, Firearms and Explosives, and eight with the Secret Service, until a back injury had knocked her into early retirement. She was 44 years old, with a cluttered house, a bit of a shopping problem, issues with her dead mother, and a ten-year-old minivan with a broken air conditioner—but she was quite sure that Mooky's new toy had not fallen off a deer carcass.

CHAPTER 2

Mooky had been drawn into the woods by a magical smell guiding her to the best bone of all. Now her tail wagged a bit faster as she looked up at Vivien, who was calling her name and moving closer to her. Vivien wanted the bone. But the bone belonged to Mooky. This could only mean that a rousing game of "Get-the-Thing" was about to begin.

The rules of this game were very simple. Mooky had a thing that belonged to her. Vivien wanted the thing. To get the thing, Vivien would have to chase Mooky, catch her, and try to pull the thing out of her mouth, signaling the beginning of the "Pull-the-Thing" game.

As Vivien got closer, Mooky lowered her shoulders, shifted the bone slightly in her jaws, and began slowly turning away from the group of people who were now trying to coax her closer. This was part of the game. One of the people lunged out for her, reaching for the thing, and Mooky made a hopping turn that she'd been doing since she was a puppy—a half-bouncing, half-jumping spin powered by an instinct that pushed her quickly away from everybody.

She dug her claws into the soft ground and stretched her body into a full sprint up the hill. Some of the other dogs in the park watched her streaking past. Several joined in the chase, and now the game was on.

"No," said Vivien. "Mooky, you drop that right now."

Mooky knew her name and the word "no," but it was too late.

She lowered her body closer to the earth and pointed her beautiful tail straight back for maximum speed and balance. Shaking her head from side to side, she flashed by the rest of the dog pack. She ran at full speed up the hill, the grass under her feet flying by in a blur. She growled to let the other dogs know that she had the thing, the most wonderful thing in the world, and it belonged to her.

One of the dogs she knew closed the gap by running beside her. Polly the poodle fell into perfect stride with her, matching her speed and gait. Polly clamped her jaws onto the other side of the bone and now they ran together, attached by the thing.

"Mooky!" said Vivien. Mooky knew that this tone of voice was not to be ignored. She was being "bad," and if she kept it up she would not get to "go," which would be sad. Mooky instinctively reacted to the word and the tone by stopping her run and releasing her hold on the bone. Polly also let go, dropping the bone on the ground. Mooky turned to look at Vivien, wagged her tail, opened her mouth, and panted for a few breaths. She picked the bone up, then peed on the spot where the bone hit the ground, thereby claiming it as her own.

Polly saw this, smelled the same spot, and then peed to override Mooky's claim to the spot. Mooky began walking back towards the group of people at the picnic table. She didn't want to be bad, but the bone was hers and she could not refuse its extraordinary aroma.

It was an intoxicating smell of dirt and flesh with a few hints of the animals that lived in the woods. Mooky now imagined the treat that she might get for bringing the bone back. Get-the-Thing might be over, but the bone still belonged to her. It would always belong to her.

CHAPTER 3

"Good girl. Mooky, come on . . ." Vivien held out an empty hand. Mooky stopped where she was standing, dropped the bone, put her nose into the air, and sniffed with flaring nostrils.

Vivien approached the dog slowly, not wanting to spook her into picking the horrid thing back up and taking off again. For a split second, she considered how she looked from behind. She had never been skinny, growing up in a household of third-generation Croatians in the upper Midwest. The steady diet of sausages and pierogies had settled in her butt and breasts, giving her ample cleavage and a pleasantly round rear end. She had been consistently strong on her physicals before her injury and she'd done a lot of walking since then to keep the extra pounds away, but she was not as thin as she was in her working days.

Vivien reached around her waist like she was going for the SIG Sauer 9 mm she used to carry when she was with the Service, but instead of feeling the cool, steel handle of the pistol, her fingers found the corner of a plastic Safeway bag that she always carried for doggie droppings.

"Good girl, Mooky. That's a very good girl," said Vivien, as she walked carefully up to where the bone lay in the grass. She used the bag as a barrier between the evidence and her fingers. She picked it up and was surprised by the weight—it was heavier than she'd expected. The bone was smooth as glass and ivory colored, with some bits of dirty flesh still clinging to the joint ends.

Vivien looked at Mooky, who now sat on her haunches and watched Vivien's hands. Vivien knew without looking that she didn't have any of the organic dog treats she often carried in her pocket, so Mooky's reward would just be praise. Vivien stood up straight and looked towards the hill just in time to see a few of the other dogs charging towards her, their eyes focused like lasers on the bone.

"No," said Vivien, as she held the bone over her head. It felt naturally balanced in her hand, like a nightstick, and she could see why cavemen would use it as a club. It was a potentially deadly weapon, but it was also evidence. It belonged to somebody—somebody who had died here in Rock Creek Park, a swath of diagonal green shooting up inside the third baseline of the geographic diamond that defined the District of Columbia.

From where she stood, Vivien faced the shadowy woods and she could hear the traffic on Military Road behind her. This main artery of civilization and the slice of the wilderness she faced were separated by a gently sloping field that belonged to the dogs and those who walked them, a place known to the locals as "Doggy Hill."

Vivien walked towards the picnic table doing half-turns and pivots to avoid the dogs jumping at her hips and trying to get closer to the bone.

"Stop, Mooky," she said, as she placed the bone in the middle of the picnic table.

"Jesus," said Walter, "I think it is a leg bone."

"No shit, Walter," said Vivien.

"Oh, this is bloody awful," said Sasha, turning her head to avoid looking.

From the parking lot came the unmistakable slam of a hatchback. The regulars turned their heads to see Linda Jackson, another dog park regular, getting out of her white Jeep Cherokee with her Great Dane. "What's up, dog people?" said Linda. She was a large black woman who worked as a catering chef and wrote screenplays on her days off. So far, none had been produced. She was in her mid-30s, sturdily built, and somewhat abrupt.

"Keep her away from the table," said Vivien, holding her arms like a crossing guard, again surprised by how shrill she sounded. She pulled another Safeway baggie out of her back pocket, gently laying it across the bone just as Linda reached the picnic table.

"Oh my God," said Linda, "it's Chandra Levy."

Vivien shot her a look and said, "Don't even say that."

"Seriously," said Linda, "they found her right over there. That's probably a piece they missed." The reference was a familiar one to anyone who frequented Rock Creek Park and read the paper. Several years earlier, the body of a murdered intern was found in the woods, which caused a national stir and forced the resignation of an implicated yet innocent Congressman.

"Good lord," said Sasha as she shielded the view with her hand.

"That's bullshit," said Walter. "They found her clear on the other side of the park."

"Bullshit on you, Walter—it was right on the bottom of the hill down there," said Linda.

"Somebody got a phone?" asked Vivien.

"Who you gonna' call? Ghostbusters?" asked Linda. "or maybe the CSI team?"

"Funny," said Vivien. "Real funny. How about the Park Police, since we have a human bone that could be evidence to a murder or God knows what?"

Lenny approached the table, looked down, and said, "Well now, this is interesting, isn't it, gang?"

"It's bloody awful," said Sasha. "Just put the dogs in the cars and throw it back into the woods."

"You can't do that, they'll just find it and carry it back out," said Vivien. She walked up to Lenny and began patting his pockets, looking for the cell phone he always carried. Lenny raised his hands to let her, lewdly rolling his eyes and swiveling his hips like he was enjoying the procedure. Nobody seemed to notice.

"It's evidence, Sasha, and besides that, it's what's left of a person." Vivien found the phone in Lenny's pants pocket and pulled it out. Sasha stood up in a most regal manner, slowly turned towards the table, and gazed down at the earthly remains draped by the Safeway bag. She slowly brought her hands to her cheeks and said, "My God, what if it's Phyllis?"

For a full two seconds, there was an unrehearsed moment of silence in the dog park. Vivien saw a flash of Phyllis's face before her eyes. Phyllis Pennybecker, whose married name was long and Indian, was considered by the regulars to be the queen bitch of the dog park. She was missing and believed to have run off to the Caribbean with a Latino lover. Or she was gravely ill, hiding in reclusion, or on vacation in India.

"Bullshit on that, too," said Walter. "Why would you even think that?"

CHAPTER 4

Vivien sat at the picnic table biting her lip, her eyes fixated on the bone sitting in front of her, still covered by the Safeway bags. The highlight of her career in law enforcement was taking down a paranoid schizophrenic man near the U.S. Capitol building who was armed with a .22 caliber Beretta. She considered herself a good cop, but she'd never fired a shot on duty or led any big-time crime investigations.

During her career, she'd shown up on time and had been a bit smarter than the average bear. She was competent and loyal—but she'd also gone off the reservation more than once. Even now she was wondering if maybe Walter was right about the bone not being human. Guys in lab coats would be able to tell if the bone was male or female, the age of the victim, and how long it had been in the ground. All the clues would lead towards answers that Vivien, even now, longed to have. Old feelings and emotions came sliding back as she pondered the possibilities.

She could smell the burnt coffee in the squad room and hear the sound of weapons sliding into holsters. She missed the dirty jokes, the sense of duty, the feeling of doing the right thing for a greater good. She longed for the feeling of being part of something bigger than herself.

"Probably some kind of Santería thing," said Linda.

"They use chickens for that, not humans," said Walter. "Plus, I'm still not convinced it's even human."

"It's horrible, whatever it is," said Sasha. "Put another bag over it, won't you?"

"Well, how does one tell, anyway?" said Lenny.

"They do forensics. They'll find out pretty fast," said Vivien. "The guys coming out might even be able to tell us."

They had already been waiting for the Park Police for forty-five minutes. When she'd called, Vivien had told them that it wasn't an emergency. The subject wasn't going anywhere. She was told that everybody who had witnessed the incident should wait till officers arrived for some routine questioning. She loved that phrase. Routine questioning.

It was getting dark, the light slowly dissolving from the sky, the traffic noise gradually subsiding. It was near seven o'clock, the time when the regulars would usually be back in their homes, preparing their versions of evening meals, and, of course, feeding the dogs. Vivien looked towards the gathering of beasts.

Mooky was lying nearly motionless but looking up, waiting for the signal to jump into the minivan and head towards supper. The others lay scattered around the picnic table, their noses pointing towards the woods, which made Vivien think there was still more waiting to be discovered.

"Well. I'm not sure how much longer I want to wait here—I gotta be up tomorrow at six," said Linda.

"Really, this is typical District of Columbia-style police efficiency here . . . not," said Lenny. "I gots to get home and feed this animal. Don't we? Huh, buddy?"

"Nobody can leave," said Viv. "That's what they said. Wait. Here we go . . ." She stood up as she saw a car heading their way. A beige Crown Victoria with stock wheel covers and three antennas mounted on the trunk pulled into the lot, parked, then sat there idling.

"God, they're taking their sweet time, aren't they?" said Lenny.

"I don't think I've ever been questioned by the police in this country," said Sasha. Vivien snorted and then faked a cough to disguise her amusement of Sasha's slightly stuffy nature. "Still the diplomat's wife, after all these years," she thought to herself.

After what seemed an eternity, the doors popped open. A black man emerged from the passenger side. He was dressed all in black. Black shoes, pants, shirt, tie, jacket, and a black straw fedora. He was large and methodically made his way to the picnic table with no wasted movement. The dogs all turned their heads when the car doors slammed, and they watched the man approach.

Nearly lost in the entrance was another guy who got out of the driver side. He was shorter and white, and he moved like he was in a hurry to keep up, using quick steps to close the gap between himself and his partner. He was wearing a gray suit over a pale blue shirt, striped tie, and a gray straw fedora. Vivien stifled a laugh. They looked like two cops out of a bad movie. But as they got closer she looked into their eyes and saw an unmistakable trace of hardness.

These guys didn't give a shit about what anybody thought about them. She could see a thousand tragedies in their eyes. Things they had seen and things they tried to forget. Their external appearance was merely that, a façade they wore for the public. The real stuff was kept inside, hidden away from the witnesses, crooks, lawyers, and probably each other.

The man in black stooped to scratch the ears of Walter's dog, Lucky. "Hey, boy," he said. "How's everybody?" He directed the greeting to nobody in particular. It went out to canines and humans alike, as the other cop, the white one, reached the picnic table, gave everybody a nod and then turned his attention to the bone. "Is this all that was recovered?" he asked.

"So far," said Vivien, as she watched the black guy make his way patiently through the pack of dogs, petting or addressing each one in turn. Polly the poodle got a "Hey, you," the Great Dane received a "Whoa," Louie, the cocker spaniel, got a ruffle on the head, and when he got to Mooky, he bent over, scratched her ears, and said, "Is this our bone finder? Huh?" Mooky's tail swished majestically as Vivien got up and approached him. "That's right, uh, Detective. How did you guess?"

"Labs got the best noses," said the cop. He gave Vivien a quick wink and then stood up to reveal his whole height. He was over six feet and had to weigh at least 250 pounds. Vivien prepared to introduce herself and already had her hand out to shake, but the cop turned towards the table to address the regulars.

"Okay, I'm Detective McCain and this is Detective Evans; we both work for the D.C. Natural Death squad. You've been asked to remain here while we determine whether there is any need to conduct an investigation into what our little friends found." McCain's eyes flitted quickly around the table, not settling on anyone, but then landing on the bone hiding under the Safeway bags, which were now dancing in a slight breeze.

McCain pulled the bags away, exposing the bone to the darkening sky. "Hmm," he said.

"It's a deer, right?" asked Walter.

"Too big," said McCain while tilting his head, "and the color is wrong."

Evans pulled a tattered spiral notebook out of his inside jacket pocket and said, "I'm going to need everybody's contact info. I'll take business cards if you got 'em."

Vivien knew that none of the regulars had real jobs, otherwise they wouldn't be hanging around in the park every day during the time that most people were struggling through their commute. She doubted if any of them had a business card.

"Which direction did the dog come from carrying the bone?" asked McCain. He was looking right at Vivien, who stood up and pointed towards the path into the woods.

"Right up there, Detective," she said. She wondered if she looked fat from this angle and then sat down on the bench.

Detective Evans began working his way through the regulars' contact information, starting with Lenny, who introduced himself as "Dr. Leonard Thomas." Vivien always had to remind herself that her slightly goofy friend Lenny was actually a well-educated, practicing psychotherapist.

While Evans scratched things into his notebook, McCain turned his back to the table, pulled out his radio, and began speaking into it as he walked towards the woods. Vivien heard snatches of the chatter, picked up the word "coroner" and the police code for a possible homicide. She glanced at Detective Evans, who was making his way over to Walter.

She figured she still had a few seconds before it was her turn to be questioned. For the first time in her life she would be on the other end of an ongoing investigation. It probably wouldn't go anywhere. It was probably just an accident. A mountain biker going over the handle bars, a Alzheimer's victim who'd wandered into the woods and died of exposure, or maybe, just maybe, some actual foul play.

She looked at McCain, who was still talking on the radio, walking slowly towards the path where Mooky had exited. He was looking down at the grass like he'd lost his car keys. A scrap of flesh, a tear of clothing—anything could be a clue. It seemed so random and haphazard. The earliest stage of an investigation was just some guy walking through a field looking at the ground.

Vivien slowly pushed herself to her feet without making eye contact with anyone. She looked down at the table and made a little hopping motion to get her legs out, favoring the bad side of her lower back. Nobody said a word, which was what she was hoping.

She did see Detective Evans glance at her under the brim of his hat. He had gray eyes that showed nothing, and that's what his glance conveyed. He noted her leaving. He said nothing and continued his work—but it was noted.

She pretended to be scanning the ground around the picnic table like she was looking for a lost dog toy. Mooky watched her and stood up, mimicking her master's motions by sniffing the ground where Vivien walked. Vivien didn't have much time and McCain had a twenty-yard lead on her. She didn't want to be too obvious, but she also didn't want to be called back to the table before she had a chance to speak to McCain alone. She wanted to be out of earshot of the people who just assumed she was a washed-up law enforcement officer with a bad back and a dog. She wanted to talk to the detective, alone, cop to cop.

She kept her head down and trailed after him, meandering a bit but steadily closing the gap. He stopped at the opening in the tree line where the path led into the woods. He finished talking into the radio, casually dropped it into his jacket pocket, turned around, and locked his eyes onto her.

"Um, Ms.?"

"It's Vivien, Detective, Vivien Szabo. I'm retired Secret Service." She so wanted to flash a badge, but she had nothing left but the title and her voice. "I just wanted to let you know that I'm at your disposal for any ongoing investigations and Mooky is, too, in case you need a DNA sample from her or anything like that. I know how these things work."

She was standing close enough to see the moustache hairs curling around McCain's full lips. His jowly face showed no indication of concern or interest. Vivien couldn't really get a reading on him and knew that was on purpose. He was wearing his poker face—and observing.

"Well, thank you for your cooperation, Ms., um, I mean, Vivien. That probably won't be necessary, but we certainly appreciate that. What'd you do for the Service?"

He was stopped at the edge of the field, now guarding the path's entrance. This was as far as she was going to get. She should have poked around in there before these schmos showed up. If she was going to find anything, that would have been the time to do it.

"Capital area security, mostly. I got to meet President Carter once," she said "I mean, after he got out of office. The ex-presidents still get protection after they leave."

"Our tax dollars at work, huh?" He smiled and looked her up and down. "Did you take an early out? You still look good enough to serve."

"Oh, thanks," she said. She felt herself blush and looked down at her scuffed sneakers. "Disability. I ruptured a disk in a training exercise."

"Damn, Viv, isn't that always the way? You get hurt in practice, not even doing your job." He laughed, a sound that started somewhere deep in his chest and then bubbled up through him, coming out as a "Heh heh heh." Vivien smiled and laughed with him. For a second she felt like she was home, like she was back to where she was supposed to be after a long trip away. She let the feeling wash over her in the fading sunlight of the dog park. It was her and the detective swapping war stories and feeling connected but then, just as quickly, it ended when she heard Sasha crying out.

"It's her! It's Phyllis!" Sasha yelled. "I just know it is!"

McCain's eyes lifted as he looked back towards the picnic table, the smile and the poker face now replaced with a look of mild curiosity. Vivien half turned, following his glance and even from this distance she could tell that some kind of incident was still under way.

"Oh, God," said Vivien.

"What's that about?" asked McCain.

"She thinks it's Phyllis," said Vivien.

"She thinks who's Phyllis?"

"The bone," said Vivien. "She thinks it belongs to her friend. A woman we all know named Phyllis, whom we haven't seen in a while."

"Why would she think that?" asked the detective.

Vivien could feel the weight of his gaze leaning in on her as she looked back towards the picnic table. Sasha's head was in her hands and even from this distance, Vivien could tell she was sobbing. The rest of the regulars were sitting around the table looking uncomfortable. Evans rested his hand on Sasha's back, his notepad temporarily held at parade rest. Vivien snapped a picture of the scene in her mind and held it, feeling that her life was turning some kind of a corner.

"Why would she think a random bone found in the woods would belong to someone she knew?" asked McCain. "Or was this someone you all knew?"

"Yes," said Vivien. "We definitely all knew her."

CHAPTER 5

Mooky watched the people milling around, talking to each other as day began melting into night. She knew it was past the time when she normally ate, and she was getting anxious. She looked at the other dogs, their heads laid on their paws, also waiting for the natural routine of the day to re-establish itself. It was now time to "eat."

As the sun set, the pressures of the earth changed slightly, which caused the wind to switch. It had been blowing in from the street, carrying a rather boring mix of car exhaust, grass, and a few traces of the fruit trees over on the far side of the field. Mooky could see that all the dog's noses were twitching ever so slightly, their heads swiveling towards the edge of the field.

The aroma was coming from the woods, in the same area that Mooky had found her magical bone that now lay on the table. An irresistible, taboo mixture of rich earth and rotted flesh wafted in on the breeze. Mooky instinctively got up and began padding back towards the path that led to where her bone came from. She was getting closer to the dark shadows of the woods, but Vivien and the large man who smelled like smoke and oil stood between Mooky and where she wanted to go.

The special place was close to where she'd chased and almost caught a squirrel one day. She knew that a patch of dirt at the bottom of the hill, where the leaves had been pulled away, was the spot with a lot more of the magic bones.

"Mooky, come," said Vivien, as she grabbed her collar and pulled her away from the trail of the scent. This was disappointing, but on the other hand, now it was time to eat.

CHAPTER 6

Vivien couldn't believe she had given the cop one of her old Secret Service business cards. She had been caught up in the excitement and now she felt embarrassed. She always kept some of the cards in her wallet in case she ever felt the need to trade her past for some professional courtesy, but this was a bit over-the-top.

She'd scratched out the address and numbers on the front of the card, scribbled her home phone onto the back, then pushed it into the beefy palm of Detective McCain, who had looked at it, nodded, and shoved it into his front pants pocket. She immediately decided that he would never call and she felt a little silly about it.

She found herself back in the park the next morning. Yellow police tape had been pulled across the entrance to the pathway and she fought the urge to ignore it and plunge into the shadows to see the crime scene. She left Mooky at the house, which made her feel guilty, but it was bad enough she was here at all—let alone her and the dog.

She stood at the edge of the woods, the yellow tape now close enough to touch. It represented a barred gateway, the slight path crowded-out and overgrown by greenery, but still visible and leading to something. Out here in the field was one place; there beyond the tape was another. Vivien craned her neck trying to see something—a mound of dirt, shovels propped against trees, anything. She felt like a little girl trying to see the circus without a ticket.

She folded her arms in front of her, fighting the urge to plunge down the path. Charging in wouldn't be professional at all. If she was going to go she would have to pick her way carefully to avoid disturbing any potential evidence. She turned towards the picnic table and began walking slowly back the way she came.

She reached the table, plopped down, and noticed that the charms of the dog park were lost without the presence of any dogs or people. It was now just a picnic table in a field. Freshly dug holes pocked the ground and the faint odor of dog poop drifted over from the trash cans.

Her thoughts returned to Sasha's outburst. Anybody who hung out at the dog park for any length of time had a "Phyllis story," including Vivien. Hers happened here at the picnic table a few months ago. Vivien showed up early that day because it was supposed to rain later. Phyllis was already seated by herself with her bichon, Boopsie, asleep on her feet.

Vivien wasn't sure why Phyllis brought the dog to the park since all it did was sleep. Vivien was convinced that Boopsie was the most antisocial dog in the park, even worse than some of the poodles—and the breed tended to be standoffish, anyway. Vivien greeted Phyllis that day and started making small talk that quickly and suddenly moved into forbidden territory.

"So, you miss being a cop?" said Phyllis.

"Sometimes," said Vivien, as she watched Mooky sniffing the grass.

"So were you the only woman?" asked Phyllis.

"No. There were a few others in the outfit. I was the only one in my detail," said Vivien.

"All dykes, huh?"

"What?" said Vivien.

"Carpet lickers. That's what Harish calls them," said Phyllis.

Harish was Phyllis's husband, an aloof but very successful

19

chiropractor who did his own TV commercials. Harish was Indian and a bit arrogant with most of the regulars at the park, but Phyllis never missed a chance to sing his praises.

Phyllis had a wide-angled, camera-ready face with slightly unnatural looking blonde hair cut short for easy maintenance. She was shorter than average height and gradually thickening into her golden years. Nobody understood the attraction between her and Harish.

"Why do people think that every woman in law enforcement is gay?" said Vivien. She felt the side of her neck flush with anger.

"Hello?" said Phyllis. "Maybe because they are?" She cackled the irritating laugh that every regular at the dog park knew and could imitate. A loud, vulgar hackle dripping with derision.

"That's not true," said Vivien. "Everybody thinks that. There are no more gays in law enforcement than anywhere else, and anyway, who cares? If they can do the job, it doesn't matter." Vivien's views on homosexuality had changed after moving to Washington and making friends with guys like Lenny, who didn't try to rub his lifestyle in anybody's face. He wasn't a gay guy, he was a guy who happened to be gay. She now found herself standing up for gay rights, a position that would not have been so popular in her Midwestern past.

"Mmm-hmm," said Phyllis. She was looking at Vivien in a strange way, like she'd lost something and the map was on Vivien's forehead. "To be honest with you, Viv, I always thought you could swing both ways. Can't ya, baby?" Phyllis cocked her head, smiling a crooked little smile that made it look like she was flirting. Vivien couldn't tell if it was real or if Phyllis was baiting her.

It took Vivien back to a time in Milwaukee where an older officer, who was clearly lesbian, used to look at Vivien in the same way. Nothing happened, but the woman did invite Vivien out for coffee once. The consistent glances Vivien had fielded from her registered in her mind as flattery, curiosity, repulsion, sadness, shock, and anger stacked up on top of each other like breakfast pancakes at the IHOP.

Phyllis held the look, but now cocked her head at an even more acute angle and made a kissing gesture with her lips. "Want to kiss me,

Viv?" Then the laugh broke out and the intention was clear. This obnoxious housewife who didn't know anything about serving or sacrificing as an officer was making fun of her.

"You're an asshole," said Vivien. She stood up, instantly wishing for a more original and withering insult. "Come on Mooky, let's take a walk." She would normally wait for the regulars to show up before taking her walk with Mooky. They would walk together, two or three abreast down the wide parts of the path, single file in the narrow sections. But on this day Vivien and Mooky would push on alone. Anything to get away from Phyllis.

"Hey, where ya goin', baby?" Phyllis called from the bench. Vivien refused to turn around or look at her but could hear Phyllis making kissing sounds with her lips and laughing that horrible cackle. Phyllis was an obnoxious, socially awkward person who had a bad habit of saying the wrong thing to the wrong person at the wrong time. Everybody knew it. Everybody had a reason to avoid her.

Pulling herself back into the present, Vivien rose from the table and walked back towards the yellow tape. She glanced behind her and watched an SUV passing by, the driver yakking on a cell phone as she took the turn too wide and crossed over the center line. In the District, it was illegal to talk on the phone while driving, but they didn't enforce it.

"Oh well, that's DC," said Vivien. She stepped around the tree, brushing past the yellow tape and walked into the cool, dark shadows.

CHAPTER 7

The knock on the front door stunned Vivien. She rarely had unannounced visitors show up at her front door in the middle of the afternoon. Mooky barked like crazy as Vivien shuffled towards the foyer, mentally preparing to chase away the Jehovah's Witness or the confused homeless person who had wandered onto her porch. She was actually dressed, so she didn't have to worry about meeting the public in her bathrobe or something worse.

She glanced down at her bare feet, put her hand on the doorknob, and checked to see if the brass chain was in place. She looked out the small side window next to the door and was surprised to see Detective Evans, the salt of the salt-and-pepper detective team that had shown up at the dog park. Her face flushed as she considered putting on some sandals to hide her unpainted toenails. Then a pang of panic shot through her. Someone must have seen her go into the woods yesterday and called the cops. She was so busted.

"Oh," she heard herself say as one hand went to the door chain while the other turned the knob. She glanced down at her breasts to remind herself what she was wearing and saw a blue cotton top—no cleavage.

She wondered if she was in danger of turning into an old lady before her time, stole a glance towards the top of the armoire where she had put the shoe she'd found in the woods, told Mooky to be quiet, pushed her away from the door with her knee, and said, "Detective . . ."

"It's Evans, ma'am—we met at the dog park."

"Sure, I remember," said Vivien. Her hand went to the second button on her top. The first was already unbuttoned. "What can I do for you?" Mooky stuck her nose in the crack of the door, trying to wedge it farther open for a better sniff, but she stopped barking, which surprised Vivien.

"Mind if I come in for a second, ma'am?"

Vivien took a quick look at the cluttered house, seeing Easter baskets stacked on top of Christmas decorations, boxes from QVC that she hadn't opened yet, and travel books from Amazon still unpacked.

"Um . . . yeah. I mean, the place is kind of a wreck. I really need to straighten up in here. I haven't had a chance since my mother passed away to really, you know, give it a good cleaning."

"I understand, ma'am. It piles up fast, doesn't it?" He was rubbing Mooky's head and stepping through the door. "How long has your mom been gone?"

"What? Oh, two years," said Vivien. As soon as she said it she knew she sounded like a crazy person. Who goes two years without cleaning her house? She stepped back away from the door, then half-turned and guided him towards the only two seats in the house that weren't stacked up with boxes, piles of clothes, or holiday decorations.

Vivien sat in the armchair that had been in her parent's living room since she was a little girl. Her mother wasn't much of a trendsetter in home décor, and housework wasn't really her bag. She did manage to find time to play golf twice a week, hitting from the men's tees. Vivien was still piloting her mom's mini-van with the "I'd Rather Be Driving a Titleist" bumper sticker.

Detective Evans did his best to gracefully squeeze his large backside onto the open section of the couch. Vivien took note for the first time of how he was built. Medium height and stocky, with a square jaw. She pegged his height at five nine, and he probably weighed one-ninety-five, maybe two hundred pounds. His movements were sparse and sure—

like he knew right where he wanted to go and what he was going to accomplish once he got there.

"So, can I get you something to drink? I have water, juice . . . I could heat up some coffee?"

"No, ma'am, I'm fine, thanks." He made a shifting motion and Vivien expected to see the pad and pen come back out, but then she realized he was probably just sliding his holster around to make it easier to sit on her broken-down couch. Now he sat forward, took off his hat, and held it between his knees.

"I just wanted to bring you up to speed with what's going on with the investigation, ma'am."

"Detective. Please, call me Viv or Vivien—'ma'am' makes me feel like an old lady."

A quick smile flashed across his lips. "Right, sure," he said, and his shoulders slumped the slightest bit, like he had just relaxed—but only half a notch.

"Anyway, Vivien." He said it like he was trying it on for size. "The thing is, I heard from Detective McCain you were ex-Secret Service. I have a lot of respect. I tried out a couple of times myself. I just thought you might like to know we did find other bones in that location. Department is still trying to decide whether to pull Homicide in on it or whether it stays with us, Natural Death. In the meantime they're running tests on the bones. I just thought you might want to know, seeing how, you know, we're kind of on the same team and all."

"Sure, sure, I certainly appreciate that," said Vivien. She studied him as he sat there on her couch. He was obviously uncomfortable but trying hard to play it cool. But this was about the most uncool cop she had ever seen. This dude was a by-the-book, quote-the-regs, stand-up-and-salute kind of guy, and yet here he was sharing information about an ongoing investigation with a civilian. Sure, she was ex-Secret Service, but still. She glanced towards the dining room. She should just give him the shoe she had found in the woods and be done with it, but something held her back.

"Detective, are you sure I can't get you something? How about lemonade? I just bought some organic lemonade from Trader Joe's."

"You know, that's the thing, isn't it? I mean how can we live in a world where lemonade can't be organic?" he asked. "I mean it's just lemons and water, right?"

"And sugar," said Vivien. "But I know what you mean. I'm going to have a glass—let me get you one."

"Well," he said and started to get up.

But she stepped in front of him and touched his shoulder. "Sit. Please. I'll get it. You stay right there."

"Yes, m— I mean Viv."

He had excellent manners, but most men do on the first meeting, she thought. She was grateful he had taken her suggestion. She really didn't want him to see her kitchen.

"I'll just be a minute," she called over her shoulder, now wondering if he was using the seconds alone to snoop around in her house. Maybe the whole thing was just a ruse to investigate her. Maybe she was a suspect.

"So, who determines if it's homicide or natural death, the chief?"

"More like a deputy chief," his voice had naturally raised, allowing him to talk to her in the kitchen and still be heard.

"And if it's natural, will you and McCain handle the investigation personally?" She found two glasses, broke some ice out of the trays, and dropped three cubes into each glass.

"Yes," he said and Vivien jumped.

He was standing in the doorway of her kitchen.

"Oh!" said Vivien, her hand going to her throat. "You scared me."

"I'm sorry, ma'am. I didn't want to yell."

"It's okay; I'm just not used to having guests over." Vivien gave the carton a shake and poured two glasses, trying to make them close to even.

"Thank you," he said as he took the glass. Vivien then tried to conceal her shock as she watched him drain the whole glass in five swallows. She counted them.

"Wow," she said. "I thought you weren't thirsty."

"It's good," he said handing the glass back to her. "But I still don't know about the whole organic thing."

Vivien took a sip, letting the tart and sweet flavor soak in as she studied his hands. The fingers were sturdy and rounded on the ends. Was that supposed to mean something? She couldn't remember. She didn't see a wedding band. "I don't know about the organic thing—maybe it's all about how they grow the lemons—but it is pretty good," she said.

"Yep," said the detective. "Well, I gotta be on my way. I was supposed to be over at the lab ten minutes ago." He turned away from her and Vivien felt sad that he was leaving. She followed him as he walked back through her cluttered dining room.

"Are you going to the lab to see about the bones you found?" she said.

He stopped with his hand on the front door. Mooky had reappeared and sniffed his leg.

"Bones?" he said.

"Didn't you say you found more?" she said.

"Yeah," he said, "I did. But this trip to the lab is for another case. We won't have any results on your bone for another couple of days. DC, you know?"

"Yep. I know," she said. "Well, listen, thanks for coming by and filling me in. I hope I'm not getting you into any trouble."

"Oh, don't worry about that, Vivien. I'm sure I can trust ex-Secret Service. But there are a couple of other things I wanted to ask you."

Vivien's eyes shot to the armoire again. This would be a good time to just hand the shoe over and confess that she'd revisited the crime scene. He popped the screen door open a crack, being mindful to keep himself between the opening and Mooky. The big Lab was looking out into the front yard, swooping her tail and hoping for an opening to bolt outside. Vivien felt her face heating up. Somebody must have seen her walk into the woods. Somebody must have seen her carry out the shoe. She was sure that's what he was about to ask her—this whole scene was obviously a set-up for the questions that were coming. But why was he asking questions on the way out? It didn't make any sense.

"Are you Polish?" he said.

"What?"

"Your last name—it sounds Polish. My mother's Pollock and you look like one of my cousins. No offense or nothing; I mean, I'm half myself."

Vivien heard herself laugh. A nice sound, which made her realize she hadn't laughed much recently. It sounded a little nervous to her, and now the cop had a funny look on his face like he was trying to decide whether he should laugh, too.

"What?" he said. "Is that funny?"

"No, no," she said, "I thought you were going to say something else. I'm Croatian, third generation; my whole family is from Wisconsin."

"Hey, no kidding. I got family in Minneapolis."

Vivien stopped herself from telling him that Minneapolis was in Minnesota and that she'd worked there for a few years. She felt herself smiling at him.

"Oh, and listen," he said. "That woman who used to come to the park, um, Phyllis—did you know her well?" He was now outside the door but his foot was still in the crack. His leg was blocking Mooky's access and giving him enough room to look at her face without a door between them. His eyes had suddenly gone from laughing windows of light to gray circles of intense concentration. He was looking right through her. She met his gaze and then looked away like she had to think about the answer to the question.

"Not real well. Why?" she said.

"We have to follow up on everything, ma'am. Just procedure. But don't leave town, okay?" He was serious when he said it, but then his face broke into a grin. He turned away and said over his shoulder, "Well. See ya." The exit seemed abrupt, like something still needed to be said. Something unfinished hung there between them. Vivien watched through the side window for a second, the purposeful walk propelling him towards the sidewalk and the unmarked car across the street, the walk taking him back to duty, back to his place in the universe.

Vivien closed the door, feeling the weight of the dog against her thigh. Mooky was now panting softly, the activity around the door indicating that she might be going out. "No, Mooky," said Vivien, "we're not going anywhere. Not yet."

Vivien leaned her head against the front door, looking down at the worn rag rug lying across the hardwood floor. She needed to get the floors sanded and refinished. She could use some new throw rugs. She really needed to get her life back in order. She felt like she'd been stuck in the same place for a long time: Held in time like an insect in amber. Held in place by the weight of the house and the furnishings, the goals unrealized. It was all feeling burdensome and heavy, and she felt like she needed to take a nap, or maybe watch some TV, or maybe just sit down and cry for a while. Then there was another knock at the door.

"Oh God," said Vivien and her hand went to her throat. How long had she been standing at the door looking at the floor? Had they seen her? She was visible through the side windows by the door. Now what? She repositioned her body so it would look like she had just walked to the door, and looked outside. It was Detective Evans again. Shit. Now she was sure she was busted.

She stole a quick glance at his face, her hand felt for the knob, her other hand checked the button on her top, and without knowing why, she unbuttoned the second button. What did the look on his face mean? He looked uncomfortable, almost nervous. He was going to take her in for questioning. She casually flipped the neckline opening in her top and felt the air on her chest. She stole a quick glance at the armoire. She couldn't even see the shoe from here. She decided she was acting paranoid and cracked the door open.

"Hello again," she said. "Forget something?"

"Ma'am, I mean, um, Vivien. Would you ever want to have coffee or a drink or something? I mean, not now—unless you wanted to go now—but I mean, you know, sometime?" His eyes glanced at her top, noting the change. He was a trained observer.

"Um . . . sure, Detective, I mean, yeah, I'd love to." He was asking her out. She couldn't believe it. She didn't even need to unbutton the button.

"It's Will," he said. "My first name is Will." She decided that sounded right. He looked and sounded like a Will. A force of will. Willful intent. He was a willful man.

"So, can I call you?" he said. "I mean, I already have your numbers."

"Yes," said Vivien, "you certainly do."

CHAPTER 8

Mooky knew that it was time to go to the park and see the rest of the dogs. She sat by the front door guarding against intruders. The spot also allowed her to make sure that Vivien could not leave without her knowing. From here she could look out the window to watch for the squirrel that lived in the tree. She'd once seen a raccoon climb up the same tree, so she looked for him, too.

She also knew that the cat that lived up the street liked to pee under the bushes in front of the house, so that was another good reason to watch from the window. Mooky didn't hate the cat, but she liked to chase it and instinctively knew how to kill it. She'd been scratched on the nose by a cat when she was a puppy and had been looking for a chance to get even ever since.

Mooky was also very anxious to get back to that wonderful place in the woods where the special bone came from. She knew there was more to discover there and also that Vivien had been back to that place without her. Vivien had left the house the day before and came back with that same smell on her clothes.

Mooky licked her lips from the remembrance of the damp earth, the hard bone, and the traces of aromas that danced around the spot. Much had happened there and she was anxious to go back and see what else she could find.

Mooky also knew that Vivien had found a shoe near that place.

She'd seen her bring it into the house. Since Vivien had found the shoe, it belonged to her, but Mooky was sure she could take it away from her if she got the chance. It would be another game of Get-the-Thing. She knew where the shoe was—on top of the big box in the corner.

Earlier, a man who smelled like leather, oil, and wool came to the house. He tried to claim Vivien for his own and Mooky was sure he would be back. Mooky was surprised that Vivien hadn't shown the shoe to the man—a sure sign that she was keeping it for herself.

Mooky stood up, put her nose to the window, and scanned the front yard, but she saw nothing. She looked at the how the sunlight was lying on the floor, sniffed her paw for a trace of the dog food that had fallen on it earlier, but smelled nothing.

She looked into the living room and saw Vivien sleeping on the couch. Before she lay down, Vivian had pulled things off the couch. She removed boxes and clothing that smelled like dust and old fabric. Mooky watched this process very closely to see if any of her toys were hiding on the couch, but it all belonged to Vivien. Vivien laid most of the things on the furniture, but some of them were lying on the floor, which meant they now belonged to Mooky.

She couldn't pee on them to mark them properly since they were in the house, but whatever was on the floor instantly became hers. After Vivien finished clearing off the sofa she went to the big box in the corner and took the shoe down. Mooky tried get closer for a good smell and start the game of Get-the-Thing, but Vivien pushed her away, looked at the shoe for a while, and then put it back.

Then Vivien sat down on the couch that she had cleared off and cried. Mooky had seen Vivien crying many times lately and this cry was no different than the other times. Then Vivien fell asleep. Mooky considered jumping up on the couch with her, but there wasn't enough room, so instead she poked Vivien with her nose.

It was time to go to the dog park and see the pack, run in the woods, and get back to where the bone had come from. If they didn't get there soon the other dogs would take what belonged to Mooky. Mooky nudged Vivien with her nose again and now whined for added emphasis.

It was time to go. Now was the time of go.

"Stop," said Vivien. She shifted a bit on the couch as Mooky stared at her closed eyes and began panting until Vivien opened her eyes.

"What?" said Vivien.

Mooky glanced towards the back door, which led to the car that would take them to the park. Then she could run into the woods, which is what she really wanted. In her mind she'd already answered Vivien's question by looking towards where she wanted to go.

"It's not time yet," said Vivien. Mooky didn't know what these words meant and didn't care. She increased her rate of panting as she became anxious about going to the park. She used her paw to scratch the couch next to Vivien.

"Stop, Mooky."

But Mooky would not stop since she was quite sure it was time to go and she scratched again, this time catching the edge of Vivien's face with her nail.

"Ow!" said Vivien. "Okay, okay—we'll go, we'll go."

"Go" was a good word and meant they would soon be in the car or outside or someplace with new and different smells and this made Mooky very happy. She twirled in circles, delighted to see the tip of her marvelous tail flashing in front of her nose but always just spinning out of reach. This caused her to bark. Vivien told her to be quiet, but Mooky would not be quiet because they were now in the time of go, a very happy place to be.

CHAPTER 9

Vivien didn't know if the shoe she had found in the woods belonged to the bone that had been recovered from the site, but it was definitely in the same vicinity. She was now trying to decide who she was going to tell—if anyone. The day she'd decided to ignore the yellow tape barring entrance to the path was now covered over by her rationalizations for venturing into the woods and underpinned by the white lie she planned on using if she had been caught in the act.

She would say she had come into the woods from the bottom of the hill where there was no police tape and was unaware that she was intruding on a possible crime scene. In Vivien's eyes, the fact that the police had never blocked off the other entrances to the path was another fine example of typical DC un-professionalism.

Why she didn't turn the shoe over to Detective Will Evans when she had the perfect chance was another question. She asked herself if she was better equipped to handle the investigation than the actual investigators, but she refused to answer her own question. She asked herself if she was using the flip-flop as a way to ease herself back into a life of fighting crime and chasing bad guys, but there was no response. She decided to tell Will on their date, which he had yet to call for. That way, if he didn't call, she had an excuse to call him.

She side-stepped Mooky, herding her towards the direction of the back door. They were a few minutes early for the dog park and would probably be the first to arrive. Mooky was now barking like crazy and running in circles around Vivien's legs, actually slowing down the process of getting in the car. Dogs were so silly that way.

"Stop, Mooky. We're going, we're going," said Vivien. She was looking forward to talking to Lenny about her impending date with the police detective. Hot gossip became enhanced by telling people at the dog park. She sampled some fantasy date scenarios floating through her brain as she climbed into the van and backed out of the garage.

She pictured her and Will at Listrani's, a nice little Italian joint down by the canal that served excellent homemade bread. He'd said he was half-Polish; what did that mean? Brats and kraut with warm potato salad? Would he wear his hat on a date? Would he be carrying his weapon? What did they use in the District? Berettas, maybe? What about his other weapon? What would that look like? She thought about his rounded fingers and brushed a hand through her hair.

She pictured the police detective naked, seeing his muscled shoulders, thick upper arms and thighs. He was built like a fireplug and she imagined his beefy torso with a nice package downstairs. She snapped her eyes back to the road and put a hand to her throat.

"Oh Christ," she said to herself. She concentrated on her driving while deciding that Will was attractive in an ugly dog kind of way. He was cute like a bulldog or maybe a pit bull, his features rendered appealing by their own plainness.

Although she had never married or had a relationship last longer than a year, she genuinely liked men. There had been a few half-hearted attempts at coupling during the twenty-five years since high school. A few boyfriends, some flings, and a number of bad dates. She'd gone out with three different guys from the dog park—dates that never amounted to anything beyond rehashed conversations about the dogs. The bachelors and some of the married guys at the park still hit on her on a regular basis.

She had let her hair revert to its mostly natural strawberry-blonde color and an easy-to-maintain, medium length. Her face was an attractive amalgam of her parents, who were both good-looking people. She looked into her rearview mirror, thought briefly about lipstick, pulled onto Military Road, and ticked off how many months it had been since she had been properly laid.

It was around the holidays last year with a guy she met at a party who was ten years younger than her. She was flattered at first. He was Latino with a nice body and an engaging laugh. He worked as a waiter and dreamed of being a professional photographer. He was not her type, assuming she had a type, but she had her way with him for a few weeks. She made him wear a condom and deferred going down. He painted her bedroom ceiling and fixed the valve on her leaky downstairs toilet. For a while it felt like they were turning into an unlikely but happy couple.

Within a month he asked her if he could borrow a thousand dollars so he could go to Mexico on a photo shoot and take pictures of bikini models. She refused, and things went downhill from there. A couple of times since then she'd gotten drunk and caught herself with her finger hovering above his number on her phone. She was proud of the fact that she had never pressed the button.

The Will situation was a different kettle of fish, but she didn't want to get her hopes too high. He was probably married or gay—or a drunk or psychotic. But he was a police officer with a steady job and a purposeful way of moving. She liked that part.

Lenny offered good perspectives on what men were thinking and why they did certain things, advice that Vivien considered crucial at times like these. She made the turn into the parking lot and felt her heart lighten as she recognized Lenny's Volkswagen.

She turned off the van and grabbed the leash and a few poop bags. She picked up a chewed-up tennis ball, popped the door open, and said, "Hey," in the general direction of the picnic table. Mooky bounded out and glanced at Lenny's Portuguese water dog, "Buddy," who was already loping towards her to say hello.

Vivien watched Mooky put her nose in the air and sniff deeply while Buddy nosed around nearby. "Mooky . . . " said Vivien. But it was already too late. Mooky stole a quick glance at the picnic table and then took off running towards the woods like she'd been shot out of a cannon. Buddy lowered his head and streaked after her.

"Hey!" Vivien yelled, "Lenny! Grab them!"

The dogs ran straight as an arrow towards the yellow tape stretched across the path on the other side of the field.

"What?" said Lenny. "Oh shit."

"They're running into the woods," said Vivien who had now started after the two dogs. "They're not supposed to go down there."

"Oh jeez," said Lenny as he stood up and yelled, "Buddy! Come on, boy." The dogs were across the road, picking up speed and showing no sign of turning around. They were running at full speed, bounding for the yellow police tape, with Vivien and Lenny now trotting behind them. Vivien broke into a run, feeling the muscles in the backs of her legs firming up. The movement felt great and getting a legitimate excuse to go back into the woods excited her. She could hear Lenny huffing behind her, occasionally calling out to the dogs as the yellow tape got closer.

She reached the opening and stepped around the tree that the tape was attached to as she watched Lenny put a hand over his chest, faking the symptoms of a heart attack. "You know," he said, exaggerating the effort of the run, "jogging is not my thing, darling. I believe I'm having a mini-stroke." Vivien couldn't help laughing. She waited for him at the edge of the woods until he caught up, as she slid her finger along the edge of the tape, anxious to move farther into the shadows.

"God, I hope there aren't any, like, body parts down there," he said.

"Don't worry; it's all cleaned out," said Vivien.

"And how would you know that, young lady?" said Lenny.

She walked ahead of him towards the spot and said. "Well, actually, I came down here yesterday and looked around a little."

He touched her shoulder lightly with his fingertips and said, "Oh no, you didn't." He said it with an accent, like he was a black girl, and this made Vivien laugh again.

Lenny was 58 and half-Lebanese. He'd grown up gay in a small town in South Carolina that wasn't Charleston and split for the big city as soon as possible. He got his master's in psychology from George Washington University, after giving up on being a lawyer. He counseled HIV patients in a program funded by a non-profit. It was a not-too-demanding job that left him plenty of time for puttering in his garden, watching tennis matches on TV, and hanging out at the dog park.

"And what happens if the police find out about that and, more importantly, what did you find, darling?"

Vivien pushed her lips together and made a snap decision.

"I didn't find much. But I did get a surprise visit from one of the police detectives."

They reached the clearing and she stopped at the edge, looking at the dirt as the dogs sniffed their way around the patch of bare earth. "I figured they'd be here. Bad dog, Mooky!"

Lenny came up beside her, touched her again on the shoulder, looked at the ground, and said, "Oh really? Now are we talking about the big black man in the fedora?"

"No," said Vivien, "the shorter white guy who was writing everything down."

"Oh honey, he was cute in a very butch, Dragnet kind-of-way."

"You think so?" said Vivien.

"Well, I can see why you said 'yes' to that. I'd let him put the cuffs on me once or twice."

Vivien giggled again and looked at the dirt. The ground looked different from how she remembered it. She wrote it off to her own altered perception, since she was so nervous the first time.

The whole site was on the side of a gently sloping hill, but the patch of dirt occupied a flat spot, partially shielded from the path by a mound of earth. Vivien could see why the location made perfect sense for a murder. The victim was probably grabbed on the path and then pulled to the small, flat spot and then . . . Who knows?

"See?" said Vivien. "No blood. No body parts. No bones.

Mooky, get out of there!" The Lab's nose was glued to the dirt as Buddy walked the perimeter and occasionally stopped to lift his leg. "Come on," said Vivien, as she grabbed Mooky by the collar and started guiding her back up the hill. Lenny did the same thing to Buddy as they headed back to the opening in the woods. They emerged into the field just as Sasha's ten-year-old Mercedes sedan was pulling into the parking lot. Other cars had also appeared in the parking lot and the hillside was dotted with people and dogs.

"Ah," said Lenny. "Her majesty has arrived."

As they walked towards the parking lot, Vivien watched Sasha exit the vehicle, walk around to the passenger side, and open the door for Polly the poodle, who gracefully hopped out and sniffed.

"Do you mean Sasha or Polly?" asked Vivien.

"Both, darling," said Lenny.

Even from this distance, Vivien could tell that Sasha looked a little uneasy on her feet. She was a well-preserved seventy-something and was known to enjoy a cocktail after her daily visits to the park—and sometimes before as well.

"And a pleasant good morning to you, Ms. Sasha."

"Afternoon, isn't it?" said Sasha.

"Indeed it is, mum, indeed it is," said Lenny.

As they moved to the picnic table, Sasha said, "So, I think you should know I had a visit from the Washington DC Metro Police Department. I swear this country is turning into a fascist state these days." The clipped accent sounded a bit muddled. Vivien watched the way Sasha's head was moving, listened to the slight slur in her words, noted the aside remarks, and picked up a slight odor of gin. Sasha was clearly tanked.

"What?" said Vivien. "One of the detectives?" She also noted that her stomach had done a quick back-flip thinking of Will Evans visiting someone other than her.

"Yes," said Sasha, "it seems they are trying to locate Phyllis."

Sasha stared off towards the woods and sniffed.

"Maybe they should just call her," said Lenny, "or haven't they thought of that yet?"

"Oh, they've thought of it," said Sasha, "but obviously they need a last name, don't they? And for whatever reason I seem to be the only one who knows her last name."

"It's Penny something, isn't it?" asked Lenny. "Pennybecker? . . . Or was that her maiden name?"

Vivien waved him off. "Which detective?" she asked Sasha.

Sasha ignored the question. "They wanted to know how long she'd been missing, where she lived, her phone number, what kind of dog she has—everything."

"I don't even know her last name," said Vivien. And then she reviewed something she always found quite curious about the dog park regulars. The same group of people met at the same time at the same place every day and shared small talk while their dogs played together. But there was also a kind of invisible force field around their social lives outside the boundaries of the park.

Vivien could provide a detailed history about the veterinary background of every dog playing on the hill. She knew how old they were, and how they came to be united with their owners. She knew that Polly only had four toes on her right front foot and Buddy was deaf in his left ear. She didn't know where Lenny's office was located but she did know which cabinet he kept his wine glasses in. She couldn't tell you the name of Sasha's dead husband, but she did know that Lucky Dog once had a bad case of mange. This was the curious thing about the dog park—it was all about the dogs. The humans were the sideshow.

"So did you tell them she was a rather unpleasant individual who was hated by all who knew her?" said Lenny. He was wiping some dirt off Buddy's nose with a bandana that he pulled out of his back pocket.

"She wasn't hated by all, at least not all the time," said Sasha as she shifted around on the picnic bench.

"Which cop was it?" said Vivien.

Sasha ignored her again and said, "We all had our dealings with her, didn't we, pretty Polly?" She was fluffing the hair on the top of the black poodle's head. "The police seemed to be especially interested in that day with Linda and the knives."

"Ah," said Lenny. "'The Infamous Knife Incident.' I remember it well. Now, who's walking?" This was the signal for all those regulars who walked their dogs in the woods to rise as one and start the mile loop through the woods that would mark the only exercise some would get for the day. The dogs would run between the trees and drink from muddy puddles, and some would venture down the hill at the half-way point to dunk themselves into the branch of Rock Creek that ran through the valley. Sasha was not a walker; almost everybody else was, including a few of the other semi-regulars who had wandered over towards the picnic table.

As those who walked began assembling leashes and leads, questions shot through Vivien's brain like lightning in a summer thunderstorm. Why would Sasha tell the police about the Knife Incident? How well did Sasha know Phyllis? Why was she still holding onto this crazy theory about the bones in the woods? Did any of these people actually have a serious beef with Phyllis? But one question was more important than all the others. She walked to Sasha's side where she would be impossible to be ignored.

"Sasha, which detective was it? Was it somebody from Homicide?"

Sasha's hand went to Vivien's wrist. Her face came in closer and now Vivien could really smell the gin. She tried looking through the older woman's sunglasses to determine her level of impairment. Maybe she had a touch of Alzheimer's.

Sasha leveled her gaze at Vivien through the smoked lenses. "It was the black one," said Sasha, "the darky who was here."

CHAPTER 10

The day known as "The Knife Incident" started off very unremarkably. It was spring at the dog park, the ground still moist from the persistent showers of April. Things were starting to bud and bloom, which meant the regulars who had avoided the park due to inclement weather were coming back out of hibernation and reestablishing their positions at the picnic table.

Vivien arrived with Mooky at her regular time and pulled in, seeing Sasha's and Phyllis's cars in the parking lot. That meant the two of them would be huddled in a conversation that didn't hold much interest to Vivien. It would be mostly health issues—health issues of the dogs—and then on to who-said-what at last month's dinner party.

From the general gossip around the park, Vivien knew all about the marvelous dinner parties hosted by Phyllis and her back-quack husband, but was never actually invited. Apparently, Sasha was a semi-regular guest.

The Knife Incident occurred after The Lesbian Incident—which was how Vivien referred to her own brush with Phyllis. Ever since then, Vivien kept her distance from Phyllis while trying not to look completely antisocial.

On the day of The Knife Incident, Vivien had been milling around the table, staying out of conversations and waiting for Lenny to signal the beginning of the walk. She heard a car pulling in and saw

41

Linda's Jeep Cherokee, with "Zena," her Great Dane, packed into the rear compartment.

In many ways Linda was just as controversial as Phyllis. Linda's history was forever rooted in the time when Zena got into a fight with a white German shepherd owned by a woman named Estelle, a manic-depressive, semi-professional dog walker. The dog fight, which didn't amount to much, escalated into Estelle dousing Linda with pepper spray and threatening to call the police. Even though Linda was clearly the victim, she was still seen as a suspicious character by some of the regulars.

Vivien never had an issue with Linda or her dog and was always happy to see her. Linda feared no one and didn't care what anybody said about her. Because she was African-American, everybody assumed she was a DC native, but she actually grew up in central Pennsylvania with a family of five brothers. Her father was a brick mason and Linda was her father's daughter.

"Hey, girl," Linda said to Vivien as she climbed out of the Jeep and walked to the back of the vehicle to release the dog. Zena bounded out as Vivien relived her amazement at the dog's size—like a small pony, really. Even though she knew the huge dog was a loving and sweet animal, having that giant nose poking around above her waistline always shot a pang of fear through her.

"Hey," said Vivien, "what's up?"

"I gotta show you something," said Linda. She oozed excitement and shot her eyebrows up and down, her wide face in a full grin. She was walking towards Vivien, as the dogs sniffed and circled. Linda had something in her hand that looked like a rolled-up placemat tied with a string.

"I just bought 'em. Come on." She walked right past Vivien and headed to the picnic table.

"What is it?" asked Vivien. But Linda was already past her. The other women said "hi" to Linda as she laid the object on top of the table. Vivien caught up and watched Linda pull the string that untied the knot and the fabric unfurled to reveal the stainless steel handles of a set of chef's knives. The fabric was divided into a series of pockets and sleeves, with each pocket holding a knife, a set of tongs, a meat tenderizer, a long handled fork, or some other kitchen tool that Vivien couldn't identify.

"They're German, all hand-honed with balanced handles. I just picked them up at the supply house," said Linda.

"They're knives, then?" asked Sasha.

"Chef's knives," said Linda. "I got a whole set: bread knife, carving knife, filet knife, paring knife, heavy bladed knife for chopping, boning knife. Check it out." Linda grabbed one of the handles and pulled out a ten-inch knife with a triangular shaped blade, the kind the maniac always uses in the slasher movies.

"Nice," said Vivien while trying to think of something better to say. "Really nice, Linda."

"Yeah, and they come with a lifetime guarantee. If I ever break one they give me a new one for free—forever," said Linda.

"I got a set of Henckels when Harish and I got married and they've never broken," said Phyllis. "Henckels are the best. Are these Henckels?" She reached for one of the handles and pulled it a few inches out of its pocket while absently looking at the blade.

"Henckels are good," said Linda, "but these are professional."

"Oh, Henckels are professional, too," said Phyllis, "Harish has a friend . . . I can't remember his name—something Indian. Anyway. He just opened that new place on Connecticut. What's it called? Can't remember. Anyway. He uses Henckels and he just opened this place and it's packed every night. What do they call it? New Age Indian or something. It's like the hottest thing in town and Harish knows him. They have vindaloo to die for. Oh my God. Can you make me some vindaloo with these knives?"

"Vinda who?" said Linda.

"It's a dish, sweetie. Indian dish. Very popular. Really, Linda, if you're going to play chef you really need to learn to cook Indian; that's all anybody eats anymore."

"Play chef?" said Linda.

Vivien was aware that the mood at the table had changed very quickly. Linda and Phyllis were never close and less than friendly. They routinely ignored each other. Vivien thought it was a little rude on both their parts, but she refused to get involved. Phyllis was also known to make vaguely racist remarks from time-to-time. Vivien knew Linda pretty well—at least in a dog park kind of way—and she could tell from the tone that the discussion was taking a bad turn.

"What do you mean, 'play chef?'" asked Linda. She was still holding the big slasher knife. "Who's all these people eating Indian all the time? You're not Indian, Phyllis." Linda looked away from the table, turning her face towards the woods. She dropped her voice slightly and said, "This bitch is crazy." With one hand she started flopping the canvas carrier closed. The knife show was over.

"What did you say?" asked Phyllis.

"Now, come on," said Vivien she held her hands up and moved closer to Linda, getting a shoulder in between her and Phyllis. Her old training kicked in automatically but she couldn't believe she was one snide comment away from breaking up a cat fight between two grown women in the middle of Rock Creek Park. Only thing was—Linda was armed with a very sharp knife.

"I said you're crazy, bitch. Nobody's eating Indian but you, and you're not even Indian. And you don't know shit about nothing, but you think you do," said Linda. Now she was pointing the knife in the general direction of Phyllis's upturned nose.

"All right ladies, that's quite enough," said Sasha and she gave her head the slightest royal shake to emphasize that she had quite enough. For once, Vivien was in agreement.

"She's right," said Vivien. "Let's all just take a breath here."

"Oh please," said Phyllis. "She thinks because she bought herself some knives she's a gourmet chef now. You're just a caterer, Linda. Wake up. Be smart for once in your life and learn to cook Indian." Now it was Phyllis who turned her head towards the woods and said, "I'll bet she financed those stupid knives."

Vivien felt herself cringe at the insult and then sensed that Linda was no longer standing beside her. With three quick steps Linda propelled herself around the table and was now standing in front of Phyllis. She held her arms stiffly by her sides, the big knife still clenched in her right hand.

"What's it to you?" asked Linda. "What's that supposed to mean?"

Phyllis made a face like she was smelling something foul and said, "Oh, nothing, Linda. I just know how you people are with your money."

"You people?" said Linda. Her voice became louder as she towered over Phyllis. Vivien began moving towards her, wishing she had some cuffs or a radio to call for back-up.

"Come on Linda, let's walk," said Vivien. She approached her from the back and put a hand on her shoulder while keeping an eye trained on the hand holding the weapon.

"You're an asshole, Phyllis," said Linda, pointing at her with the knife, "and one of these days somebody's going to deal with you once and for all. You watch your ass around me, bitch."

"All right. Come on, Linda," said Vivien. She pulled gently on Linda's upper arm, feeling the mass of it. Linda would crush Phyllis in a fight if it came to that. She could easily drive that slasher knife right through her.

Phyllis was now silent and looked towards the woods, waiting for the scene to end. Maybe she was finally realizing that it was in her best interest to pipe down. Much to Vivien's relief, she felt Linda take a step back as she slid the knife back into the pocket, rolled up the case, tucked into under her arm and said,

"Come on, dogs, let's get away from this racist bitch." Then she and Vivien walked to the car in silence, locked the knives under the front seat, and walked into the woods without waiting for Lenny.

On that day, as on a few others scattered through the calendar, Vivien saw the thin wall of tolerance and acceptance that surrounded the dog park regulars crack into an ugly, distorted pane of mean. They were all from different racial and socioeconomic backgrounds. Some drove Mercedes, some piloted busted-up minivans and first-generation SUVs.

But all this diversity and grounds for potential disagreement was pushed aside for the one thing that bonded them all together— the love of dogs. On that day, the good vibes of planet canine failed. They were outmatched by a quick shot of hatred and ugliness that Vivien now wished she could forget.

CHAPTER 11

Mooky sat in her regular space by the front door watching for squirrels, dogs, cats, and raccoons. It was after supper. She'd chomped down a treat and had already been outside. The rest of the evening was devoted to napping in the room with the noisy box until it was time to go to bed. She'd get to go out at least once more, maybe twice, which would give her a chance to look for animals in the yard. But something was up.

Vivien was in her closet rooting around, trying on different kinds of shoes and clothes, which was stirring up all kinds of smells. Each pair of shoes had their own aroma and even from here Mooky could tell at least four different pairs were being tried on and then slipped off. Some of the shoes hadn't been out of the closet for months. Hearing the closet noises—squeaks, thumps, and bumps—probably meant Vivien was going somewhere without her and Mooky started to pant.

She didn't hear any of the good words. She didn't hear "go" or "park." She didn't hear "walk" or "ride." She lay by the door without making any noise. When the door opened Mooky planned to bolt out to join Vivien in whatever was about to happen. In the meantime, she rested, watched, and waited.

Through the vibrations on the floor and the sounds, Mooky knew that Vivien was out of the closet. Out of the side of her eye, she watched Vivien reaching for the shoe that she had brought home from the woods. It was on top of the big box in the corner. The shoe had come from the place in the woods where Mooky had found the most beautiful bone ever, and her tail wagged at the memory. Vivien had one of the bags used at the park and this made Mooky's tail wag a bit faster. They usually didn't go to the park in the dark, but she would certainly like to so she could chase the animals that came out at night. Mooky sat up, turning to face Vivien. She watched her looking at the shoe and Mooky's mouth began to water.

"No," said Vivien, "Mommy's going out. I have a date and you need to stay home and guard the house." Mooky watched Vivien put the shoe into the bag and laid it on top of the table. "Mommy may even get lucky," said Vivien. She laughed a little, a nice sound that Mooky liked to hear. Mooky opened her mouth slightly and began panting while looking at Vivien and then seeing the shoe on top of the table.

The other smells came next, smells Mooky hadn't experienced in a long time—but she still knew them. Smells like fruit and flowers that meant Vivien was definitely going somewhere and Mooky was probably not. Noise from the street outside drifted into the house. Mooky ignored most of it, but the slam of a car door was a different thing. This sound meant somebody was going for a ride. Mooky barked at the sound and turned back towards the door. She used her nose to move the cloth by the window so she could see who was going for a ride. At first she couldn't see anybody but then he appeared. She recognized the shape of the man but would need to get a smell to make sure it was the same one.

He moved in the same way and her tail wagged when she saw him come through the gate and walk to the front of the house. Maybe he was coming for the shoe and maybe he would want to play "Pull-the-Thing." Mooky's tail wagged harder as she thought about that. That was a fun game that Vivien didn't really like to play.

She whined a bit as his scent began to arrive through the door. Leather and oil, maybe some fruit and flowers on him, too. He knocked and Mooky barked in response. She could smell soap and some fear coming through. What was he afraid of? Her? She barked louder.

"Hey," said Vivien. "Be quiet, Mooky. Come on. Back up, back up." Vivien was pushing her away from the door with her knee, digging it into Mooky's ribs, which meant Mooky's part of the game was to get past the knee and give the man a good sniff.

"Hi, Will. Come on in. I'm not quite ready. Mooky, stop. Jeez, I'm sorry. She gets really excited when new people come over," said Vivien.

"It's okay," said the man. "She's fine. Just let her go. I was on K-9 detail for 18 months a few years ago. I love dogs."

Vivien stopped trying to hold Mooky back. Mooky was happy to hear the word "go." She went to the man, nose down, tail wagging. She went to his knee, checked the fabric and the flesh, and determined it was the same man. That was good. She felt his hand on her back, smoothing the fur and feeling the muscles in her shoulders.

"Really?" asked Vivien. "Do they use shepherds for that?"

"Mostly shepherds," said the man. "But also a few rotties and some dobies."

"Sure." said Vivien. "Dobermans would make sense, but I didn't know they used Rottweilers."

"Oh yeah," said the man. He worked on Mooky's head while the dog made a careful inspection of his shoes to see if he'd been around any other animals. "You take the Rotties over to the projects in Southeast you get instant respect."

"I'm sure," said Vivien. "Just make yourself at home and I'll be right out."

Mooky watched Vivien walk out of the room, leaving her alone with the man. This was perfect. Now she could start the game. The man stopped petting her and began walking around the room looking at things. Mooky sat on her haunches and waited for him to look back at her so she could show him what she wanted. It didn't take long.

"What's on your mind, girl?" His voice was low so only the two of them could hear. He wanted to play. She wagged her tail, opened her mouth a bit, made sure he was looking at her, and then looked towards the top of the table, then back at him. But he looked the other way. He was teasing her, so she waited till he got through looking at something else and looked back at her. She looked him in the eye and this time more slowly, she turned her head and looked at the top of the table. This time he looked where she was looking. Perfect. He was catching on and wanted to play.

"What?" he said.

She looked at him and began panting a little, waiting for him to pick up the shoe so she could pull on the other end of it.

"You want water?" he asked, look briefly at her and then looked away. She whined a bit to get his attention, waited till he looked at her, and then once again looked to the top of the table. This time he looked. "What?" he said. "Something up here you want?" The man walked towards the table and Mooky became more excited. She was finally going to get the shoe and this man would probably want to pull on it with her.

She wagged her big tail harder and stood up to point with her nose to where she had seen Vivien put the bag down. She moved closer to the table to show the man right where it was—and to get a good hold on it as soon as she got the chance. He was looking at the top of the table.

"What?" he asked. "The bag?"

"Ready?" asked Vivien as she walked into the room smelling like flowers and fruit.

"Yeah," said the man. "She was acting like she wanted something."

"Well," said Vivien, "that's nothing new; she always wants something. Mooky, you stay here and be a good girl. Mommy will be right back." The flower smell was all over Vivien's fingers and it made Mooky sneeze. She knew for sure now they were going somewhere together. Unless she could sneak out, she was going to be left here alone. She made one more attempt to get the man to pick up the shoe. She looked at him, her head half under the table as he glanced down at her. She saw him look back at the top of table, but they were leaving and Mooky was nudged back into the house. Lights were turned out and the door was locked.

Mooky was alone in the house with the shoe. She had taken an entire roast beef off that table once when she was a puppy by climbing up on a chair. She got into big trouble. As a full-grown black Lab she could rest the bottom of her chin on the table with a little stretching. One half-hop and she could have most of her body on top of the table. She knew that whatever was on the table was off limits, but the shoe came from the same place as the best bone ever.

CHAPTER 12

Prior to Will's arrival Vivien had done something that she normally took great pains to avoid: standing naked in front of her full-length mirror. She sucked her stomach in, cupped her breasts, and fluffed up the downy pillow of hair between her legs. She did a half turn and looked over her shoulder at her ass, flexing her glutes, spreading her thighs, running her hand across the gentle curve, before giving herself a playful slap on the cheek. She liked the sound as she turned around to face her desires and herself. She was solidly in her 40s but still looked halfway decent as a bare-naked lady.

She had always attracted attention from men. Her mother was skinny as a rail her entire life, probably due to genetics, a constant buzz of activity, and two packs of Virginia Slims a day. Emphysema did her in at 72; her father had died from a stroke at the age of 50.

As she stared into the mirror with Mooky locked on the other side of the bedroom door, Vivien licked a finger and traced it around her nipple imagining what it would feel like with Will. He seemed confident, which was a good sign, and yet a little unsure of himself around her, which she found endearing. Her body responded to its wake-up call as she felt the nipple stiffen and become more sensitive.

She ran a hand down her tummy, smiling a small grin as it came to rest between her legs. She was always a little embarrassed about playing with herself but it had never stopped her. She had a vibrator in the drawer but not one shaped like a giant dick. It had a handle and a large round button, and it plugged into the wall, so she never had to worry about batteries. She'd let an ex-boyfriend use it on her once, but had decided that toys and men were better if used separately. She looked at the clock and jumped into the shower.

Now as she sat in the restaurant she could still smell the soap on her body and the spritz of perfume on her wrist. She had thought about Will as she stood in the shower, thought about them together under the warm spray, lathering each other up. She'd found her hand back between her legs.

"Oh boy," she said to herself, while shaking her head and grabbing a breadstick out of the green glass jar on the table. "I need to focus." She said it low since she was at the table by herself. Will had gotten up to wash his hands. She decided to focus on telling him about the flip-flop she'd found.

Going into the woods, picking up the shoe, disturbing a crime scene, and bringing evidence home was way wrong every step of the way and she knew it. She wasn't a cop, she was a citizen, and the correct thing to do was to keep her nosey-Parker nose out of it. But she hadn't been able to stop herself, and it was time to confess. Maybe he'd want to punish her. She squirmed in her seat a bit and took another bite of breadstick.

She had been careful about the transgression. The flip-flop was wrapped in a Safeway bag, she hadn't touched it, and she had been careful with how she handled it to avoid leaving any prints. So she would come clean, say she was sorry, say she got carried away, here's the evidence, no big deal. It probably didn't even belong to Phyllis and the bones probably didn't, either. It was all a big zero and meant nothing.

A flash of movement on the other side of the room caught her eye as she watched Will walking towards her. He moved gingerly, maneuvering around the tables, and Vivien thought he resembled a bear on roller skates. A big, cuddly bear. He hadn't worn his hat and Vivien was grateful to see a full set of blonde hair manicured into a crew cut, with every hair standing straight up at full attention. He wasn't completely graceful, but he oozed discipline.

He folded himself into the seat, looked her in the eye, and said,

"Sorry. I had to make a stop before here and didn't have time to get cleaned up."

"Oh," she said. "Crime scene?"

"No. On Natural Death, we don't call them crime scenes. I mean, if it is a crime scene, it goes to Homicide. Which I actually wouldn't mind doing someday."

"Sure," said Vivien. "It's probably more exciting or interesting, anyway."

"Yeah, maybe," said Will. "From what I've seen, Homicide is mostly about dumb-asses shooting other dumb-asses. People fighting over sneakers, cell phones, card games, bicycles. Mostly stupid shit, you know? Ooops, sorry. Didn't mean to say shit."

Vivien touched his hand and said, "It's okay, Will. I was in law enforcement. I've heard all the naughty words."

"Right, yeah, I know," he said. "But still. Hey, did I tell you the lab rats released some stuff on your bone? It was from a female—no determination on how old or how long in the woods yet."

"No. You didn't tell me that." Vivien swallowed hard as the possibility of the bones being Phyllis quickly flashed back.

Will snapped a breadstick in half and stuck a piece in his mouth. While looking Vivien in the eye, he said, "And McCain talked to the English lady . . . what's her name?"

"Sasha?"

"Right, Sasha. Anyway, he got a last name on your missing friend Phyllis, called the house, left a message, nothing. So he tracks down the husband, right? He's a chiropractor, does those stupid commercials you see on Saturday mornings. McCain called his office, but the guy's been in India for a month."

"Oh," said Vivien. "Well, that solves the case, doesn't it? They're in India. That's why nobody's seen them."

Will raised a finger and tilted his head slightly sideways. "But here's where it gets interesting," he said. "The girl who answers the phone at the office tells McCain the doctor's wife didn't go with him to India. She says he went by himself."

"Really?" asked Vivien.

"Really," said Will. "What do you think of that?"

"Hmm," said Vivien. "Could be suspicious."

"Yeah," said Will. "The English lady also said this Phyllis had a beef with the black chick. What's her name?"

"Linda?"

"Right, Linda. Says Linda threatened her with a knife."

"Oh, that's kind of an exaggeration, Will. 'Threatened with a knife' is kind of over-the-top." Vivien felt a flush of anger towards Sasha. What a bitch.

"Yeah? What would you call it? You were there, right?" He was looking right at her and she felt the lasers boring into her. How had the conversation gotten here? She was feeling like a suspect again. She needed to tell him about the shoe she'd found as soon as possible.

"It was nothing, really. Phyllis had issues with a lot of people. She was a, um, difficult person."

"Mmm-hmm," said Will and looked her up and down as she sat there mulling over the calamari. The conversation changed course after that, but Vivien could tell that the subject wasn't completely closed. He was investigating her. And she was interviewing him.

She found out he had been married once, to a librarian, but it didn't last very long. He owned a small house in the Northeast. His parents were retired and lived in Florida. He didn't have any kids; he bowled in a league on Tuesday nights in the winter and played on a softball team in the summer. Both leagues were run out of the precinct, so even when he was off-duty and having fun he was surrounded by cops. A hard life for a woman who wasn't a cop or a lover of all things cop.

His table manners were in place but a bit rusty, and she could tell he was trying hard to be on his best behavior. He was wearing one of those fake 1950s open collar shirts that looked like it belonged at a luau. He had on dark pants—not jeans—and black lace-up shoes with thicker-than-normal soles. Totally cop-like. The shirt tail was worn out over his pants and Vivien assumed he was armed. She assumed there was a 9 mm tucked into the small of his back, or maybe a .380 in an ankle holster. Most of the career officers that she knew always carried weapons in public.

Her thoughts turned to how the evening would end. Would he want to kiss her and would she let him? She would. What if he wanted to come in and go further than she wanted? She would ask him to leave. She doubted that things would go that far. It was a non-issue. They finished the meal and he paid after she made a half-serious protest and a suggestion about splitting the bill. At least he wasn't a cheapskate.

They rode home, talking about how neighborhoods in the District were changing practically in front of their eyes. She'd had three glasses of wine with dinner, which was one past her limit, and he'd plowed through three light beers. When he pulled up in front of her house, she made the move that was supposed to put her back on the straight and narrow. She was going to confess about the found shoe and turn it over.

He pulled up to the curb, stopped, and said, "Well . . . "

He was giving her the chance to get off the hook without the awkward kiss in front of the door routine. Or maybe he didn't want to pursue it. Maybe she had blown the deal. She was seized with a moment of panic and looked into his face. He was staring down at his lap and she could tell right away that he was just shy and unsure of himself around her. He didn't want to make a mistake.

"Will," she said. She liked the sound of her voice saying his name. "I want you to come in for a minute, there's something I have to show you."

She thought she saw the slightest movement of one corner of his mouth shoot up and he hunched forward to unsnap his seat belt. "Okay," he said with a smile.

What a dog, Vivien thought, grinning to herself. They stepped out and she waited for him to walk around so they could walk up to the house together.

"Do you think you're going to want coffee or anything? I'm not sure I even have any," said Vivien.

"No," he said, "I can't drink it this late, unless its decaf, so what's the point? I mean really, coffee with no caffeine, beer with no alcohol, organic lemonade—I don't get it."

"Well, you know some people just like the taste," she said.

"I guess."

They were filling in the gaps of silence as she unlocked the door, told Mooky to be quiet, pushed her away, dropped keys and purse on the table, and went towards the bathroom. "Be right back," she said over her shoulder. She liked how she felt comfortable enough to walk in with him and leave him alone in her home. It was a nice feeling. She rehearsed what she was going to say while she checked her teeth for stuck food, ran her fingers through her hair, and tilted her face in the mirror.

She came back out and he was standing in the dining room petting Mooky. "Oh, she has to go out, hang on a sec." She let Mooky out, came back, and stood to face him. "So," she said.

"Yeah," he said. "Listen, I have to tell you something."

She felt her heart dropping through the floor and knew this was where it would all go wrong. He was married, impotent, gay, or had a terminal illness. He was a serial rapist, lived with his parents, or liked to dress up as a woman. There was something terribly wrong with him and he was about to reveal it to her.

She braced for the impact and told herself it was better that she find out now. But she had her own little secret. If she went first, that would give her a few more precious moments to collect her thoughts and prepare for the horrible way this precious little romance was about to end.

"I know; I have to tell you something, too." Her eyes went to the top of the table, looking for the Safeway bag, and she felt a slight pang of confusion when she didn't see it. She could have sworn she'd left it on the table. She must have put it back on top of the armoire.

"Well, let me go first, okay?" he asked.

She could tell that he was stressed about whatever it was that he was about to say. "Okay," she said. "You go first."

He half turned away from her and it looked like he was pulling something out of a box on top of her table. He picked something up and put it on his head. When he turned back towards her he was wearing a fake Abe Lincoln beard and a cardboard stovepipe hat that she had bought for President's Day.

"What the hell is this?" he said, as a big grin opened up across the bottom of his face. He looked insanely funny as Abe Lincoln, and Vivien cupped her hand over her mouth and laughed till she started to double over.

"I mean really, Viv. You like guys to dress up like Abe? Is that what you're into?" This only made things funnier as she nodded her head, now pretending to admit to the fact that she had a fetish for Lincoln.

"Oh God," she said in between laughs. "I bought this for President's Day. They had a George Washington wig, too; I think it's in the other room. I really need to straighten this house up. Oh shit."

He was smiling at her, looking extremely goofy in the Lincoln garb. He had a nice smile, good teeth, and a devilish sense of humor. She touched his upper arm and bounced her head lightly against his shoulder.

Then she felt his hand on her shoulder and she looked up to see him looking at her in a very serious way. Or was trying very hard to look serious. He was still struggling to stop laughing.

"Hey. I know we just met and all. But I'm very attracted to you, Vivien," he said between laughs.

She was still giggling and it came out of her mouth before she knew she was going to say it.

"Well, why don't you do something about it, Abe?"

He looked hurt for a second, like he'd just been challenged by a schoolyard bully and was now facing his deepest, darkest fears. But then it was gone and the face showed something else. Willfulness. Without bothering to remove the hat or the fake beard he kissed her full on the lips. She felt his lips on hers and was surprised by how soft they felt. Such a hard man with sweet, soft lips. She fell into the kiss without a protest and kissed him back as he gently pulled her closer.

She felt his mouth open and didn't resist. Their tongues swirled around each other, flicking and twisting as she immediately felt a flush of heat between her legs. In that instant she decided she'd fuck him on top of the dining room table if that's what he wanted. She'd climb on top of him, spread her thighs, and ride him until they broke all the furniture in the house.

His arms went around her, squeezing her as he kissed her neck then took a couple little bites. She felt goose pimples rise on her shoulders as she imagined those lips and teeth biting her all over. She let out a little sigh, shuddered a bit, ran her hands up his back, feeling the material of his shirt and wishing it was skin.

He wheeled her around, pinning her back against the wall. She felt his hands go to her waist. Their strength circled her rib cage and for a second she wondered if the hands would go up, down, or if they should stop here and call it a night.

Her mouth went to his ear. She sucked the lobe between her lips and bit him back. Take that, Abe. With her nose she could feel the plastic ring that went around his ear holding the fake beard in place. It was too silly now, a funny distraction that had to go. She gently pulled the beard away and said, "Oh. It's you, Detective."

She took his chin in between her fingers and pulled his mouth back towards hers. His tongue worked its way back into her mouth; she sucked it gently and felt herself opening her thighs. Her hands went to his rump and she squeezed his cheeks, wondering what they looked like from behind. His hands were moving up towards her breasts and she couldn't wait for his touch. She thought about shoving him away from her and ripping her own blouse apart to expose herself to him.

"Wait," she said. And he instantly stopped. She realized the top of his thigh was between her legs. In this position she could wiggle her hips and take things to another level. She brushed a hand across her lips getting a whiff of her own lipstick or what was left of it. "Wow," she said. "Lose the hat, Abe."

He stepped back for a second to remove the hat as she felt his weight come off her body and she immediately wished it back. There wasn't going to be time to go upstairs.

"Come here," she said and she led him towards the couch in the living room. She heard him kicking his shoes off as she pulled the meaty hand along behind her, the fingers like little sausages curling slightly around her own. She stood in front of the couch and looked at the small pitiful cushion that had been cleared away. She had napped here a few days ago, cried, made a decision to clean the house and then had refilled the couch with piles of stuff. Just moving piles from one place to the next.

She grabbed a pile from the cushion and tossed it towards the far wall. Christmas lights coiled inside an Easter basket landed in the far corner. She grabbed a second pile and flung it across the room. Crepe paper bunting celebrating the 4th of July unfurled itself across the TV as it flew. Shoes, pillow cases, TV Guides, empty shopping bags, socks, rolls of duct tape went flying. After two more handfuls the couch was bare.

She turned to face Will and saw him pulling his shirt off. The chest hair was blonde, short and curly, not unattractive. She stepped towards him, kissed his neck and face. She felt his hands on the buttons to her top. And she intended to have him right here on the couch like they were high school kids. The fabric fell away from her breasts and the bra quickly followed. His mouth returned, found her nipples and played tag with them. She pulled him down onto the couch, reaching for his belt, anxious to see more of him. The belt hit the floor with a tinkling thud, followed by the pants, and she felt his hardness through his underwear. She rolled her hips to pull off her own jeans as she watched Will try to remove his skivvies and socks gracefully while balancing on one foot then the other.

The lights were off in the living room but there was enough

illumination coming in from the dining room to get a quick look at him, and she liked what she saw. And then he was kneeling in front of her reaching for the top of her panties. Did she want this to really happen? Now would be the time to say something. He was looking at her, moving his hands slowly like he was sensing the moment of decision. She felt his fingers on her waist, the material starting to slide down around her as she lifted her hips to make it easier.

She angled her hips towards him and pulled on his upper arm, easing him towards her. His fingers found the inside of her thigh, stroked it and then explored that area where her legs joined. He rubbed her in circles as she bit her lip to stifle a moan, which only partially succeeded. The rubbing continued as she sensed herself getting wet. A few more nibbles on the neck and she felt herself coming while mumbling, "Oh god, oh shit, it's been too long."

He pulled her close for a few seconds, giving her a chance to recover before moving between her legs.

"Are you okay with this? I'm healthy, but I didn't bring protection," he said.

"I don't care, Detective, just fuck me."

He pulled her hips to him and slid his length into her. Her back was on the cushion of the couch, her legs held open, her knees pointing up at the ceiling as he thrust into her, his hard belly slapping against the backs of her thighs. He grunted as the thrusts came quicker and deeper. She heard herself making sounds she didn't recognize. The window of pure animal pleasure swallowed her and she lost herself in the rutting. With a final heave, she felt him shudder and stop.

CHAPTER 13

Mooky lay on the porch in front of the door, keeping a sharp eye out for the animals that came out at night. Her vision was limited in the dark, so she pointed her nose in different directions to pick up anything that might increase her chances to find a raccoon or opossum, or the cat that lived down the street.

She occasionally let out short, grunty barks at the noises that were coming from inside the house. The new man was still in there and she assumed they were looking for the shoe that she had taken off the table and hidden in a special place. If they found it they could play Pull-the-Thing, which was one of her favorites. Vivien didn't like to play Pull-the-Thing, but Mooky was pretty sure the man would play.

After a while the bangs and bumps from inside the house stopped and Mooky was delighted to think that she might be allowed to stay outside all night and look for animals. But on the other hand, she wanted to go back in and see what she was missing. She missed Vivien and she wanted to see if the man was ready to play with her.

The door then opened and the man came out, moving a bit hesitantly, like he had just woken up. Mooky sniffed him for the shoe she'd hidden. A variety of other smells inside the house rushed out to meet her; she detected excitement, warm flowers, fruit, sweat, and something musty and earthy that she hadn't smelled in a long time. Apparently Vivien kept it in the closet with the old clothes and shoes. Mooky got between the man and Vivien to give her a good smell, but

Vivien grabbed her collar and pulled her into the house.

"Go lie down, Mooky," she said. Mooky knew the word "down" but chose to ignore it based on the tone of Vivien's voice. Mooky could tell she didn't really mean it. Instead, she stood inside the door panting, watching the man and Vivien touch noses.

"I'll call you," said the man. "Good night."

"Okay," said Vivien. "Good night, Abe."

And then she laughed a little. Mooky watched Vivien watching the man walk towards his car. He opened the gate in the fence, waved to them, and climbed into his car. As he closed the car door, Vivien looked at Mooky and said, "Oh my God." Her hand went to her face and she said, "Wow, I wasn't expecting that to happen." She ruffled the fur on Mooky's rump, which made her leg move in a scratching maneuver even though it wasn't close to scratching anything.

"Mommy just had some naughty fun, Mooky," said Vivien as she stopped the scratching.

Mooky didn't know any of these words and she wondered if they would be going into the kitchen now. It was the time of night when Vivien liked to eat ice cream and sometimes Mooky would get to lick the spoon or even get a few bites. She did know the words "ice cream," and she looked at Vivien and then looked towards the kitchen to tell her that she'd like some ice cream now. Her tail wagged slowly in big arcs as she moved her shoulders around so her body was pointing towards the ice cream—but Vivien was already walking through the house and turning off lights, which meant the day was over and it was time to sleep.

Tomorrow it would start all over again. There would be eating in the morning, looking for animals in the yard, napping, going to the park, and eating again, and then maybe the man would come over and Mooky would show him where she had hidden the shoe so they could play Pull-the-Thing. Mooky had already made up her mind that she would not show Vivien where the shoe was hidden, but she would trade it for the most wonderful bone in the world.

CHAPTER 14

Vivien called Lenny the next day and told him a few juicy tidbits about her date with Detective Evans. Will. His name was Will. She didn't want to recount the whole story blow by blow. He got her to reveal a lot of the details later as they walked through the woods while the dogs did their doggy thing. It was huge news at the dog park when somebody started having sex with somebody else, but Vivien wanted to keep this between her and Lenny. She would tell Linda at some point, but when it came to talking about these kinds of intimate adventures, Lenny was her go-to guy.

They strolled along the trail as a few stray cicadas buzzed somewhere in the trees above them.

"So, how was the meal?" He was imitating the voice of a Jewish mother, one of Vivien's favorite fictional characters that existed inside her friend's shiny skull. At any given time Lenny could change his voice to sound African-American, or drippingly gay, or he would imitate Sasha's clipped British accent. Vivien was amused by all of them, but the Jewish mother was one of her favorites. She tried to imitate him by using it back.

"Fine. The meal was fine." She tried drawing out the sound of the "i" while hunching her shoulders and using her hands like she'd thought she'd seen famous Jewish mothers doing on TV, but she wasn't very good at it. There weren't many Jews in Wisconsin. She had never actually met one till she moved to Washington. She wasn't really sure what all the fuss was about.

"And the dessert, darling—how was that?"

Lenny could make anything sound dirty by changing the inflections of his voice, which made Vivien cross her arms over her chest and giggle. They were walking with the dogs, just the two of them, on a level part of the trail that cut across a great rounded hill in Rock Creek Park. She looked down and saw glimpses of houses half-hidden by the trees. She assumed the houses belonged to rich people or old-time Washingtonians who were shrewd enough to buy homes that backed up to the park when nobody wanted to live in the District of Columbia. Now with the changing tide of real estate values, they were millionaires. Some of them, anyway.

"Fine, the dessert was fine." She tried the accent and the hand gestures again, this time picturing Joan Rivers in her head, but she knew she still looked and sounded like a slice of white bread from Wisconsin.

Lenny stopped, touched her forearm, cocked his head like some of the black chicks do when they're getting ready to say something important, and said, "Girl, are you goin' to give me some details or do I have to go upside your head?" Lenny was black now and Vivien had to stop walking so she could laugh with him. She loved Lenny like a sister even though he sometimes drove her crazy.

He rarely called her; she always had to call him. He used his answering machine to screen calls—she'd seen him do it to other people—and every time she called him and he didn't answer she pictured him standing there, looking at the phone and deeming it not important enough to pick up. In spite of the quirks, they shared many secrets, including the story of Lenny's most poignant lost love. He liked younger men with boyish good looks, tousled hair, and tight jeans. They couldn't be too effeminate. He enjoyed lavishing attention and gifts to any that he found worthy.

The one that did him in was an ex-patient he'd started having a relationship with—a big taboo right from the beginning. His name was Michael, a gorgeous but disturbed young man who died of a self-induced drug overdose on his 27th birthday. Lenny had to call the kid's parents and give them the bad news. He had never really recovered from the ordeal. Lenny turned his excess of affection to his dog, Buddy, a typically goofy, playful, and socially gifted Portuguese water dog that everybody found perfectly charming.

The park was a pleasant blur of greenery as a slight breeze

puffed across their faces. Vivien took Lenny's arm and said, "I can tell you that he is good with his hands."

"Oh no, you didn't," said Lenny, still black.

"Um-hmm," said Vivien, letting the hazy images of what happened on the couch hang out there like a juicy headline on the cover of a grocery store tabloid. She liked keeping him on the edge, making him work for the information. He was still too much of a southern gentleman to just blurt out exactly what he wanted to know. They reached the halfway point of the walk, a rounded hilltop that looked down on the creek. The dogs plunged down the hill, sensing the cool water below.

Vivien smiled, watching Lenny watch his dog, and her mind slipped back to thoughts of Phyllis, now possibly in India or maybe lying in the refrigerated dark confines of the DC morgue. Lenny suffered a run-in with Phyllis just like everybody else. Vivien flashed on the possibility that one of the characters living in Lenny's head could be capable of ending Phyllis's existence. It didn't seem plausible, but he did have a slow burning temper about certain things.

It was in between Thanksgiving and Christmas, the time when everybody's calendar filled up with holiday parties and informal gatherings. There were gallery openings to attend, concerts to experience, and events that required an appearance. The holidays would end with a bang on New Year's Eve and the District would go back to work until summer.

Since the dog park regulars were all, in their own way, social misfits, their calendars were not as full as those of the lawyers, journalists, lobbyists, or government workers that filled the neighborhoods of Washington. The dog park regulars were all from someplace else, their families and original social groups sequestered in the deep south, or out west, or hidden away in corners of New England. Because of this, the parties the regulars were invited to took on a deeper meaning. Invitations that were expected but never came drove home the fact that they were people who, for whatever reason, had an easier time dealing with canines than humans. They were by their nature dog people. Except for Phyllis.

Phyllis took a lot of heat behind her back for the fact that she didn't pay much attention to Boopsie, her bichon. Boopsie never ran or played with the other dogs, choosing instead to sleep on Phyllis's feet under the picnic table. Nobody was really sure why they even bothered coming to the park in the first place. Phyllis was more of a people person than any of them. She seemed to know everybody and dropped names like so many breadcrumbs in the woods.

She seemed to be on a first-name basis with lots of people who were nearly famous. In Washington that group included judges, congressional aides, and gobs of lawyers. Vivien never knew the people Phyllis was talking about and assumed she was totally out of touch with the movers and shakers. It didn't really bother Vivien that much, but Lenny was different.

For some reason that Vivien couldn't define, Lenny held onto Phyllis's description of her stuffy cocktail parties or dinner engagements like they were the crown jewels. Lenny would question Phyllis on the names and locations like he was chronicling her adventures through the District social scene. At first Vivien thought he was just being polite, but after a while she could tell that he was genuinely fascinated.

Vivien learned Phyllis's celebrity stories by heart after hearing them told over and over again by Lenny. She claimed to have met Chief Justice Rehnquist at Café Milano. She said she saw Wolf Blitzer having lunch at The Palm. She'd spotted James Carville at DC Coast and had seen Bo Derek at a fund-raiser in Great Falls.

Some senator's ex-wife came to dinner at Phyllis's house for Easter and some VP from AOL had once attended her Sunday brunch. Vivien typically yawned her way through the retelling of these tales, but Lenny was clearly enamored. The culmination of Phyllis's social season every year was what she called her "Winterfest Fantastique."

To avoid offending any particular religion or lifestyle she went overboard to make the celebration as non-denominational as possible. Although Phyllis mercilessly tormented individuals she considered to be her inferiors, she bent over backwards to honor large groups of people that contained those she wanted to impress.

Vivien remembered seeing Lenny and Phyllis sitting at the picnic table on that crisp day in late fall, the sun already hanging lower in the sky and providing a hint of the dark days of winter to come.

"So we're expecting forty-eight people, but I wouldn't be surprised if we ended up with closer to fifty-two," said Phyllis. "I was going to do something more continental this year, but Harish likes the Indian menu so much . . ."

"Fifty-two. Wow, and these are most of the people that you normally have?" said Lenny. "I mean, you know, your regular crowd?"

"Oh, yeah," said Phyllis. "All the regular suspects, along with a few special guest stars we're bringing in for the occasion. This year will be truly fantastique."

"Really?" said Lenny. "Well, do tell, darling, who's coming?"

Vivien cringed at Lenny's dying curiosity. He was such an old lady sometimes. Loved the gossip.

"Oh, no one you would know," said Phyllis. She had him right where she wanted him and began hanging him out to dry. Vivien felt sorry for him and was about to jump in and change the subject to something more dog-centric before he got hurt, but it was too late.

"Well, can you at least give us a hint—is there anybody coming from here?" asked Lenny.

Vivien suddenly realized that he was angling for an invitation, hoping against hope that by paying close attention to Phyllis he would somehow find his way onto her guest list. With his last remark, he had left himself wide open. Vivien waited for the axe to drop, hoping for mercy.

"Oh, please," said Phyllis. "This isn't a party for dog people."

There was silence at the picnic table except for the whish of traffic going by on Military Road. Vivien was aware that she had just been insulted, too, but didn't really care. She'd take a polka dance party over cocktails with Phyllis anytime. But Lenny was furious and he was now barely concealing it behind his broad southern smile.

"I see," said Lenny. "So, what kind of party would dog people be invited to?" He wasn't black or Jewish or British when he said this. He was playing it straight down the line.

"Beats me," said Phyllis. "Who would want to throw one of those? Maybe a keg of beer, dirty dungarees, and plenty of monogrammed poop bags, I guess." And then the cackling laugh came out, ringing into the dead air around the picnic table. Lenny's face went blank as Vivien watched him politely end his conversation with Phyllis, looked at Vivien with arched eyebrows and said, "Walkies?"

"Certainly," said Vivien. They both knew it was pointless to invite Phyllis to walk with them through the woods. Phyllis was not a walker, nor was her little white dog. They were sit and yakkers. As they walked out of earshot from the picnic table, Lenny called Buddy behind them as Mooky led them towards the shadowy confines of the trail to the point.

"You know," said Lenny, "there are times when I would really enjoy pulling Phyllis into the woods and snapping her fucking neck like a chicken bone."

The words had always stuck in Vivien's head. Lenny could curse like a sailor, and he harbored grudges, but she didn't consider him to be a violent man. Her thoughts returned to the present as she looked down at him kneeling over Buddy, fussing around with wiping the dog's mouth with a napkin from Popeye's Chicken.

He was an average height and powerfully built. He'd once told her that his father owned an industrial roofing company in the small town where he grew up. The summers of his youth were spent pouring asphalt and gravel in the hellish environment of flat roofs in South Carolina. She was sure that under the right circumstances Lenny was more than physically able to kill.

He already had a motive and the means, and had told her in anger that he was looking for the opportunity. She looked away from Lenny, looked away from the spot where the bones came from and back towards the millionaires' homes. Lenny was a lot of things but he wasn't a killer. The whole thing was just a stupid misunderstanding, just like all the other stupid misunderstandings that people had with Phyllis. She was pretty much convinced of that. Pretty much.

CHAPTER 15

Vivien eventually did finish telling Lenny as much as she was going to about her tryst with Detective Will Evans, which was everything except the part about removing a flip-flop from near the spot where the bones were found. She wanted to tell Will about it, she really did, but then their clothes flew off and the focus changed. She also knew she was out-of-line by withholding evidence, but she wanted to stay involved. The shoe kept her in the game even if she was currently watching from the sidelines.

These feelings were compounded as she cleared off the dining room table for the third time in two days. She pulled a dining room chair over to the armoire, stood on top and performed a thorough search but couldn't find the flip-flop. Mooky watched her, sitting by the front door. She looked at Vivien until she made eye contact and then looked towards the door, indicating that she wanted to go out.

"All right, all right, we're going," said Vivien as she looked for the leash and stuffed Safeway bags into her pockets. "I just wish I could find that damn shoe. I can't really confess to tampering with evidence if I can't find the evidence, can I?" She walked aimlessly through the rooms, occasionally stopping to lift a magazine or a pile of laundry to see if it had somehow gotten buried during the scene on the couch.

Will called her the next day, acting a bit sheepish about how things had gotten what he called "hot and steamy." She told him it wasn't his fault and to not feel guilty about it. It had just happened, that's all, and they'd both enjoyed it. She had learned to compartmentalize things in her life from the years of being in law enforcement.

Besides that, what was the big deal? They were both adults. They hadn't used protection, and she was a little concerned about that, but she also knew cops had to get physicals on a regular basis and Will seemed to be the type of man to take good care of himself. The chance of an unwanted pregnancy at Vivien's age was a possibility, but she considered it remote.

On the phone they decided to try again to have a normal date without screwing on her couch like a pair of horny high-schoolers. He was currently working double shifts to make extra money, so they decided when his schedule returned to normal they would take another shot at it.

Vivien found Mooky's leash and she snapped its fastener, a sound that Mooky recognized as "go-outside time." The Lab came to her, the great tail swooshing through the afternoon sunbeams piercing the windows, creating happy dog shadows on the floor.

"That's right," said Vivien, "we're going." The "go" word intensified the dog's movements as she went to the back door. Vivien picked up her keys, looked again at the top of the dining room table, then at the top of the armoire, searching for the Safeway bag that would reveal the missing flip-flop. The top of the table showed the same thing as before—nothing. She looked at Mooky, who stood by the door with her nose touching the knob, making it impossible to enter or exit without her knowing about it.

As Vivien looked at Mooky and then back at the table, a stab of realization shot up her spine. "Did you take something off this table?" she asked Mooky. Vivien looked at the dog, searching for a clue, but all she saw was a dog who wanted to go to the park. Mooky had taken a roast beef off that table as a puppy. Vivien had punished her severely for it and was relieved that the habit seemed to have been nipped in the bud. Or had it?

"Did you?"

"Mooky?"

CHAPTER 16

Mooky looked at Vivien, knowing that she suspected her of having something to do with the disappearance of the shoe. Vivien was looking at the top of the table and then back at Mooky. Mooky knew that she had been caught and acknowledged the fact by dropping the corner of her left ear just slightly. She began panting, glanced upstairs towards where the shoe was hidden, then looked back at Vivien. Then she looked back to the door to tell Vivien she didn't want to talk about the shoe right now, because it was time to go to the dog park.

Vivien looked away from Mooky and back to the table, the place that Mooky was forbidden to go. She was not allowed on top of the table, but the lure of the shoe was too much to resist.

Mooky had no intention of showing the shoe to Vivien. She was saving it, hiding it in the special place where it would remain until the man came back. The man would play Pull the Thing with her and Vivien would not. Therefore Mooky would ignore Vivien's requests for the shoe. Her voice tone gave no indication that she was serious about the shoe and besides, it was time to go to the dog park. Vivien had the car keys in her hand.

Mooky stood her ground, put her nose back on the cool, brassy door knob, swooped her tail, and waited. She did not look at Vivien, or where the shoe was hidden, or towards the table. She pointed towards where she wanted to go and waited for the situation to resolve itself. She heard Vivien sigh and say, "You better not have." Mooky didn't know any of these words and soon she began hearing the sounds of leaving for the dog park—the magical time of "go."

Keys rattled, locks turned, and the door opened. The smells of the outside rushed in to greet her. There was grass and garbage, flowers, and a fresh scent from the cat up the street. Animals had walked through the yard the night before, leaving small traces of smells from the woods. The street brought her car exhaust and warm motor oil. The van door opened and she smelled herself, dust, newspapers, and the old lady who used to own the car. There was still a trace of tobacco smoke and her scent.

They were moving and the window jumped down, letting in the wind from outside. Fruit trees and the earthy wet smells from the woods told her that it was time to run in the park. The door popped open and smells of many dogs that played here blew through her nostrils. She leaped out into the wide world as the past fell behind her. She ran free into the sounds, sights, and smells found in the time of go.

CHAPTER 17

"Shit," said Vivien. "Walter."

She recognized his minivan when she pulled in, but was hoping he was in the woods with Lucky Dog. Walter was an inconsistent walker. He seemed to go through phases where he would walk every day for a couple of weeks in a row before lapsing back into the sedentary life spent around the picnic table. Like all the other dog park regulars, Walter had his own set of quirks and somewhat disagreeable personality traits.

He was a cynical smart ass with the intellectual capacity to cut swift and deep. He liked to drink. Upon spotting the Titleist bumper sticker on Vivien's car, he claimed to be an avid golfer. He was married to a Korean woman who had made a career working for the federal government and probably brought home enough dough to support Walter's always sketchy writing career.

He had an opinion on everything and didn't mind sharing it with anyone who cared to listen. For a while last summer he had taken to bringing plastic pitchers of horrible margaritas to the park and dispensing tastes in Styrofoam cups to anybody brave enough to sample his brew. Vivien was one of the chosen few and this was how the problem with Walter got started.

She closed the back door of the van and looked around the trees towards the picnic table. Sure enough, there he was. Sitting at the table by himself, staring towards the woods at nothing. She could pretend that she hadn't seen him and just head down the path by herself, but she didn't like to walk through the woods alone. The social aspect of the walk was important for Mooky and herself as well.

She was sure he had seen her pull in and it would be rude to just ignore him, even though he probably couldn't care less. She was raised to be a polite person, so she walked slowly towards the picnic table, already thinking of a quick conversation that would lead to a smooth getaway. She kept Mooky close to prevent another bolt into the woods. She looked over her shoulder hoping to see Lenny or Linda pull in behind her, but the parking lot remained empty.

She walked towards him trying to figure out the power he held over her. How was it that he was able to get her to reveal intimate details about herself that she normally didn't tell anybody else? It happened that day when he was going through his margarita phase as Vivien sat there and drank three of the horrible things.

Maybe it was the tequila that made her tell the story about how as a high school junior she was caught on the couch with her boyfriend with her panties around her ankles. Her mother came home from a bridge game earlier than expected and found her daughter in this compromising position with the captain of the junior varsity basketball team.

Vivien's mother called her a slut, slapped her face, and threatened to throw her out of the house. Things were never quite the same between Vivien and her mother after that. Over the years her emotions about the incident evolved from guilt to shame to anger that was eventually numbed into nothingness. As she watched her mother's strong personality wither into dementia while she struggled through her final days, Vivien reflected back on the incident and sadness for an opportunity lost. That piece of emotional wreckage was over and done, it couldn't be repaired and the scar still remained.

For reasons Vivien still couldn't explain, the only person on the planet she had ever told this to was Walter. He had listened with typical non-reaction as Vivien amped up the details, trying to get a rise out of him, but he remained nonplussed through the entire performance. Even now, a year after his margarita period, Vivien caught herself telling stories around Walter and watching his face to gauge his reaction. There never was any and this drove her crazier than anything.

"Fucking Walter," she said under her breath as she approached the table. Physically there was no attraction, a fact confirmed as she approached the table. He had strings of long hair swept back across his skull and a face that perennially looked sad with age and worry. There were bags under his eyes and jowls hanging from the sides of his oversized head.

"Viv . . ." was all he said, which said so much more.

"Walter . . ." said Vivien while making a conscious effort to keep her guard up. "How are you?"

"Swell," said Walter. "How goes the criminal investigation?"

"What investigation?" asked Vivien.

"The mysterious case of the missing deer bone," said Walter.

"Actually, it's human. The detective told me they're still running tests. I also found a shoe in the woods." As soon as she said it Vivien had the urge to clamp her hand over her big mouth like the kids used to do in the Little Rascals. What the hell was the matter with her? What strange powers emanated from the guy at the picnic table with pizza stains on his Penn State t-shirt?

"A shoe, huh?" said Walter. "Well, that should prove things beyond a shadow of a doubt."

Vivien felt a moment of relief like she'd just caught herself from falling. This was why it was okay to tell Walter anything—because he didn't care about anything. It was all a big joke to him.

"Prove what beyond a shadow of a doubt?" asked Vivien.

"Well, aren't you and Sasha entertaining the notion that the alleged deer bone is all that remains of our missing and presumed dead Phyllis?"

"Sasha said that, not me," said Vivien.

"Yeah, well, whatever," said Walter as he called Lucky Dog back towards the table. "Did you turn the shoe over to your buddies in blue, like a good girl?"

He wasn't looking at her, which was good, because she was sure her face was registering shock. And then she remembered the bad thing about telling Walter anything. He had an uncommon knack for getting to the heart of the matter very quickly and exposing things for what they really were. All the time you thought he wasn't paying attention he was actually two steps ahead of everybody else.

"I don't think it's hers anyway," said Vivien. "The shoe or the bone. I don't think humans decompose that fast. I mean, how long has it been since anybody's seen her?"

Walter squinted into the sun and said, "Probably a couple of weeks for me. But if somebody threw an accelerator on the body, you know, lime or something like that, it could go to bone pretty quick."

He paused for a second, sucked a tooth, and looked like he was thinking about something far away. "Good riddance either way, I say. She was a cunt with a capital K."

"Walter! That's a horrible word. I can't believe you said that."

"Yeah, well. Sorry, but she was."

"What did she ever do to you?"

"You weren't here that day?"

"What day?"

"The day she tried to run me over with her car."

"Um, no," said Vivien, hoping against hope that there was more to the story and that Walter would tell her so she would at last have something to stack against the secret things that he knew about her. The big head turned towards her, the eyes gone to slits as he looked at her like he was examining a bug.

"The bitch tried to kill me. Sasha was here. She saw the whole thing. I was going to press charges, but Sasha talked me out of it. Said Phyllis was off her meds or something."

"Off her meds?" asked Vivien.

"Yeah, you know. Antidepressants, mood levelers, whatever you want to call them. Phyllis was like a walking pharmaceutical experiment gone haywire. You didn't know that?" Walter made the tooth sucking sound again. He was so gross and he stopped talking, now stringing out the juicy details.

"So what happened?" asked Vivien.

"Nothing. Bunch of shit over nothing."

"Tell me, Walter."

He exhaled louder than what was necessary and turned to face her, straddling the bench. He looked around like he wanted to make sure they were alone, which seemed a little melodramatic to her. They were in the middle of the field at the picnic table. He dropped his head, looked Vivian in the eye and said, "Phyllis wanted me to fuck her."

"What?" said Vivien. "Oh, please. She's married to Harish."

"No shit. Only thing is Harish won't, you know, go down on her."

"Oh, come on, Walter." Vivien felt dirty and guilty listening to the baloney coming out Walter's mouth, but she was hoping he would continue. Could any of it be true? Was Phyllis on drugs?

"Swear to fucking Christ, she sat right here on this bench, told me she and Harish or whatever his name is hadn't had sex in eight years and said she wanted me to, um, service her." Walter was holding his hand up like he was being sworn in, but technically it was the wrong hand.

The pictures running through Vivien's mind were too bizarre to be believed. Walter and Phyllis? Granted, neither one were what you would call beautiful people, but she had a hard time believing there could be an attraction between them.

"So what did you tell her?"

"First of all, I told her I was married. And second of all if I was going to risk blowing my marriage for a fling, it would have to be something very special—more, um, special than her."

"And?"

"She took a certain amount of offense to that," said Walter. "She turned her back to me and I said good-bye. I was putting the dog in the car when I hear a car start on the other side of the parking lot. I'm walking around to get in my car and here comes fucking Phyllis in her Volvo. She just misses running me over as I jump out of the way. She's going so fast, she hops the curb and hits the tree that used to be right there." Walter pointed to a line of small saplings lining the parking lot and sure enough, there was one missing. A gap in the smile of baby oaks ringing the asphalt.

"The Park Police shows up. Phyllis's trying to pull the tree out of her grill. Remember when her car went to the shop for a month? Sasha's crying and telling me to not say anything. It was fucked up, man."

"Wow," said Vivien. "I never heard about any of that."

"Yeah, well, nobody did. That was the point," said Walter. "Serves her right if somebody conked her over the head and dragged her into the woods. Maybe they gave her some before she died, so she went out with a smile on her face."

"Stop, Walter. That's terrible."

"Yeah well, she isn't a nice person, Viv. There's a lot of people out there we'd be better off without." He went silent as the big head dropped towards the ground and he seemed to study the patch of bare ground under the picnic table. Then it rose again to face her, the squinty eyes boring in.

"I think she and Sasha were fucking, too."

"What?" said Vivien and once again she felt the earth move under her feet.

CHAPTER 18

Vivien spent the rest of her time that day at the park in a disconnected daze. She caught herself looking at Walter sideways, trying to picture him smashing Phyllis in the head with a rock as they struggled through a murder scene that could have happened in that place in the woods. She watched Mooky to see if the dog had picked up on the weird vibe she was feeling, but the black Lab appeared perfectly normal in her routine. Sasha arrived and Vivien tried to picture her and Phyllis in bed together doing god knows what. She shuddered and looked back at Walter, now talking to a radiologist about how the Chinese were screwing up HD television standards. He was so full of shit.

Everything seemed perfectly normal, but it wasn't. Everything was in fact spinning slowly out of control for Vivien. Her compact, predictable little world was ripping apart, one snapped thread at a time, and so far she was enjoying every second of it. She watched Linda throwing a dirty tennis ball to her Great Dane, who pounced and loped after it, occasionally pausing to sniff and scratch the ground. She panned her head to watch Sasha showing pictures of the dogs to some other semi-regulars at the picnic table. Vivien felt herself floating above the scene and watching it like a trained observer.

Distance was what she needed. Some perspective would be nice. She vowed to get her ducks in a row and then shoot them in the head, as one of her ex-sergeants used to say. She must find the flip-flop that had somehow vanished in her mess of a house. She had to figure out how to handle this Will situation, and she wanted to find out Phyllis's last name. With a name she might be able to run down a phone number and an address. With an address she could do a little surveillance, maybe talk to some of the neighbors, see if they had seen anything unusual going on.

She caught herself hovering above the table and forced herself back to earth. What was she thinking? Talk to the neighbors? Is this what she had turned into? A neighborhood vigilante running around half-cocked and interfering with a police investigation? She felt herself slipping into an imaginary universe where she was Agatha Christie and everybody around her—the people she saw on a daily basis—were murder suspects. Colonel Mustard in the drawing room with the lead pipe? Linda and the chef's knife? Lenny with his strong hands wrapped around Phyllis's neck? Walter with a bloody rock in his hand, "giving her some" before he finished her off? Isn't that what he said?

It was stupid. None of this could have happened. It was all in her imagination. Except the bone was real. And the shoe was real but maybe not related. What happened on the couch with her and Will? Probably a mistake, but real. One thing was for sure, she wasn't Agatha Christie. She had never read any of the books. She shuddered at the thought that she was turning into an aging spinster. The kind of women who vanished into senility with a house full of cats—except she had a dog.

Vivien physically drifted towards the picnic table, tuning into the conversation as the words registered in her brain. The topic was familiar. Vets. Some were expensive and some were arrogant. Some were way out in Virginia and some also worked on horses. Some did acupuncture and some recommended raw meat diets. Blah, blah, blah—she had heard it all before. She watched Sasha out of the corner of her eye while drifting towards Lenny. He was talking to a woman who owned a clothing store about baseball. From what Vivien could gather, neither one of them had been to a game in a long time, but they might like to go someday.

There were lots of those conversations at the park. Ideas and notions that didn't get acted on because they would upset the daily routine, which was comfortable and predictable. Everybody talking about what they should do or could do or ought to do one of these days when they could get around to it.

"When's the next game?" asked Vivien.

"What?" asked Lenny.

"The next baseball game, when is it?" she said.

"Well, I don't know, Viv. Why, you wanna go watch some boys play baseball?"

"Sure, why not?" said Vivien. "Let's get a group and go. Maybe me, you, Sasha, Linda, Walter; I could even ask Will. He likes sports." And so just that fast, a plan was hatched. Not much of a plan, but still, it would give Vivien a chance to circulate among them and provide an opportunity to get them all away from their home base. Maybe a few beers at the ballpark, a little distraction mixed with a little boredom, could open up a world of possibilities.

"Who has a paper?" she said to nobody in particular. She scanned the top of the picnic table. Sometimes people would bring a newspaper to talk about a restaurant review or, more likely, a column about dog food or training methods, but Vivien didn't see one.

"What do you want to know?" asked Linda, who paused in her ball throwing to look at Vivien.

"Baseball," said Vivien. "We're going to see a game."

"Who's we?" asked Linda.

"All of us—you, me, Sasha, Walter and Lenny," said Vivien.

"O's or Nats?" asked Linda.

"Whoever is closer," said Vivien.

"That would be the Nats," said Linda. "They're starting a three-game series with the Mets, so they'll be playing on Saturday. Want to shoot for that?"

Vivien remembered that Linda played catcher in a women's baseball league. "Fast pitch, hardball," as she liked to point out, not softball.

"Perfect," said Vivien. "I'll find out about tickets."

CHAPTER 19

Mooky sat on her haunches in the dining room, sensing that something had changed. Vivien had pulled the trashcan into the house. The can was a source of many strong smells—she had never seen it in the house before. Vivien then brought in two other plastic containers, one of which was also used outside to hold cans and bottles, but it rarely held any good smells. The third one was brand new and it just smelled like plastic.

Mooky watched Vivien struggle to bring in all the cans since there wasn't much room in the house to start with. Vivien started picking things up, looking at them, and putting them in one of the cans.

The game began to take on new interest for Mooky when lost dog toys began to appear from beneath the piles. For a long time the toys had lain hidden under piles of newspapers or other stuff, but now they were returned to Mooky. Once again, they were hers. She piled them between her paws, sniffing them to see where they had been, as her great tail occasionally thumped against the floor, making happy dog sounds.

While this was going on the ringing machine went off on a regular basis and Mooky heard Vivien using the magic word by saying things like, "It would be fun; do you want to go?" Of course Mooky wanted to "go" and this caused her tail to thump louder on the floor. Then Vivien would say, "It's Saturday night at seven and I figured we could just go in one car." Mooky was excited about going in the car and wondered if it was time to go to the park and see the dog pack, but the sun didn't look quite right.

Then Vivien put down the ringing machine and went back to her work of putting different things in the cans. She started making a sound with her mouth, a sound she made when she wanted to play—and Mooky's tail thumped a bit stronger in response. She was fun when she was happy, and this made Mooky even happier. Mooky thumped her tail and occasionally captured a toy between her jaws, gave it a shake to make sure it was dead, and then dropped it back between her paws as she watched Vivien making her way around the living room and working her way towards the dining room.

As Vivien started picking things up that were on top of the table, Mooky's tail stopped thumping and her ears dropped. She lowered her head onto the pile of toys between her paws and watched Vivien continue to examine objects that sat on top of the table. Some things went into the garbage, some went into the one that held the bottles and cans, and many went into the new container, as Mooky became more anxious.

Vivien worked her way to the spot where the shoe used to be. This was a cause for concern, since the shoe belonged to Mooky and she was saving it for when the man came back so they could play Pull-the-Thing. If the game continued this way, Vivien would eventually make it all the way upstairs, look under the bed, and find the shoe. This would not do. Mooky got up very quietly and walked into the kitchen. She sniffed at the water bowl to see if anything had changed about it, checked the food bowl to make sure Vivien hadn't put anything in it while she wasn't looking, and then walked to the back door.

She sniffed around the door to make sure nobody had come in while she wasn't looking and then nudged it around the handle. Sometimes when she did this the door would open and she could let herself into the back yard. The back yard was fenced, but there were lots of good places to hide things outside. The nudge on the door worked. It opened a crack and Mooky got a whiff of the outside air. It was warm out there and she could smell flowers, the cat from up the street, and freshly cut grass.

Mooky walked out of the kitchen and watched Vivien still playing the can game with the things on the table. She stopped for a second, looked at Mooky and said, "Did you take a shoe off this table? Did you?" Mooky kind of knew the word "shoe." She raised her ears and tail as she went on alert and started to pant. She tried not to look upstairs towards the shoe. She didn't want to give Vivien any hints, since the shoe still rightfully belonged to Mooky.

Vivien stared at her for a second and Mooky did her best not to look guilty by not really looking anywhere specific. "You better not have," said Vivien, and returned to her can game. Mooky dropped her ears and tail while working her way around the cans and climbing the steps as quietly as possible. She nudged the bedroom door open and dropped to her belly, extending her paws under the bed. When she was a puppy she slept under here, but as she got bigger it was harder to fit. She'd gotten stuck once and now avoided going all the way under. She flopped onto her side, scooched her head under till she could see the shoe, and then used her paws to pull it close till she got a grip on it and pulled it out.

She used her jaws to change her grip a few times till she felt like it wasn't going to fall out, and walked quietly to the top of the stairs. Gauging the sounds of the room, she waited until Vivien was far away. As she climbed down the steps she could hear things being flung into the cans and for a moment she considered starting a new game where she would try to catch the things in the air as they were headed towards the can. This would be an excellent game since anything that Mooky could catch would become hers. But first she had to finish the shoe game.

She reached the bottom of the steps and looked towards where the sounds were coming from. Vivien had her back turned, so Mooky made her move. With ears down and tail held very low, she slinked towards the back door with the shoe held in her mouth. Mooky nudged the door with her nose just as something large crashed into a can. She squeezed herself through the crack of the door.

The door closed behind her as the latch snapped shut and Mooky headed towards the row of hedges that lined the house. There was a small opening in the hedges—too small for Vivien—and she pushed herself through. Once she was all the way behind the bushes, Mooky dug a hole in the sweet moist earth and buried the shoe.

CHAPTER 20

Vivien was feeling pretty good abut what she was calling in her mind "the Baseball Game Plan." After a set of selective phone calls, the suspects that she wanted to observe or interview had committed to attending the Washington Nationals versus the New York Mets. She reconsidered including Will in her plans, but he was working nights, which made him unavailable.

Besides that, she still hadn't told him about the shoe, or resolved how she was going to deal with the fact that they had sex on their very first date without even making it to the bedroom. She really wanted to tell him about the shoe in person, so she put off the conversation and concentrated on her investigation. The other problem was that even after a pretty extensive house cleaning, the shoe was still missing.

The search-and-sort mission did turn up a moldy salami sandwich, large stacks of now recycled newspapers, eight half-full bottles of body lotion, five dead batteries, two television remotes, and a variety of decorations from six different national holidays. The good news was that for the first time in two years, Vivien's downstairs looked presentable. She was even able to run the sweeper and do some dusting.

All the cleared space caused a headful of mixed emotions. She felt a sense of accomplishment . . . but also anxiety, since the upstairs and basement were just as cluttered. She shoved the holiday decorations into the small shed in her backyard, cringing about the fact that it was overflowing, too. Still, she had made a sizable dent in the piles and had successfully organized a group activity that was about to commence. The plan was to drive over to Lenny's house and have a drink before picking everybody else up for the game.

Lenny was actually the lowest suspect on her list, since Vivien didn't really believe he was violent by nature. The reason she hadn't completely ruled him out was his remark about snapping Phyllis's neck like a chicken bone.

She was driving with the windows open in the minivan, partially because she enjoyed the feeling of wind blowing on her skin and partially because the van's air conditioner was broken and had been for at least three summers. It needed something that cost eight hundred dollars to fix. Vivien didn't do that much driving, so it remained broken.

She parked in front of Lenny's house, let herself in through the open front door and yelled, "Hellloooo . . . "

"Be right down," came the reply, as Buddy the Portuguese water dog bounded down the stairs and greeted Vivien with a wet nose.

"Hi, Buddy, let's see what Daddy's got in the kitchen, okay?"

Vivien walked towards the kitchen hoping to find an open bottle of chilled white wine. As she walked through the house, she scanned Lenny's belongings: familiar piles of unopened mail, the TV schedule with tennis matches circled, and the most recent copy of "Opera Magazine."

She heard Lenny come down the steps and noticed he was wearing the male version of her outfit.

"Darling," he said while opening his arms. "How are you, sweetie?" He kissed her delicately on the lips and said, "A cocktail to start things off?"

"Absolutely," she replied, "but not too many, since I'm driving."

"Of course," he said. "I have a bottle of California grig—will that do for you?"

"Sure, that's fine," said Vivien. She felt the slight embarrassment about not really knowing if she liked California grig or any other kind of grig, but she was pretty sure it was a white. She relaxed her shoulders as she watched him go towards the fridge.

"I forgot you like opera," she said.

"Mad for it, sweetie," he said, "always have been. When I was a kid I listened to 'Live at the Met' on NPR. My parents knew there was something different about me, even at a tender age."

Vivien smiled at the way Lenny made everything sound dramatic as the cork popped out of the bottle.

"Operas are bloody, aren't they?" asked Vivien. "Isn't there a lot stabbing and sword fights and stuff?"

"Well, there can be, Viv, it just depends on the opera. Poisoning is pretty popular, too."

"I guess it's mostly about the singing, right?" asked Vivien.

"Exactly, darling. Here we go." Lenny handed her a glass of wine with some room left at the top. She watched him take a quick sniff from his glass and raise it to his lips. She mimicked his movements.

"Why?" said Lenny, "Do we have murder on our minds?"

"Well, I can't stop thinking about the bone and Phyllis and all that," said Vivien.

"Honey, we are better off without her, wherever she is," said Lenny. "And I have a hard time believing that bone belongs to her." Lenny then cocked his head, wagged his finger in her face, and became a black girl. "Put that stuff out of your mind, sugar. We about to go watch some boys play baseball in tight pants, and that's all that you should be thinking about."

"Who's that voice?" asked Vivien.

"What voice?"

"That voice you just did. Does that girl have a name?"

Lenny fanned his fingers over his chest and became Scarlet O'Hara, a new incarnation that Vivien hadn't seen before.

"Well, I do declare, darling. Whatever are you talking about?" asked Lenny.

"That. See? You're doing it again. You probably don't even know you're doing it. Do you have names for all those different voices in your head?"

Lenny bent at the waist and made a big show of laughing. "My mimicry? Oh, sweetie, those aren't voices in my head, I'm just imitating people I've heard all my life. Everybody in my family does it. Didn't yours?"

Vivien tried to remember her parents talking in funny voices, but knew before she started that it was a waste of time. Her parents didn't do funny. She liked to laugh and would pick a romantic comedy over a drama on TV anytime. Maybe that's why she liked Lenny so much—he was funny all the time. "So you don't think you have multiple personalities or anything like that?" asked Vivien.

Lenny turned from her, topped off his wine, and turned back while cocking his head. "Multiple? Um, no, sweetie, nothing as dramatic as all that."

"Well, let me ask you something else," said Vivien. "If a person had multiple personalities, could one of them be a violent psycho-killer without the person knowing it?"

"Oh, I see where you're going with this," he said. He pointed a finger towards the ceiling, paced in front of the couch for a few steps with his head down, and then said, "I'm a suspect, aren't I? You're playing police detective, aren't you? You can't let it go, can you, sweetie?" He was pointing at her and she felt herself blush.

"No. It's not that. I mean, I just think it's funny the way you can do those voices and I've seen movies about people with more than one personality and I . . ." she trailed off as he gave her a dismissive wave and brought a finger to his lips like he was thinking about something.

"Viv. Come on. But I know what you're talking about. The whole *Sybil* thing," said Lenny. "*The Three Faces of Eve*. It's actually extremely rare, multiple personality disorder. I don't have it, by the way. But I do like this parlor game of discovering the murderer—assuming she's actually been murdered. And I'm a suspect, because why?"

"You said you wanted to snap her neck like a chicken bone."

His eyebrows shot up. He approached her and touched her forearm with outstretched fingers, looking like he was struggling to swallow the wine in his mouth without choking.

He swallowed hard and said, "I did say that, didn't I? Because that bitch snubbed me over her stupid party. Oh, this is good. Who are my fellow suspects?"

"Well," said Vivien. "There's you, Linda, Walter, and maybe Sasha."

"Sasha? Her majesty? But she and Phyllis were thick as thieves. What would be her motive?"

"Walter says they were lesbian lovers."

Lenny sprayed wine out of his mouth like one of the Three Stooges and stomped his foot on the floor like he was trying to put out a fire. This caused Buddy to bark and run to the front door. Lenny started choking as he waved his hand in front of his mouth and did half turns in the living room looking for a towel or something to wipe his mouth on.

Between chokes he said, "Lesbian . . . lovers . . . Sasha . . . Phyllis . . . shut up, Buddy! . . . Walter said what?" Lenny walked out of the room, doubling over from laughing, choking, yelling at the dog, and trying to talk, while Vivien collected herself.

Had she tipped her hand? Not really. Confronting the suspect with suspicions was always part of a standard investigation and she had taken note of his reactions. She knew he didn't have multiple personality disorder, but he was intrigued by his inclusion in the suspects. He admitted to threatening Phyllis in an offhand way and he seemed to be skeptical about Sasha and Phyllis.

He came back into the living room holding a damp paper towel. Sitting on the couch, he pulled Buddy towards him and dried his eyes. "Oh my god, that's too much," said Lenny. "Now why (cough) would Walter think that?"

"I don't know," said Vivien, "but I intend to ask him."

"I see," said Lenny, while again pointing his finger to the ceiling and looking a bit like Sherlock Holmes. "So you've gathered your suspects for a night of questioning at the ball game—very clever, darling." He was the Jewish lady at the end of the sentence. "But aren't you forgetting somebody?" he asked.

"Who?"

"Well, as I recall there was no love lost between you and Phyllis," said Lenny.

"But I know I didn't do it, so I'm ruling myself out," said Vivien.

"Ahhhh, but here's the thing Viv: If you had multiple personality disorder you wouldn't know it, and maybe one of your other personalities did it."

"Then how do you know *you* don't have it and that one of *your* other personalities didn't do it?" asked Vivien.

"Because to be a psychologist requires years of rigorous self-analysis . . . but that doesn't matter. Here's the point, Viv." He pulled himself forward on the couch and looked right into her eyes. "I want to play, too. In fact, I insist on it—otherwise I'll spill the beans to the other suspects and the jig will be up."

Vivien couldn't resist including him in her game. On the way over to Sasha's house, Vivien filled him in on the story of Phyllis allegedly trying to hit Walter with her car. She told him about the smashed tree, the Park Police, everything. They batted around a theory about why, if in fact Phyllis and Sasha were lovers, one would want to kill the other.

"Maybe Sasha wanted her to leave her husband," said Vivien.

"Always a possibility, darling; that happens all the time," said Lenny.

They were driving through the park with the windows open as the light began to soften in the western sky. Vivien could feel the air getting warmer and thicker with each passing day and already felt a sense of dread about the wet blanket days of August, even though they were still weeks away. "I just don't understand," said Vivien. "If they were both gay, why would they get married to men?"

Lenny looked at her sideways, turned into a black girl and said, "Honey, where did they find you out there in Wisconsin? Under a cabbage in the cabbage patch?"

"Mmmmmm, I like cabbage, actually. My mom and grandma used to make homemade pigs-in-a-blanket out of fresh cabbage every Christmas. It would go on for days and the whole house would smell like paprika and cabbage"

"Mmmm-hmmm," said Lenny. "Well, you're not in Kansas anymore, baby doll."

They came up with a plan that put Vivien to work on Walter and Linda, while Lenny would zero in on Sasha. They figured that if anybody could pick up a positive reading on "gaydar" from Sasha, it would be Lenny. The two rode in silence with their arms resting on the open window frames, their eyes looking straight ahead.

Vivien thought about a time in Milwaukee, before she became a cop, when she got a chance to go on a ride-along with two metro police officers responding to a domestic dispute. She was in the back seat watching the officers, feeling a sense of importance about what she was doing. It was meaningful and gave her a purpose for existing. A trace of that feeling came back to her now. For a few seconds she felt a sense of relief move through her. The mess at the house, the missing shoe, and the screwed up way she had entered into her latest possible romance all went away, evaporating like summer rain puddles.

She tried to focus on what would happen next. Proper preparation was the key to a successful interrogation. She planned a few questions out ahead of time and worked the seating arrangement around in her head so that she and Lenny would end up next to the people they wanted to talk to. Vivien began steeling herself for dealing with Walter and again asked herself about the strange effect he had over her. This time she would stay in control, find out what she needed to know, and move the case forward. It was time to go back to work.

CHAPTER 21

Vivien was sitting next to Walter at the ball game telling him all about the time she almost had an affair with her boss at the ATF. Her supervisor was married with four kids but would screw anything in a skirt. He was an older, attractive man, and Vivien found herself drawn to him the day they met. She knew it was wrong and resisted the temptation, but still found herself with his tongue twisting around in her mouth as they hid in one of the back evidence rooms, standing up against a filing cabinet grinding their hips into each other. Even now, she could feel his hands on her, remembering the feeling of running her fingers across his gray, short-cropped bristle. Any time she got a whiff of Old Spice, his preferred scent, her face flushed.

She had stopped it before it went much farther, a fact she was proud of—for once she'd exercised a bit of self-control. But she was equally disappointed in herself as she sat here in the ballpark listening to the words spill out of her mouth into the visibly unmoved ears of Walter. Goddamn Walter. She was supposed to be probing him for clues about Phyllis's disappearance, but once again he had managed to turn the tables and trick her into revealing another one of her most closely guarded secrets.

But as she finished the story, she got a brainstorm. Maybe she was unconsciously playing the oldest game on the books between men and women. I'll show you mine, if you show me yours. "Has anything like that ever happened to you, Walter? Ever done something that you ended up regretting later?" He made a face like he was actually giving it some consideration and Vivien once again felt the fleeting warmth of self-satisfaction. Finally, she had him where she wanted him.

"Well, being a freelancer I don't really have a boss to sleep with," said Walter. His face pushed closer to hers to compensate for the bad acoustics in the stadium. Maybe this wasn't such a good venue choice for her investigation. She could smell the beer on his breath and could practically feel herself falling into the creases of his face. "I can tell you that me and the old lady almost got caught in a, shall we say, delicate situation on a beach in Costa Rica, when these two German tourists came out of nowhere, just as she . . ." The unmistakable sound of a hardball cracking against a wooden bat and the roar of the crowd drowned out whatever sordid detail Walter was about to reveal.

Everybody's eyes turned towards the field as a home run sailed over the wall in deep right center. The fans rose as one to cheer as Vivien glanced down the aisle to see Linda, on her feet, program in hand, half a beat ahead of everybody else. She was probably the only one in the group who knew what was actually happening in the game.

Walter stood and clapped politely, his face held in a casual grimace like he felt bothered by the whole thing. Vivien followed the lead of the masses, putting her hands together and watching the tiny figures below striding around the bases. She breathed out heavily, accepting the fact that her investigation was going nowhere fast. She glanced down the aisle to where Lenny was sitting next to Sasha, who appeared to be weeping uncontrollably. Lenny had his arms around her, pulling her close like a child.

Vivien struggled to make sense of the pictures in her head. Sasha was a Brit. She had no stakes in the game. No horse in this race. That was something her ex-boss said once. She liked the phrase and always looked for the right time to use it but it never came. This would be the perfect time. Lenny looked at Vivien. He looked deadly serious and he nodded to her as he continued to console Sasha.

The nodding was slow and deliberate, acknowledging something to be true. It was true. She got it right. Something was going on. Vivien nodded back, a slight almost imperceptible nod. Very professional. As Sasha pulled her head away from Lenny's shoulder, Vivien looked away to see if Walter and Linda had noticed the situation.

They all clapped and watched as the runner tagged home looking very confident and casual about it. The batter was just doing his job, that's all. Knocking small balls made of horsehide and string over a wall with a wooden bat. It happened all the time in baseball stadiums all over the world. Just some guy doing his job. Vivien clapped louder, stood up and stepped up towards the seats in front of her to further distract Linda and Walter. She assumed that Sasha weeping in Lenny's arms represented a break in the case and she didn't want things to get fouled up now.

She glanced at Linda and Walter, put her fingers in her mouth, and whistled so loudly that Walter covered his ears. Her father had taught her to do that when she was a little girl, before he disappeared in an ambulance and never came back, leaving her alone for a lifetime with her uptight mother. Linda looked at her and smiled, happily surprised by Vivien's hidden talents.

"Woooo-hooo," Vivien shouted and stole a glance down the row as Sasha stood, dabbing at the corners of her eyes. For all anybody knew, the reaction could have been caused by dust falling from the rafters of the stadium, an allergy, a yawn, a burst of emotion for a scored run by the home team, anything. Lenny now stood also, clapping and looking forward as some in the crowd began reseating themselves. He looked down the row at Vivien, wiggled his eyebrows and gave her another nod.

CHAPTER 22

Mooky positioned herself in her favorite spot on the porch, knowing that something was about to happen. During this time of day, the sidewalk near the front gate was her preferred place to lie. By now, the concrete would be nice and warm from the sun. But the smell of coffee brewing changed that. Vivien had coffee every morning and Mooky looked forward to the aroma that marked the time of day when she got her first meal and was allowed out. Coffee was a wonderful smell that changed slightly depending on various things, but the heavy, roasted-toasty flavor was a delightful constant in her life every morning. Smelling it now, in the middle of the day, meant something exciting was about to happen.

Somebody was probably coming to visit, and once the guests started drinking the coffee, the activity level would rise. There would be talking and laughing, maybe some yelling, and everybody would be in the mood to play. The smell of coffee always triggered good things. She hadn't smelled this aroma recently, but the memory hadn't faded.

From this spot on the porch, nobody would be able to get in or out the front door without her seeing them. If they came to the back door, Mooky would hear the sounds—from this location, sounds from the back yard bounced off the house next door and ended up here on the front porch.

She was, as usual, in an excellent position to watch for squirrels working the oak tree in the front yard, and for keeping an eye out for the cat that lived down the street. The street itself was an object of mild interest as the cars drove by each other, sometimes honking or waving. Mooky watched the cars, waiting to see somebody she knew. It didn't take long. A car pulled to the curb and a shape got out that she recognized. She recognized his walk and would confirm his identity as soon as she could get a good smell.

She watched him go to the back of the car and open the big door. Then she saw somebody else she recognized. Buddy! She was on her feet, tail wagging, now that she could see why the coffee was being brewed at this time of day. Her ears came up to full attention as she whined and trotted down to the gate. She sniffed the air looking for confirmation, caught a whiff of the leather seats in the car, exhaust fumes, motor oil warming on the pavement, and maybe a bit of Buddy. He was still too far away and the wind was blowing the wrong way, carrying her own aroma to him.

She looked through the wire diamonds of the chain link fence and saw Buddy looking at her, his stub of a tail twitching back and forth. The man was pulling things out of the car, gathering up the leash, and talking to himself and Buddy in a funny, high-pitched voice. More fun was about to start. Mooky bounced her front half into the air so that her paws came down on top of the fence.

She barked a greeting to the visitors and wagged her magnificent tail as far as it would go. She pulled herself off the fence, twirled in circles, stopped for a second to attend to an itch in her butt and then resumed spinning and barking. Vivien came to the front door and said, "Okay, okay, I see them. Hi, Buddy. Hi, Lenny. Come on in."

She was in her bare feet, which meant she probably wasn't going anywhere. Instead, everybody was coming here, which was just as exciting. The front gate squeaked open and Mooky got a good sniff of Buddy and the man to make sure everybody was who they appeared to be. "Stop, Mooky, stop. Let them get in the gate, for God's sake," said Vivien. "You would think she hasn't seen you in weeks."

"Well. You know how they are," said Lenny. "Hi, honey."

He put his arms around her and gave her a hug while patting her shoulder. Then he ruffled the fur on Mooky's head and said, "Hello, Mooky Mooky."

"Okay," said Vivien. "Back. Back. Back. You guys stay out and play while us grown-ups talk." Mooky heard the "play" word and that's exactly what she intended to do. Buddy wasn't much of a runner, and she couldn't ever remember getting into a good game of Pull-the-Thing with him. But she remembered that he did enjoy Find-the-Thing.

Find-the-Thing was a very simple game. Mooky knew where a certain thing was that belonged to her. Mooky would lead Buddy towards the object to see if he could find the thing. If Buddy could find it, he would naturally think the thing belonged to him, which could lead to a rousing round of Pull-the-Thing, which was the game that Mooky really wanted to play.

Mooky let Buddy get settled first as he sniffed and peed in various corners of the yard. She followed him, watching to see where his nose would lead him, which turned out to be the places in the yard that Mooky already knew. Eventually, Buddy seemed to lose his motivation and began sniffing in random areas that were basically barren of any good smells.

Mooky walked towards the bushes near the place where the cat liked to pee and also close to where the shoe was buried. She didn't have to turn around to sense that Buddy had followed her into the shady area behind the shrubs. The smells of the stony house foundation were back here, musty and mossy, mostly covered in cool, black dirt. Mooky walked past the cat spot to where the ground was still moist from where she had dug it up a few days earlier. Mooky sniffed the spot, gave the earth a cursory scratch, and turned to see if Buddy's nose was good enough to get it.

Buddy sniffed where Mooky had scratched, looked like he wanted to pee on it, but instead, scratched across Mooky's scratch. Mooky's jaw opened and her tongue poked out, now tasting the warm smell of the fresh dirt. She sniffed Buddy's neck, gave him a push with her nose, and scratched over his scratch. That was all it took.

Both dogs now went at the hole, knowing there was something desirable under the dirt and knowing that whoever got there first would own whatever was in there. Of course, Mooky already knew it was the shoe that Vivien had brought back from the place in the woods where the special bone came from. Buddy had no clue what he was digging for, but could tell from Mooky's desire that it had to be something extraordinary.

Almost simultaneously the white and red rubber of the flip flop emerged as Mooky and Buddy both sunk their teeth into it. Both dogs growled fake warnings at each other, and Find-the-Thing quickly spilled into Pull-the-Thing. Both dogs had a good grip on it as they maneuvered themselves out of the shrubbery, herking and jerking out into the sunshine and the more open confines of the yard.

CHAPTER 23

Lenny was driving Vivien crazy by teasing her with little morsels about the conversation that had happened between him and Sasha the night before. He was now preparing to start their debriefing, which Lenny insisted they have over coffee and donuts.

"That's a stereotype, Lenny," she told him on the phone. "Cops don't really do coffee and donuts, except in the movies." But he wasn't having any of it. He called her from work, told her he was getting off early, coming over, and bringing donuts. All she had to do was brew the coffee. He would bring Buddy, the dogs would play, he and she would dish, and then they would go to the park together to stage the next phase of the investigation into the possible disappearance of Phyllis, queen bitch of the dog park.

It wasn't really possible for her and Lenny to talk during the baseball game, as Lenny seemed to be uncovering secrets and Vivien didn't want to interrupt the flow of information. All Lenny would say at the game in response to Vivien's queries was, "Shhh . . . I'll tell you later." Then he rolled his eyes and put a hand to his face like he was bearing a terrible burden by keeping it quiet. He was so very dramatic.

Convinced that she now had a bird in hand, Vivien put the kibosh on her own assignment of interrogating Linda and Walter at the game. Walter reacted to her inattention by slumping back into what appeared to be a state of mild interest in the game, as she watched him guzzle four stadium-sized cups of beer. Linda routinely checked her game program and monitored the out-of-town scores flashing by on the scoreboard while booing at strikes against the home team and cheering the hits.

They all got home before 11:30 and Vivien went to bed excited about what would be revealed the next day. She still hadn't found the shoe—which was a problem, since Will had been calling about setting up their second date. She felt like an idiot for not turning the thing over to him in the first place, and now even more stupid that she couldn't find it. Even the day of extreme house cleaning hadn't produced it. She was now convinced that Mooky was the key suspect in the shoe's disappearance.

She sat at her small table in the kitchen tapping her fingers, waiting for Lenny to emerge from the powder room. She looked at the box from Dunkin Donuts and the coffee she had already poured herself. Lenny had asked her if she had any Styrofoam cups they could drink out of for added realistic effect. Vivien ignored him, now thinking he had taken the "playing policeman" gag far enough.

She sat and tapped, staring into the coffee like it might reveal a clue about the stories that Lenny was obviously enjoying keeping from her. Finally she heard the door open and he emerged wringing his hands. "You're out of towels in there, darling," he said.

"Yes, I know, Lenny. Now please sit."

"Right," he said, while lifting the tape on one end of the doughnut box and pouring coffee. "So," he said. "Here's the deal. Sasha went to an all-girls boarding school just north of London."

Vivien studied Lenny and scooped some sugar into her cup. "And?"

"Well. You know, nothing helped promote queerness in the world better than a stay at an English boarding school."

"And so, they were . . . ?" asked Vivien.

"They were what?" said Lenny.

"Sasha and Phyllis. Were they having an affair?"

Lenny poured a dab of milk into his own cup and said, "Oh, heavens, how would I know that?"

"That's what you were supposed to do, Lenny. That's why you were talking to her."

"Oh, I know that, but you just can't come out and ask somebody a question like that, especially not her majesty."

Vivien pressed her hands against her face like it might fall off.

"Lenny, that was the whole point of you sitting next to her—why was she crying, for Christ's sake?" asked Vivien.

"Oh, that. Well. She started talking about her husband and how he had an affair with a bank teller he met while buying traveler's checks. She really loved him and somehow she got onto that and she just bawled, sweetie. Well, you saw. Apparently he was killed in a fall, some kind of freak accident at home. She was the one who discovered the body. Kind of gruesome, actually."

Vivien pulled her hands down her face and felt a wave of depression wash over her. This was what she'd been waiting for? She cursed herself for allowing a civilian to compromise her investigation. Her investigation? She was clearly losing it. For the first time in quite a while she considered the possibility of getting a part-time job.

Her disability pension from the Secret Service was enough so she didn't really need to work if she was careful. But she was not careful. She walked into a store and felt compelled to buy something, sure that she would eventually find a use for the item. At this moment she saw herself working at a bookstore or a pet shop just to get herself out of the rut she was calling a life.

"Oh, and you know what else she told me?"

Vivien looked out the window at nothing in particular. From here she could see the private school on the hill just beyond Utah Avenue. On warm days she could hear the kids outside at recess. Maybe she should have married a cop, had a few kids, and been done with it.

"What, Lenny? What else did she tell you?" Her voice sounded dejected and hopeless.

"She told me that that bitch, Phyllis, invited Sasha to every goddamn one of those fucking parties that you and I are excluded from."

Vivien felt her attention returning to the immediate. "The Winterfest Fantastique ? Sasha was invited? And she went?"

"Every goddamn year," said Lenny while taking a pull from his coffee cup and making a face like it was a shot of rye.

"Really?" said Vivien. "It's funny; Sasha never shared that bit of information with us."

"I don't think it's funny at all," said Lenny. He bit into a jelly doughnut like it had said something to insult him. "Goddamn sneaky is what it is. Bitch." He slurped his coffee, a sound that Vivien usually found extremely irritating; at this moment she felt herself unmoved by it. In her mind she floated out the window and drifted over the school, looking down at the playground, now emptied by the end of the school year coupled with the sultry transition to full summer.

"I wonder what else she's being sneaky about," said Vivien.

"I hate that sneaky shit," said Lenny.

"Mmm-hmm," said Vivien. She turned her head to look out the window, distracted from the conversation by growling dogs. Her heart lifted as she looked out and saw Mooky and Buddy playing tug-of-war with a stick or something. She rested her hand on her chin, absently watching the dogs jockeying for position.

She watched as whatever they were fighting over was torn into two pieces. The dogs fell away from each other, both dropped the piece they had in their mouth and then resumed fighting over the larger piece. Now Vivien could tell that whatever they had wasn't a stick, but probably a piece of plastic, kind of a pale red color.

"Hey," she said to the window. And then she got a weird feeling in her stomach as she watched the dogs tear the thing into two smaller pieces, which they dropped. They turned their attention back to the largest piece. They each got a hold of an end and quickly ripped it in two.

"Hey!" said Vivien, and now she was on her feet, brushing by Lenny and walking quickly towards the back door. The weird feeling in her stomach turned into a large black hole as she realized exactly what the dogs were playing with. She hoped she was wrong and was just seeing what she didn't want to see. She walked into the yard as the dogs spied her. They dropped their heads, lowered their bodies for better traction, and took off at full speed, heading around the house with their two mouths still clamped onto whatever it was that they were fighting over.

Vivien stood in the yard and was aware that Lenny had followed her out. She looked down and saw pieces of rubber, torn into chunks, most of them the size of popcorn kernels. She picked one up, knocked some dirt off, and turned it over in her fingers, wondering if it could be what she thought it was. Another flash of color in the green grass caught her eye. She walked a few steps, bent over, and picked up a strap that used to be attached to a flip-flop.

"Oh, shit," said Lenny. "Were those your shoes they just tore up?"

"Not exactly," said Vivien. "Damn, Lenny. I am so screwed right now."

CHAPTER 24

Mooky was a bad dog. She knew this because ever since she and Buddy had turned Pull-the-Thing into Tear-the-Thing-into-Pieces, Vivien had told her over and over again that she was a bad dog. Mooky knew the word "bad," having learned it as a puppy during the same time she learned the word "no." The two words were often used together and then usually followed by a punishment.

In this case, the punishment was to be put on the leash at the dog park. Mooky sat next to Vivien at the picnic table and panted. She noticed that Buddy was not restricted to the leash. Vivien sat and talked to the other people while Mooky listened to the words, waiting for the word "go," when she would be allowed to run with the rest of the dogs. "Car" would be just as good, since that would mean it was time to eat.

But the only words she was hearing didn't contain these sounds. Instead she heard the words "bad," "bad dog," and occasionally "shoe." It was frustrating for her. She sat on her haunches and then lay down in a snatch of shade created by the picnic table. Frustrating because as fun as Find-the-Thing and Pull-the-Thing were, neither was as fun as Tear-the-Thing-into-Pieces.

The tearing game allowed two dogs to play and the result was taking one fun thing and turning it into many, many fun things. The smaller things could be chewed into even smaller things, eaten, buried, peed on, or dropped over the fence for humans to throw back. If the human didn't want to throw the thing, there were many more pieces that could be dropped over the fence, one at a time, until somebody threw one back.

But this game would not happen, since Vivien and Buddy's owner had picked up every piece of the shoe that had come from the woods and packed them into a small plastic bag. Earlier that day, Mooky watched Vivien place the plastic bag on top of the high box in the dining room. The box was much too high for Mooky to reach, even if she were to stand on top of the table.

It was warm that day as Mooky sniffed the air and looked towards the woods where the special bone and the shoe came from. The heat from the sun was changing the pressure in the air, causing new smells to come to her, smells of flowers and car exhaust from the road. The mud and damp earth of spring was drying up, making everything more dusty and dry. The heat also caused things to rot faster, which created intoxicating aromas from trashcans, sewers, garbage trucks, and dead animals.

These were the smells that Mooky could not refuse. They compelled her to find the source and make them hers. Depending on what the thing was, once she found it, she could not stop herself from eating the source or rolling around in it to cover her entire magnificent coat in its essence. In this way she would own the smell forever.

Even now, her head pivoted and her nose turned towards the edge of the woods as she detected something wonderful hiding under the shadows of the tall trees. She whined and panted, looking at the leash as she watched Vivien talking to the other dog owners. To leave the land of "bad dog" and get back to the place of "go" and "car," Mooky knew what she had to do. She had to submit and show obedience. She had to be a good dog by playing a game with Vivien.

The game was called "Give-the-Thing." It was a simple game. Mooky would find a thing that Vivien would like, pick it up, bring it to her, and drop it. Mooky looked around under the table for a thing that Vivien would like. It could be anything. A scrap of paper that smelled like flowers or tobacco, a stick, a piece of grass, anything. But the area under the table didn't offer much.

The grass was worn down and picked clean by the other dogs playing variations of the same game. Mooky sniffed around for something that might be hiding in the grass, but there was nothing. The wind switched around as smells from the road were replaced by smells from the woods, and that's when she got it. The most amazing smell she had ever received. A smell that could not be ignored.

She stood up so suddenly she bonked her head underneath the picnic table. She turned towards the woods and was excited for a second as slack in the leash permitted her to take a step towards the place where the special bone had come from. But as Mooky tried to step forward, the leash instantly tightened. Her wonderful tail stood straight out and her nose twitched in the slight breeze. She pulled on the leash, feeling the collar digging into her skin and constricting her breathing.

"Mooky. Stop," said Vivien. And then she resumed talking. Mooky whined and swooped her tail, hoping that she would be released from the world of bad because something that Vivien would like and something that would be the best thing ever was right over there in the woods. If she could only be released, Mooky would run to the thing, find it, claim it for hers, and then bring a piece of it back to Vivien. She would drop it for Vivien. Right at her feet. And then she would be redeemed. She would be a good dog. She would no longer be a bad dog but would return to the world of go.

CHAPTER 25

Vivien sat at the dining room table noticing that some of the clutter that she had cleared out of the space was already returning. Old newspapers, boxes from QVC, junk mail, and grocery bags were accumulating on the chairs and table top. She'd cut back on her chronic shopping but the deluge of detritus never ended. In front of her lay a quart sized, zip-lock baggie. The torn-into-pieces flip flop was crammed inside.

The day before, she and Lenny had picked up every piece of the shoe they could find while wearing rubber gloves she'd found under the sink. She only had one pair, so they each wore one hand. Now she sat at the table wearing a new pair of sandals she'd found on sale at Target, a new pair of white shorts that she'd found the same day—not on sale but very cute—and one of her favorite tops, which made her boobs look bigger.

She'd done her hair, put on some lipstick, and rubbed a drop of perfume between her wrists. She felt like a little girl waiting for her father to get home. He would be angry about what she'd done. Her emotions swung from excitement, knowing that she would be seeing Will in a few minutes, to dread, knowing the conversation that they were going to have.

Mixed in with that was the dull ache of self-loathing that came from the revelation that as an investigator, she sucked. Planning the questioning for the ball game was a stupid idea. It was too hard to control because of the crowd noise and too distracting for the investigators and the subjects.

Her next major blunder was entrusting Lenny to interview Sasha. Vivien assumed that since he was a therapist he would excel at asking questions and getting to the truth. But for him, it was all about being invited or not invited to Phyllis's stupid parties. She should have handled the job herself. She then compounded her mistake by letting Linda and Walter off the hook, thinking that Sasha had confessed to Lenny.

During her career in law enforcement, actual investigation procedures were typically handed out to the rock star cops. The brightest, the best looking, the smoothest bullshitters, the ones with their noses up the boss's ass got those assignments. At one point she was up for the Special Investigation Unit at ATF.

There were four slots available for a new task force. One went to a guy whose father used to run one of the units, one went to a Joe College type, one went to a guy who was a pretty good cop but kind of a nerd, and the other one went to a woman who bore a passing resemblance to Sharon Stone. So there you go.

She told herself that she was a victim of unfair circumstances, but a nagging thought in the back of her mind told her different. She'd had a decent shot at making that squad, but she had an issue with a captain that never really got resolved.

While doing clerical duty, Vivien had spotted an anomaly in some records of a gun dealer in Richmond, Virginia. He appeared to be selling more guns than he was buying. It was probably just a bookkeeping error, but she brought it to her captain, who was impressed with her attention to detail.

She was told to visit the dealer's store and look around to see what she could observe. She would pretend to be interested in a handgun for self-defense. She stood at attention in front of her superior's desk, feeling her body temperature rise by the second.

"Technically you're not even supposed to be doing field work, so just go down there and take a look around. Look for assault weapons that may have come in through back channels. For God's sake don't say anything; just look around then come back and tell me what you found. Got it?"

But Vivien didn't just look. She started off playing the role of the confused, female, would-be firearm owner, but spied what she thought was a stack of fully automatic AK-47's behind the counter—

which were quite illegal. She identified herself as an ATF officer, drew her weapon, handcuffed the guy, read him his rights, and then determined that the AK's were totally legit. She got reprimanded and was sent back to the clerical squad for the rest of her time on the force.

Vivien faced the facts that she was a woman from the Midwest who had been hired into law enforcement because she did better than average on her tests, could speak passable Croatian, and was a crack shot. The interest in guns had started early.

Her uncle had insisted on taking her squirrel hunting when she was a little girl and Vivien had actually wanted to go. Uncle Mike had done a good job of explaining that squirrels were varmints who chewed holes in the bird feeders and there were too many of them in the woods to survive the winter. He told her that thinning the squirrel herd was the only humane thing to do.

To her and her uncle's surprise, Vivien quickly became deadly accurate with a .22 rifle after a few lessons using tin cans as targets. Uncle Mike took care of the skinning and field dressing; Vivien's job was to shoot them. Uncle Mike was a bit of a mountain man who made his own jerked venison and used the squirrels for batches of what he called "hunter's stew."

For most of her career she worked a desk job and occasionally worked security details. Self-doubts about her own abilities lay in front of her, a piece of evidence from an active, ongoing investigation that she had hidden from a police officer that was then torn into a bag of rubber confetti by her stupid dog. She was such an idiot and now the chickens were coming home to roost.

She exhaled long and slow, looked at the clock on the stove, tapped her fingers on the tabletop, and then ran them over the smooth surface of the plump baggie. She told herself that they still might be able to pull some DNA off the bits of shoe. This made her feel a little better, and just for a second, there was a sliver of hope that she was not ruined. She felt herself jump as Mooky barked from under the table.

Vivien looked at the clock again—6:59 p.m.—and got up to peek out the front door. Sure enough, the beige Crown Victoria was parked across the street and the door had already been opened and slammed shut—which must have been what Mooky heard. The compact, always-moving-forward form of Detective Will Evans was waiting for a break in the traffic to cross the street.

Assuming he didn't have to wait too long for cars, he would arrive at her door at exactly 7:00, which was when he said he would be there. She got a twinge between her legs thinking about the military precision of the act, as she noticed the fading sunlight glinting off the top of his standing-at-attention crew cut.

"Stop," she said to herself and moved away from the door before he could see her. "Lie down, Mooky. You're still a bad dog." She felt a little guilty about continuing to punish the dog, but not much. Vivien stood in the tiny kitchen, which really needed a makeover. She checked the coffee pot. It was half-full with the warmer on in case Will wanted a cup. Then she stood perfectly still, waiting for the doorbell.

The knocking and the barking started at 7:00, the time when her trial by fire would begin. She let a few seconds go by so it wouldn't seem like she'd been standing there waiting for him, and then walked to the door. "Stop, Mooky. Get back. Get back," she said as she moved the big Lab aside with her knee. She noticed Mooky's tail wagging and her ears were low, a sign of recognition. This made her feel good as she pushed the door open and looked at Will standing with his hands behind his back in an at-ease posture.

"Hi," she heard herself say while noticing how her voice came up in excitement.

"Hey, Viv," he said as he stepped inside the door and gave her a quick kiss on the lips. "How ya been, stranger?" he said.

"Been awhile, Detective," she said.

"Yes, ma'am, I've been thinking about you."

"I'm sure you have," she said. "Come on in. Want some coffee?"

"Ummmm, I'll take a beer if you have one."

Vivien felt a jolt of panic shoot through her. Did she have any beer? Why hadn't she thought of that?

"Sure, let me look; sit down at the table a sec," she said, as she flashed into the kitchen, her mind doing a mental inventory of what was in the refrigerator. She opened the door, looking past the leftover pierogies she'd found at the Polish deli in Rockville and the white cartons of Indonesian food from the place on Connecticut Avenue. She slid the milk forward and there, sure enough, were two bottles of some kind of German beer she'd bought last year for an Oktoberfest party that never happened. "Do you like, 'Bitburger Dark?'" she said.

"Yeah, sure, anything," he said. "Hey, the place looks different."

"Yeah, thanks. I finally cleaned up a little." She could tell by the sound of his voice that he was in the dining room. There was a good chance he was probably looking at the baggie with the torn-up shoe as they were talking.

"It's kind of old. I hope it's still good," she said as she fumbled with an opener, popped it open, walked back into the room, and handed it to him. "Oh, sorry, do you want a glass?"

He took a big swig, pointed at the bottle, and said, "It's already in a glass, Viv."

She laughed a nervous laugh and said, "Sit down, Will. I have to tell you something."

"Uh-oh. Sounds serious."

"Well, maybe."

They each pulled a high-backed chair away from the table and took seats while looking clumsy and official. Vivien sat at the head of the table with Will on her right. He took another swig, as she felt him watching her as he tilted his head back. She got that uncomfortable feeling again, aware that she was being looked at, but she brushed it aside. Where else would he be looking? She tugged at the front of her shirt and said, "Will, after the dogs found the bone and the forensics guys left, I went back to the site."

"The site in the park?"

"Yeah. I went back to the site and went down to where they dug and, um, poked around a little."

"Poked around?" His head was tilted back a little, his mouth slightly open. She had no idea what he could be thinking. She couldn't read his emotions at all.

"Yeah, um, a little. Anyway, I was down there poking around and, um, well, I found a shoe."

"A shoe?"

"Yeah. A flip-flop, actually."

"Flip-flop?"

"Um, yeah."

"Great. Did you bag it and turn it in?"

"Well. Um. I wanted to. I was going to give it to you, actually. But then you were doing all that overtime and I got kind of busy and I kind of lost it for a while."

"Lost the shoe?" He took another drink of the beer.

Vivien's eyes drifted from his face to the foam in the beer bottle. How long would a beer stay good in a bottle? she wondered. Stay focused, she told herself. "Yeah. I picked it up with a grocery bag so I wouldn't mess anything up, and I had it on top of the table here. I thought I put it on top of the armoire, but I must've left it on the table and somehow the dog got it and well . . ." She reached for the baggie in front of her, overstuffed with the remains of the flip-flop. She let her fingers trail over the soft contours of the plastic and looked up at his face, ready to face the music and do her time. What would they charge her with? Obstruction of justice? Interfering with a police investigation? She was ruined. And she kind of liked Will.

Will was looking at her hand touching the baggie as the realization of what she was telling him began to register on his face.

"And, this is it? Mooky did this?" he said.

Vivien cast her eyes down and nodded yes.

"Hah! Hah! Hah! You're shitting me. Hah! Hah! Hah! Oh my God. Hah! Hah! Hah! The dog ate the shoe? Oh, man . . ."

For a few seconds Vivien couldn't make any sense of what she was hearing. He was laughing hysterically and now actually brushing tears out of his eyes. She looked up, hazarding a slight smile. She flashed back to the first night they met. The night he put on the Abe Lincoln beard. He had a good sense of humor, this guy—devilish almost. She smiled, fought back her own chuckles, and crossed her legs.

"Well, it was before I cleaned the room up and she must have gotten it and taken it outside. And then Lenny came over with Buddy and the two of them were playing tug of war with it and . . ."

"And this was what's left?" he asked. "Oh my god. Too funny. Freaking dogs, huh?"

"You think I may have compromised the investigation?" she asked.

"Well, Viv, you certainly haven't done anything to help it." He laughed some more while picking up the bag and looking at it.

She felt crushed and it must have shown on her face. This was what she was afraid of, extreme disapproval and proof that she had screwed this up.

"Oh, look. I'm sorry," he said. "You probably should have turned it in as soon as you found it." He sniffed and rubbed his nose. "How far was it from the site?"

"Probably ten yards or so."

"Yeah. So it was probably too far away to be relevant. Plus, if the forensic guys missed it—that's their fuck-up, you know? I mean, assuming it has anything to do with the case, which it probably doesn't, they may still be able to pull something off. Are all the pieces in there?" He was holding the bag up towards the light, looking at it like it might reveal a clue.

"I think so," said Vivien. "We tried to find it all but I think Buddy ate a few pieces."

"Unbelievable," said Will as he dropped the bag back down on the table. "Well, you're going to have to turn it in. Just tell them that you tried to do the right thing but the dog got a hold of it, that's all. Tell them, 'my dog ate the evidence.' Oh my God." And then he was off on another laughing jag as Vivien found herself joining in. She laughed and put her hands over her eyes, trying to disguise it. She did screw up, but apparently, it was going to be all right. He wasn't mad and she wasn't going to get into any trouble. "Well, can you take it with you and give it to whoever is supposed to get it?" she asked.

His massive shoulders were still bouncing a little as he wiped the corners of his eyes again.

"Oh, shit. Um, actually, no. They pulled me off the case."

"Pulled off? Why?"

"Dunno. Department isn't saying, but I think I'm being re-assigned, hopefully to Homicide. That's what I really want to do. They have me flying a desk right now till it gets sorted out. I need the change because this Natural Death stuff is just killing me, heh, heh, heh."

"Very funny," said Vivien.

"But the real question is going to be, 'What were you doing down there in the first place, Viv?'" he said.

"I'll tell them I was walking my dog and didn't see the yellow tape."

"Mmm-hmm. I understand that part, but what *were* you doing down there, Viv? You know you can't be walking around in what could be a crime scene during an active investigation."

He was looking at her seriously and she felt the weight of his stare. She squirmed a bit in her seat. It was a fair question. A question she'd been asking herself since the day the leg bone showed up in her life. She bit her lip and rubbed the baggie with her fingertip. She said nothing as the thoughts banged around in her head.

"You miss it, don't you?" he said. He was looking at her with arms folded across his rounded chest.

She looked down at the table. "Probably."

"Yeah. Well, that's okay. I probably would, too," he said. "You know, the other thing is, they never found any more bones at that site.

They think the leg bone came from somewhere else and somehow ended up where your dog found it."

"How could that happen?" said Vivien.

"It had teeth marks in it. I mean, besides what the dogs did to it. Maybe a coon, opossum, or coyote got a hold of it from someplace else, dragged it through the woods for a while, and then dropped it where the dogs found it. So your shoe here is probably totally random and unrelated."

The vision of a coyote popped into Vivien's head for a second. She'd heard about them being seen in the park and desperately wanted to see one. "Coyote?"

"Oh, they're, in there, Viv. I got a buddy who works midnights; he sees them all the time."

"Really?"

"Yeah. Anyway, I'll tell you something else. Before they pulled me off this thing, we determined that your friend, the English lady, was probably the last person to see Phyllis before she turned up missing. And Phyllis's husband—what's his name?"

"Harish," said Vivien.

"Right. Dr. Harish is supposed to be back from his month-long trip to India late today. I'm going to call him, just to put a cap on this little caper. I'm sure his wife is with him or he at least knows where she is, but, like I say, I'm being reassigned. He's a chiropractor or something, right?"

"Yep," said Vivien, "a back quack."

"Yeah, well, some people swear by them," said Will. "You ever been to one?"

"Me? No. I don't believe in them," said Vivien.

"But you do believe in coyotes?"

"I just want to see one," said Vivien. And as she sat at the table, thanking her lucky stars for not being in trouble with the law and her new potential boyfriend, her mind was racing far, far away. She moved her ankle against Mooky's back, feeling the warmth of her. Her dog's tail was thumping in slow motion against the floor. Mooky had relaxed quickly around Will, always a good sign for new humans in the house.

Will's words permeated through her as she ignored any thoughts about why he was telling her details of an ongoing investigation. He must really like her. He considered her a colleague. They were talking shop, that's all. That's all it could possibly be. She unconsciously put her hand on her hip and thought about her bad disc. It still hurt if she stood or sat too long in the same position. It wasn't enough of an injury to prevent her from doing things, but it was enough of an insurance liability that the Secret Service had decided to put her out to pasture. A decision that she now considered a bit premature.

From that point on the date went well. They went to the Italian place on Connecticut Avenue and chatted through plates of steaming pasta and red sauce. Vivien had already decided that no matter what happened, no matter how well things were going, she was not going to sleep with Will tonight. There would be no sex on the couch, in the bedroom, kitchen, police cruiser, or anywhere else. She had done her bit as the desperate floozy; tonight there would be no nookie.

They made out in the car for a while after Vivien made her wishes clear. Will respected her desire for a platonic end to the evening. It was a challenge not to break her own rule as he pulled her close, her knee scraping the police radio mounted under the dash. She could smell his scent and feel his whiskers brushing her cheek as her hands circled his waist. But just as she was getting to the point of ripping open his shirt or hers, she pushed away and popped open the door. "Next time, big boy," she said.

"Saturday?" he said.

She slammed the door shut. "Call me," she said, making her fingers into a tiny telephone and walking around the car. The engine roared to life, the headlamps flicked on, and she was illuminated in white light. The driver side window slid down. "You can bet on that, ma'am."

"I'm counting on it, Detective."

She felt light on her feet as she walked towards her front door and she let her hips sway a bit more than usual, exaggerating her stride to give him something to remember her by. She was sure he was watching and didn't bother to turn around. She waved over her shoulder without looking, adding to her own mystery. She felt good about herself for the first time in months, years, maybe, and she intended to follow up on the feeling by calling Phyllis's husband first thing in the morning and making an appointment.

CHAPTER 26

Vivien awoke the next day with a renewed sense of purpose. The destroyed flip-flop was not going to send her up the river nor end her relationship with Will, her large, laughing policeman. If Phyllis had been in India with Harish these last few weeks, she was due back today. There was an excellent chance she would be at the dog park regaling the regulars with her travel tales—and the mystery of her disappearance would be over.

If, on the other hand, Phyllis didn't show up at the park, then there was a good chance that the DC Metro Police Department would want Vivien's help. Will, the officer initially investigating Phyllis's mysterious disappearance, had been reassigned, possibly to Homicide. Lenny had let her down by botching the routine questioning at the ball game, Sasha had reemerged as a person of interest, but Vivien still had doubts about Linda and Walter. As she punched "DC chiropractors" into the computer to find a number for Harish's office, Vivien revisited the possibility that Lenny could be more involved than he appeared.

Maybe he hadn't been completely honest with her regarding what Sasha had really said. Maybe Sasha's sobbing jag at the ball game was not related to her deceased husband.

"What's Harish's last name, Mooky?" For a second she imagined herself as a private investigator solving mysteries with the help of her faithful dog. This made her laugh out loud. She tried to picture the name of Harish's clinic from the TV commercials, but she was drawing a blank. She could see the pictures in her mind.

There was a shot of the outside of the building and then a pretty Indian girl looked up from her reception desk, smiling into the camera while the voiceover said, "Do you have chronic back pain? Have you been injured at work or in a car accident? Don't want to take the risk of surgery? Call . . . ." And that was all she could remember. She had no recollection of the practice's name, but the final shot was of the office staff, all wearing crisp white lab coats, smiling and waving at the camera. She could see Harish in the back, standing behind the pretty girl, looking a bit uncomfortable but faking a smile and waving as the words on the screen flashed a phone number, web address, and street address.

She scrolled through the listings, amazed at how many chiropractors were listed. If there were this many people doing it, maybe there was something to it after all. Maybe it could work for her. None of the names looked familiar. She looked up at the clock. It was just after 10:30 in the morning. The regulars would start gathering at the park in about six hours. Sasha was always the first to arrive.

Vivien usually timed her arrival to get there about the same time as Lenny, who generally showed up just past prime time, which was around five o'clock. Today she would change things up. She had some errands to run, and she vowed that today was the day she would take the flip-flop to the police. She wasn't going to learn anything more from it since it probably was totally unrelated to the crime. Just in case, she got out the digital camera and took several pictures of the over-stuffed baggie. She made a mental note to take the camera with her to the dog park that day, return to the site where she had found the shoe, and take a few more shots.

She would go to the dog park early to make sure she could spend some time alone with Sasha. She would ask her, point-blank, if Phyllis was in India with Harish. Vivien read the paper every day and hadn't seen any mention of Phyllis being missing. It was all so odd. A jolt ran through her as she pictured herself arriving at the park and finding Phyllis and Sasha sitting at the picnic bench chatting about the trip.

"That would put an end to the little adventure right there, wouldn't it, Mooky?" Then all this—the bone, the investigation, the shoe, meeting Will—would all change into a big charade. She pushed the uncomfortable feelings aside and moved forward with her plan. It was cool outside, so she'd take Mooky with her in the mini-van. She gathered her keys, sunglasses, wallet, dog leash, poop bags, checkbook, and the baggie with the flip-flop as she prepared to leave the house.

She loaded the dog and began moving through the day, feeling a bit of dread as she drove towards the Fourth District Metropolitan Police Headquarters on Georgia Avenue. The Natural Death Squad was based here. This was where Will worked—at least until his transfer was complete.

The precinct was a nondescript white brick building jammed between a car dealership and a convenience store. Vivien parked the minivan in a visitor slot in the shade, cracked the windows for the dog, grabbed the baggie, and walked to the front door. It was cool inside and she could smell bleach from the freshly mopped floor. There was a wide marble hallway leading to a bulletproof window with a bored-looking uniformed cop sitting behind it, making notes on a manila file. He looked up at her and said, "Can I help you, ma'am?"

God, she hated being called that, but she let it go. "Ah, yes. I need to turn this in." She placed the baggie on the narrow countertop between her and the officer, and could already see it wasn't going to fit through the little slot in the bottom. "Turn it into whom?" said the man, eyeing the baggie.

"Homicide, or maybe Natural Death—I'm not sure who's handling the investigation. Is Detective Evans on duty?"

"Who's Detective Evans?" said the officer. He was probably in his fifties and was balding, with dark skin, eyes, and hair. He looked Hispanic and his name badge said "Ayala."

"He works out of here. Natural Death Squad?" She tried to remember the other cop's name. "He works with another guy—large, over six feet, probably two-fifty, African American, wears a hat?" she said.

"Wears a hat," said the cop, and sucked a tooth.

"Yes. Actually, they both wear hats. This is a flip-flop that I found in the woods near a crime scene and I was told to turn it in."

"Mm-hm," said the cop.

Vivien bit her lip, just waiting for the guy to ask her why the shoe was torn to pieces. She fought back the urge to just tell him. He was reaching into a file cabinet, a motion that looked like he had done it a thousand times before. A form appeared on the shelf between them. It slid easily under the glass.

"Fill this out and we'll take care of it, ma'am," he said as he pushed it towards her.

Vivien resisted the desire to pepper the man with questions. She filled out the form, trying to remember the right dates. Had it only been eight days ago? It seemed like this had been going on for at least a year. She slid the form back through. "I have pictures, too," she said.

"If we need those we'll contact you."

"So that's it?" she asked.

"Unless you have something else you'd like to turn in to the police," he answered. He was looking at her with a dead look in his eyes.

She wondered if he was on tranquilizers or something. He seemed drugged. "Do you need to take a statement or something?"

"No, ma'am. No statement is needed at this time. Is this your correct phone number?"

"No. It's my incorrect phone number," she snapped. She could feel her forehead getting hot.

"Excuse me?" he said and his head cocked to the right just slightly. Finally, a reaction.

"I'm sorry, Officer. I just thought there would be, you know, more to it than filling out a report. I found this fairly close to the scene of a possible homicide."

"Yes, ma'am, and this is your correct phone number. Is that right?"

His eyes now seemed to have gained some focus. He was looking right at her and she tried to imagine herself sitting on the other side of the glass, interviewing somebody like her. Crazy people showed up at police stations all the time. People who wanted attention by pretending to have committed crimes, and sometimes actual criminals, secretly taunting the cops by showing up and acting innocent. Daring the police to figure it out and catch them. Then there were the neighborhood busybodies. The amateur detectives—like her. "Yes, Officer. That's my correct phone number." She turned on a heel and padded back towards the outside world. She wondered how long the bag of shoe pieces would sit on the shelf or if it would ever actually be "turned in."

She spent the next two hours like she was sleepwalking. She ate lunch but couldn't taste it and shopped without any passion, always keeping one eye on the clock. Seeing Phyllis sitting at the picnic table today would be like hitting the restart button on her old life. Things would return to where they were, a predictable existence of the daily routine with no cause for suspicions of foul play, intrigue, or dishonesty. Just a bunch of people meeting at the dog park, barely interacting, while the canines got some exercise. She made her usual rounds—post office, grocery store, bank—and returned home with time left to kill.

Is this what she did every day? How did she use to work forty or fifty hours a week and still have time for a life? How did anybody do it? She watched TV but couldn't sit still. She tried sitting on the porch but her IKEA furniture was uncomfortable. She needed cushions. She tried looking through catalogs, but she didn't like anything. She couldn't find the catalog she really liked. She jumped online and looked at animal-related emails that people had sent her.

She opened YouTube and watched a squirrel that could water ski and a Jack Russell terrier that rode a skateboard. There was an elephant in India that could paint pictures of elephants. Animals were quite amazing—especially considering they were animals. An hour slipped away. She decided to watch one more video—a dancing border collie. Wait. Another elephant, this one sitting on a car. Leopards lying on somebody's car hood in Africa. Okay. What time was it? Shit. She was on the verge of being late.

She quickly reassembled the personal traveling items needed for the dog park–leash, poop bags, keys, sunglasses, purse, water bottle, collapsible doggie water bowl, and sun block. She checked her watch and hustled Mooky back into the minivan. She made sure the oven was off, locked the door, and climbed into the van. She sat impatiently through the red lights and the scattered clumps of traffic that were already starting to thicken as the work day came to an end. She forced herself to come to complete stops at the intersections and resisted the urge to cross a double yellow line to pass a grandma.

She arrived at the parking lot exactly eight minutes later than she wanted to be and was already beating herself up for blowing the opportunity to catch Sasha alone. She popped open the rear door, herded Mooky away from the woods towards the field, and she walked purposefully towards the picnic table. As the days had grown hotter, a couple of the guys had dragged the table closer to a small knot of trees that offered a bit of shade. The trees were in a shallow hollow in the land that couldn't be seen from the parking lot. Vivien walked towards the table, craning her neck to see who might be sitting there. Shit. She should have checked the parking lot.

She spun around and saw Sasha's Subaru with the Union Jack sticker on the bumper. Excellent. There were other cars in the lot, but none she recognized. What kind of car did Phyllis drive? She tried to remember. SUV? She was terrible at identifying cars. Such a chick, sometimes. She tried to keep her walking speed down and nudged Mooky in the general direction of the table. What had gotten into her dog? All Mooky seemed to want to do was get into the woods.

"Want to see Polly, Mooky? Polly's here, look."

Polly was a prim and proper poodle, always sporting a fresh haircut and polished toenails. Sasha was actually a bit of an eccentric, in Vivien's book. Always had been. She craned her neck again, thought briefly of a yoga pose she used to do, and saw what she'd been waiting to see. Sasha at the table, Polly standing nearby at full attention, and somebody else sitting with her back to Vivien. Somebody wearing a floppy hat. A floppy hat because she'd had too much sun in India?

Had she ever seen Phyllis wearing a hat? She tried to remember. She looked at the person's shoulders and tried reverting to her training as a professional observer. Was the person male or female? How tall were they? How old? What color eyes and hair? Well, the hat was killing her there. She looked at Sasha instead. She had her hands on her chin, listening to something. Tales from the subcontinent? She was too far away to hear the voices. Was Sasha looking at her? It was hard to tell because Sasha was wearing sunglasses. She resisted the urge to give a little wave. She looked down at Mooky, pretending to brush something off her back.

Mooky was walking forward in a comfortable trot, tail and ears low as she pointed her nose in Polly's general direction.

"That's right, Mooky. See? That's Polly."

In her mind Vivien told herself to be quiet. She was supposed to be investigating; for God's sake. She listened to the sound of her own footsteps and walked in a more quiet way. She zipped her lip and trained her eyes on the picnic table. Was there anything on top? Pictures from the trip? Nothing. She heard Sasha laugh. A nice sound—sophisticated, almost. How could anybody laugh in a sophisticated way? She was crazy. She was losing her mind. Who was on the other side of the table?

"Hello Sasha," said Vivien.

"Viv, how are you, sweetie? You remember Susan, don't you?"

"What?" said Vivien. "Oh. Susan. Not . . . oh. Sure. Of course. Hi, Susan."

Her brain spun around inside her skull for a few seconds. She felt dizzy as she tried to get a grip on what was happening. Phyllis was not at the picnic table; Susan was. Susan used to have a cocker spaniel named Maurice. Everybody called him Moe. Moe lived to almost 15 and then Susan had to do the unspeakable. Nobody had seen her in weeks, since without a dog there was no reason to come to the park. Now she was back, but still without a dog.

"Hi, Viv, good to see you. How's our Mooky?" said Susan.

"Oh, she's fine. How have you been?"

"Eh," said Susan, "getting through it, you know . . ."

"Sure. It's terrible. I don't even like to think about it," said Vivien.

"Then let's don't, shall we?" said Sasha.

"Well, I'm off," said Susan. "Dentist appointment. Such an exciting life, huh?"

"Take care," said Sasha. "We miss you, darling."

Susan took her leave and walked slowly back towards the cars.

"Horrible," said Vivien.

"'Tis, isn't it?" said Sasha. "It's the unfortunate side of dog ownership, I'm afraid."

"Um, yeah. Anyway. I'm glad I caught you here, Sasha. I wanted to ask you—did Phyllis not go to India with Harish?"

Vivien watched Sasha's expression as she asked the question, observing carefully, looking for any reaction and she immediately got one. It was almost imperceptible, but a stoniness seemed to wash over the older woman's face. Vivien immediately doubted her own observation, but she could swear she saw Sasha's chin jut out, just the slightest bit. What was that thing about the British having a stiff upper lip?

"She was supposed to go, but I think she changed her mind at the last minute and decided not to go," said Sasha.

Vivien turned questions over in her mind, trying to figure out how to ask them without arousing suspicion or having Sasha clam up on her. She needed to play it cool. Very smooth.

"Were she and Harish having problems?" said Vivien.

Sasha didn't blink but she did pause for a second before saying, "Well, I think anybody who's been married for eighteen-and-a-half years goes through rough patches, Vivien. You've never been, have you?"

"Me? Married? No."

"Married to your job, though, weren't you?"

For a second Vivien was happy they were talking about her and wanted to share her feelings about duty and honor but then realized Sasha had flipped the conversation around.

"Well, it was a satisfying career at times. I enjoyed the sense of duty. You know? I felt like I had a place in life."

"Of course, darling. That's important for all of us." Sasha patted Vivien's hand and Vivien felt a bond with Sasha that she had never experienced before. Maybe Sasha wasn't the slightly stuck-up elitist that Vivien had always thought she was. "But I think it's even harder for those in law enforcement or ex-law enforcement like yourself. You get caught up in all that hoo-hah, wave-the-flag kind of nonsense, don't you?"

Vivien felt her face flush and she took back the nice things she was thinking about Sasha. She really was a nasty little bitch.

"So, you haven't seen or heard from Phyllis in how long?" asked Vivien.

"Oh, taking over the investigation, are you? Well. I'll tell you the same thing I told the real coppers and Leonard. I saw her the day before she was supposed to leave. We met here in the morning. She said she didn't want to go to bloody India and I haven't seen or heard from her since."

Sasha looked at Vivien like she was accusing her of something before glancing away and rubbing Polly's back as the poodle stood and looked towards the woods. "You know, she's not nearly as dreadful as you make her out to be, Viv. She's actually a very beautiful person."

Vivien couldn't see Sasha's eyes. She was wearing sunglasses and looking away. Her face showed no emotion.

"I never had anything against her, Sasha. And all this mystery or whatever it is just has me curious about a lot of things, that's all. Plus Walter has said a bunch of stuff."

"Walter?" sniffed Sasha. "Oh, please. The bald blowhard who believes he's God's gift to all womankind?"

Vivien looked over her shoulder, expecting Walter to appear upon the mention of his name.

"Wait, don't tell me," said Sasha. "He told you that he and Phyllis were having an affair."

"Not exactly. He actually told me that you and—" But Sasha cut her off.

"Let me tell you something about Walter," said Sasha. "He was here the day that Phyllis unfortunately bumped her car into a tree, and he's been making up stories about it ever since. And I'll tell you something else about Walter and Phyllis—"

Just then Vivien's concentration was broken by the sound of car tires squealing across asphalt. Her head instinctively snapped towards the sound. Somebody had just slammed on the brakes to avoid hitting something or maybe the driver's reaction was a second too late to avoid a crash. Vivien instinctively flinched, while waiting to hear the crunch of metal. She looked down under the table and felt her stomach pitch as she realized Mooky was gone.

She turned her head towards the terrible screeching sound to see an SUV stopped in the middle of the street, and she thought she saw the tip of Mooky's tail disappearing under the front bumper. Vivien scanned the immediate area as a lump of black fear seized her mind. Her hands went to her face as she hoped against hope that she didn't see what she thought she just saw—her dog being hit by a car. A dog that she had raised as a puppy, killed on the street by a careless driver? She was aware that she was now on her feet, running towards the stopped car. She watched the driver get out of the car and looked under the tire farthest from her.

Maybe it was a squirrel and Mooky was someplace else. She felt nauseous and light-headed and already decided that she would kill the driver if her dog was . . . She couldn't think about it and stretched herself trying to see what she didn't want to see.

CHAPTER 27

Mooky heard the screeching tires at the same instant that she felt the car scrape against her back. It was a loud and terrible noise very close to her ears, which made her drop her head, tuck her tail between her legs, and run faster than she had ever run before. Her back arched inward protecting her beautiful tail from the noise. Her claws slipped on the pavement, trying to find soft earth to dig into. She heard a snap and felt a twinge in her paw. There wasn't much pain, but now her foot felt slightly different.

If she hadn't been moving so fast she might have favored it or at least stopped to give it a lick. She was aware that the car had stopped and she heard Vivien calling her name from somewhere behind her. She kept her head low, ignored whatever had happened to her back and foot, and concentrated on getting her paws back onto the earth. The car had created a different smell around her when it made the loud noise, a heavy dark smell that for a second blotted out the aroma that had drawn her towards the woods in the first place.

The smell from the trees was one of those compelling smells that she could not refuse. A smell that would pull her away from Vivien's side, away from Polly and the old ladies with their smells of flowers, dust, fabric, and dog treats, away towards the woods and back towards the spot where she found the magic bone. She would return to this spot to find the source of the marvelous smell and drape herself in it. Then she would carry the thing back to Vivien and present it to her and she would be a good dog again.

Since Mooky would find the thing that made the smell, it would belong only to her. She might keep it in one piece or perhaps she would tear it into many things. Maybe she would eat it or drop it in the yard and roll around on it coating herself with it forever. The smell was just a trace now, mixed in with the heaviness from the car, but there was enough of it to get the direction. She pointed her nose at the woods, felt her paws reach the turf, and dug in as the grass rushed by below her.

She felt the sun on her back and then cool shade as she crossed the line into the thicket. The smells in here were familiar and fresh. Rotting leaves, trees, traces of the animals that came out at night, and that other smell. The smell that could not be refused. She reached the spot and stopped to scratch the earth and examine her paw.

One of her nails was cracked so she licked it and gave it a sniff. It was fine. She craned her neck to look at her back, but couldn't see much. She gave her tail a quick inspection and was relieved to see it was still attached to her. Her attention returned to the ground as she begin nosing around, trying to pick up the whiff that had carried her this far.

The smell of the bone was still there, but not as strong, as she lifted her head and flared her nostrils, trying to get a bead on where it was coming from. She heard a noise, snapping sticks and footsteps on leaves. Slight vibrations coming through the ground told her that somebody was coming towards her. She heard her name being called and turned towards the sound to see Vivien picking her way down the path.

"Mooky! Do not move! Oh my God!"

Mooky didn't know any of these words other than her name so she stopped, watched Vivien, and gently swooped her tail in long, slow strokes. The tone of Vivien's voice meant something serious and Mooky assumed that she was being a bad dog again. She hadn't taken anything off the table, she hadn't peed in the house, but she did run away. If she could find what she was looking for and give it to Vivien, the rest of it wouldn't matter. This was a thing that could not be ignored and so only Mooky knew where it was.

"Mooky. Do not move. Sit, Mooky."

Vivien was closer now and she heard the "sit" word. She

dropped her ears, began to pant slightly and considered sitting, but Vivien didn't sound that serious so she remained standing, pivoting her head, longing to pick up the scent.

"You are a very bad dog, Mooky. You sit, right now."

This "sit" sounded more serious, but Mooky refused, knowing that if she got on that smell she wouldn't want to waste any time moving from a sit to a full-out run.

"You are in such trouble. Do not move, Mooky."

She felt Vivien's hand on the scruff of her neck and then heard the sound of the leash snapping onto the collar.

"Oh my god," said Vivien. "You're bleeding. Oh, Mooky. Jesus Christ."

She felt a twinge of pain somewhere on her back and watched Vivien look at something on her fingers, Mooky sniffed at the hand but Vivien pulled her fingers out of reach.

"Stop. You're a very lucky dog, Mooky. Jesus. Come on."

She felt the tug on her collar and initially resisted moving, but Vivien was serious about leaving. She reluctantly turned her shoulders towards where the sunlight was coming from, dropped her tail, and began loping behind Vivien. The wind changed for a second as old smells were replaced by new ones and there, just for a second, there it was. She stopped in her tracks, turned towards the smell, and felt the leash go tight around her neck. "Come, Mooky."

She knew this word but didn't really care for it. It usually meant she would have to go somewhere she didn't want to go. This was one of those times. She felt the collar being pulled and she locked her legs, refusing to move.

"Come on, Mooky. You're going to the vet, immediately. And that idiot in the car is going to pay the bill."

She didn't know any of these words and she craned her neck into the position that allowed her to slip the collar if she wanted to, but then the wind switched around again and the smell was gone. She looked into the woods, then back at Vivien as she was pulling on the leash. She would go. She would be a good dog and obey, but the thing in the woods belonged to her and she would find it again, just as soon as the wind changed.

CHAPTER 28

Vivien approached the car where the SUV owner had stopped. He had pulled it to the side of the road and stood with his hands on his hips, sweating in the heat with his cell phone in his hand. He looked like a typical government worker—navy slacks, long sleeved shirt, collar undone. The tie was probably in the front seat. He looked to be in his mid-30s and totally average looking. He seemed nervous. "Is she all right? I'm really sorry. I love dogs. She just came out of nowhere."

Vivien wanted to be angry at him and read him the riot act, but he seemed more nervous than she was. She felt fairly sure her dog was fine. "Just do me a favor when you come through here. Slow down and stay off the cell phone, okay? We all have dogs running around here."

"Yeah. Sure. I mean, yes, ma'am. I didn't realize this was a dog park. Did she get out of the fence?"

There was no fence and, technically, the dog park didn't exist. The regulars played an ongoing cat-and-mouse game with the Park Police who sometimes wrote tickets for dogs who were not on a leash. Even though talking on a cellphone while driving is against the law in the District, Vivien was also legally in the wrong.

"Just slow down, okay?" she said. She walked by him without making eye contact and guided Mooky back to the picnic table, where she and Sasha inspected the dog for injuries. They both decided that a quick trip to the vet wouldn't hurt.

Three hours later she was back in her house, hungry, emotionally drained, and two hundred dollars lighter. The prognosis was good.

Mooky had a broken toenail, which looked nasty but would grow back, and a small cut on her back, which would heal. All and all she was a very lucky. Vivien moved past the feeling of being a lousy dog owner for not paying attention and rejected the notion that she owned a bad dog.

She was still angry at the bozo SUV driver for talking on the phone, going too fast in the park, and nearly killing her best friend. She was not happy with the vet who charged her a boatload of money for a spritz of antiseptic and some white medical tape on Mooky's nail. She dropped her keys on the table, examined the cut on Mooky's back for the twelfth time, and grabbed the phone to call Lenny.

She was sure this latest incident was the talk of the dog park and she was looking forward to providing her version of what happened. Since it was her dog, her version should be the only one that mattered. Plus, there was the revelation of what Sasha had said. She wanted to review the information with Lenny, even though she realized his limitations as a crime investigator. If she was Sherlock Holmes, he was not so good as Dr. Watson. She wondered if Agatha Christie had a sidekick, and as she dialed Lenny's number she made a note to herself about reading one of her books.

She tried to remember the last book she had read. Was it the one about the geisha girl in China? Or maybe it was the one about feeding your dogs a diet of raw meat? Did that qualify as a real book? Lenny's phone was ringing but he wasn't picking up. Vivien looked at the clock. Quarter to seven. He might still be at the park. Four rings. He wasn't there.

She used the phone to scratch her head and thought about changing her hair color. Maybe just cut it really short for the summer. Maybe go with a spiky look like all the kids were doing. Were they still doing that? Maybe go with something redder. Would Will like that? She should call him. She wanted to talk to somebody. Seven rings. Where was the answering machine?

"Hello?"

"Lenny, oh thank God. Did you hear what happened?"

"Well, yes, darling, of course I heard. I just walked in the door.

Is she okay?"

"She's fine, just a scratch and a broken nail, but they still charged me two hundred dollars."

"You know—they are fucking pirates. I don't know how they sleep at night. I took Buddy in there last winter for some sniffles. He was doing this coughing noise, like kennel cough but not that bad and—"

"Lenny. Listen. I talked to Sasha, and Phyllis wasn't at the park today.

"You what?"

Vivien could hear the confusion in his voice and knew that she wasn't making any sense. Her mind was going faster than her mouth.

"Sorry. I went to the park early today to talk to Sasha about Phyllis. Today is the day when Phyllis is supposed to be back from India, assuming she went to India at all, and when I went to the park I saw somebody sitting with Sasha. I thought it was Phyllis, but it was actually Susan. Remember Susan, who had that cocker spaniel that always smelled kind of funny, like moth balls or something?"

"Maurice. Moe. Sure I remember. What a sweetie. But listen, Viv. Darling. Do you think that maybe you're obsessing over this whole Phyllis thing a little too much? I mean, aren't the police looking into all of this?"

"No. Will's been reassigned. He's off the case. That's the thing. Nobody is following up on any of this." For the first time she heard a trace of desperation in her own voice.

The other end of the line went silent for a few seconds as Vivien tried to picture what Lenny was doing. She pictured him in his house with the opera magazines and the tennis matches circled in the TV listings. Was he rubbing his mostly bald skull trying to figure out what to say? Was he pacing between the matching sofas in his living room?

She looked around her own house and saw the clutter creeping back into the corners, refilling the surface areas of her tables and chairs with more piles of worthless material. Didn't she have better things to do than play detective? Maybe she should try golf. That's what her mother did.

"Why do you feel like this is your responsibility, Vivien?"

The tone of his voice had changed and it was unusual for him to call her by her full name. She was always "Viv" or "darling" or "sweetie" except for times when he was being really serious—which were rare. She was aware for the first time that he was talking to her like a therapist, which was comforting and disconcerting at the same time.

"It's not like that, Lenny. I'm just, you know, curious."

"Mmm-hmmm." He didn't sound convinced. "So what is your intention? What is it that you want to happen?" Again, with the therapist voice.

"I want to confront Harish."

"Harish? Oh come on, Viv, you don't even know the man, do you?"

"I've met him at the park a couple of times. I don't mean confront. I just want to ask him, face to face, where Phyllis is. Out of concern."

"Out of concern," Lenny repeated back to her.

"That's right. Do you know where his office is?"

"You're going to call him at his office to ask him where his wife is? Don't you think that's crossing some kind of line, Viv? I mean really, sweetie, you should take some time and think this through. I'm afraid you're overwrought."

The word "overwrought" made Vivien think of Sherlock Holmes—it sounded so British and fancy.

"Lenny. I'm not stupid. I have unspecified back pain. I'm on disability, remember? Herniated disc and all?"

"You're going to go there under the guise of seeking treatment, then?"

"Seeking treatment. Exactly," said Vivien.

There was the slightest slice of silence in the conversation. Then Lenny came back and said, "I know exactly where his clinic is; it's right down the street from my dry cleaner. What time are we going?"

CHAPTER 29

Vivien had trouble sleeping that night and woke up the next morning feeling blurry. She hadn't planned on including Lenny on the visit but she was actually glad he had inserted himself into the situation. If nothing else, he would serve as a sounding board for whatever new information was about to be gleaned. Lenny remembered the name of the clinic and she called for an appointment as soon as it opened that morning.

The woman who answered had a thick but understandable Indian accent and told Vivien there were no appointments available. Vivien dropped in the fact that she knew Harish from the dog park. She was put on hold briefly and was then told she could come in for a fifteen-minute "consultation" at 2:45.

One of Lenny's appointments had canceled so his schedule was flexible for the day. The plan was to go from the chiropractor's office to the dog park. The dogs would stay in the car with the windows down, and if they got hung up in the waiting room, Lenny could let them out, give them water, and keep them cool. Vivien fidgeted through the morning, moved some piles of stuff around in the house, watched Martha Stewart, balanced her checkbook, and looked at animal videos on YouTube until it was time to go.

She swung by Lenny's and followed his directions to the clinic, which was located in a non-descript office park near American University. They rode the elevator to the third floor and found Harish's office, which was called "American Chiropractic," which Vivien found ironic.

"I wonder why he didn't call it 'Indian Chiropractic,'" she said.

"Stop, Viv. That's not nice," said Lenny. "It's because it's close to the school."

She smiled to herself for making a joke, or trying to, anyway. Lenny was usually the funny one, while she played the straight man role. This caused her to giggle, since she was the straight one but not a man.

"Stop, Viv, it wasn't that funny."

"I know—I was just thinking of something else," she said.

"Have the giggles, do we, darling?"

He drew out the words, sounding British, as she pulled the heavy glass door open and stepped inside. It was done up in typical doctor's office décor, with magazines fanned out and a ring of chairs, mostly occupied by a cross section of everyday people, flanking a reception area. Vivien was still giggling as she approached the counter, but her smile faded as she instantly recognized the woman behind the reception desk as the pretty girl waving in the commercial.

She looked different here—smaller, with a haunted look in her eyes that bordered on angry.

"Can we help you?" she asked.

Vivien instantly recognized the voice as the one that had answered the phone and booked the appointment.

"Ah, yes, I called in this morning about an appoint . . . I mean, a consultation."

"The woman from the dog park, of course. Is it Ms. Szabo?"

"That's right—Viv. Vivien Szabo."

"Of course, Ms. Szabo. Have a seat and we'll call you when the doctor is ready." The girl seemed a bit cold to Vivien, and she wondered if she acted like this to all new patients.

Vivien nodded and sat down next to Lenny, who had already claimed a seat and was leafing through last month's edition of *Metropolitan Home*.

"She seems like a lovely and charming person," said Lenny.

"Who?" said Vivien. "The receptionist?" She dropped her voice and said, "She's the one in the commercial, waving at the camera."

Lenny touched her upper arm and looked incredulous for a second. "You're right," he whispered back, "except she looks bigger on TV."

They sat and flipped pages while Vivien practiced in her mind what she was going to say when it was her time. She hoped she wouldn't have to take her clothes off. How did they actually work? She didn't really have a clue. She leaned over to tap Lenny to ask him when she heard a door close.

She looked towards the receptionist and saw Harish come out from the back rooms. He approached the receptionist and quietly said something to her. The girl was still seated and he had to lean over to get closer to her. Vivien watched as his hand went to her shoulder and seemed to linger there, just for a second too long for casual contact.

She nudged Lenny, who looked at her and said, "Hmmm?"

She motioned towards Harish and Lenny followed her gaze. Together they watched the two of them interact. The doctor and nurse— or whatever her title was—were not looking out towards the patients. Instead they kept their eyes on each other and talked in hushed tones. Then Harish gave her a pat on the shoulder and disappeared again into the offices behind the desk.

"Did you see that?" whispered Vivien.

"That was Harish," said Lenny.

God, he could be so dense sometimes. "I know that, Lenny. Did you notice how he was touching her?"

"Who?"

"Ms. Szabo?"

Vivien jumped like she had been jabbed with a needle. "Yes?"

"He's ready for you."

Vivien gave Lenny a "here we go" face, stood up and smoothed the front of her shorts, but didn't know why. She cleared her throat and walked behind the desk while noticing the girl's icy stare—or was she just bored senseless by the typical routine of the workday? It was hard to tell.

"Back here?" asked Vivien.

"Yes. First room on your right." The girl wasn't even looking at her, but was instead focusing on the contents of a pink file in front of her. Vivien pushed the door of the room open and found a typical doctor's office except maybe a bit warmer in tone. The walls were painted a pumpkin color and there was a chart of the human spine on the wall. A small window on the outside wall provided a view of the parking lot. There was an examining table, and a fairly healthy-looking ficus plant in the corner.

Vivien resisted the idea of sitting on the examining table but she felt awkward standing around in the middle of the room and briefly considered asking the unpleasant young woman if she should sit. Instead she kind of floated around the room, looked out the window, and felt generally uncomfortable.

She was aware of movement behind her, so she turned and there he was. Harish. He was taller than she remembered and was wearing a white lab coat and chic designer eyeglass, with strands of his thinning jet black hair combed straight back. His nose was pointy like a bird's beak and his skin was a pleasant shade of mocha. He was carrying a black lacquer clipboard. His hands looked too big for the rest of his body and Vivien wondered if that had something to do with his chosen profession.

"Hello there, Ms. Szabo. One of our dog park friends, yes?"

Vivien looked at him and considered the possibility that he had no idea who she was, even though they had been introduced at least twice. Or the cool greeting was because he wanted to be in control and detached by pretending not to recognize her.

"Hi, Ha— doctor. I'm sorry. I don't know what to call you, but we've met a couple of times. I'm Vivien." She was aware of herself pointing to her chest like she was talking to somebody who didn't speak English and immediately felt dumb for doing it.

"Of course, Vivien. Please sit and let's have a chat."

That sounded nice. She could probably chat without having to take anything off and she hoisted herself onto the table as gracefully as possible. "Will it take very long? Because I have the dogs in the car," she said.

"Not long at all, Vivien. This is just a preliminary consultation to see if we can help you. Did you give the name of your insurance company to Mina yet?"

That must have been what they were talking about. The insurance forms. That's what the doctors always wanted to talk about. Getting paid. Bastards. "Um, no. But I can leave it with her on the way out," said Vivien.

"Okay, fine," he said.

She was sitting on the table, shifting her weight a bit trying to get comfortable in a situation that didn't encourage comfort.

"So do you have a history of back problems, Vivien?" He was slowly reaching towards the sides of her neck while looking down his nose at her. "I'm just going to touch you up here to see how you are aligned, okay? It won't hurt."

"Oh, sure," she said. "Yes, I'm on disability from the Secret Service. I messed up one of my discs running the obstacle course and then aggravated it on duty with the Presidential detail, and had to retire early."

"I see," he said.

His big hands were soft and gentle as he laid them on the side of her face and gently rotated her head from one side to the other. "Any pain here?" he asked.

"No," she said, "it usually doesn't hurt unless, you know, I overdo it at the park or gardening or shopping or something."

"I see," he said and dropped his hands. "Have you seen a chiropractor before?"

"No, I usually just take Tylenol. Did you just get back from

144

India?"

Vivien noticed that he cocked his head ever so slightly, like Mooky did when she heard a siren. Did that mean something?

"Yes," he said. "I go every year. Do you know which number disc you injured?"

"No," she said. "I used to. I'm sure it's in my records somewhere. I guess I should have brought them. So did Phyllis go with you?" She heard herself just blurt it out. The question hung there in the air and Vivien was aware that the answer would somehow decide her future. How could all this lead her here? What was she possibly thinking? She'd turned into Gladys Cravitz, the busybody from the "Bewitched" TV show and a terrible neighbor.

She watched him carefully, ready to hang on any word that came out of his mouth, wanting, hoping, wishing for the mystery to continue.

"No. Not this time," he said. He looked down for just a second and seemed to study her knees. "Any discomfort from walking?"

"No? I'm sorry. Walking? No. It doesn't hurt to walk. Because we've been wondering at the dog park where she's been."

"You walk at the dog park, Vivien? Into the woods?"

"Almost every day. It helps tire the dogs out, you know?"

"Of course, and exercise is good for you, too. I would suggest stretching, if you're not already, or more if you are," he said as he stood up and reached for his clipboard. "There are some yoga poses that many of my patients find beneficial. If you'd like to proceed with treatment I would ask that you bring in your records and any recent x-rays that you have, and we can work on some minor adjustments to relieve your occasional pain. I usually recommend a block of treatments—at least five to start with, maybe once a week—till we see how you're progressing, and then make adjustments from there. Any questions for me, Ms. Vivien?"

At that moment, Vivien had many questions for the good doctor, but knew she had to play it cool. "So where is Phyllis?" That's what came out.

Harish clicked his pen shut and slid it into his breast pocket without making eye contact. He placed one hand on the doorknob and Vivien wondered if he was anxious to get out of the room.

"Well, um, Vivien, if you must know, Phyllis and I are trying to work a few things out. She's staying with her sister for a while in Connecticut, which explains why you haven't seen her at the dog park. Please see the receptionist on your way out about the insurance and do let us know if we can help you, okay?"

"Oh. Sure. I'm sorry, doctor, I didn't mean to pry. Thanks." She watched him turn around and disappear through the door. She felt her face heat up again. The answer was no answer. She felt nothing. She was nothing. She had learned nothing. And this was probably going to cost her one hundred dollars. For nothing. Or was there something?

She hopped off the table, fluffed her hair, and prepared herself to deal with the mean woman at the front desk. In Vivien's mind the woman had already passed over into the realm of mean. For what? Vivien knew she was overreacting to everything. She needed a hobby. She needed to get a life. Why wouldn't Sasha know if Phyllis was at her sister's? Something didn't make any sense.

CHAPTER 30

Vivien and Lenny exited Harish's office and climbed back into the minivan. They were driving down Wisconsin Avenue. Lenny had the window open and was tilting his face into the wind, doing a pretty good imitation of a dog hanging its head out the window. "So, let's review what we've learned," she said.

"Viv. Darling. Give it a rest. Can't you see I'm trying to get some sun on my lily-white skull? Bald looks better with a tan, don't you know . . ." Lenny replied.

"No, I didn't know that. Is that what you're supposed to do? Anyway. As far as you and I know, Phyllis does not have a sister in Connecticut or anywhere else."

"If you say so, sweetie."

"And if that were true that would mean that Harish would be lying."

"That is correct," said Lenny. "He would be a big, fat liar."

"And why would he be a big fat liar to us? We're nobody, just some random people from the dog park," she said.

"Speak for yourself. I am certainly a somebody, and perhaps he lied to you because it's really none of your business where his wife is or isn't."

Vivien gave him a look as she briefly considered what he said as the truth. It really wasn't any of her business—but she couldn't really stop herself, either.

"Anyway. I'm thinking if anybody knows whether or not Phyllis has a sister, it would be Sasha," said Vivien. "Plus she was getting ready to tell me something about Walter right before Mooky almost got hit."

"Walter? Is he still a suspect in your twisted little scenario? I don't think he would haul his fat ass off the picnic table for anything except maybe one of those horrible margaritas he used to make. God, what a bore," said Lenny.

"Yeah, well, he's still on the list because he may have had a motive. According to him, Phyllis tried to run him over with her car. Linda didn't like her ever since that day with the chef's knives, and Sasha was allegedly romantically involved with her, which could have gone wrong. Maybe it was a crime of passion."

Lenny sat up straight in the seat as they pulled into the parking lot of the dog park and began ticking off fingers on his hand while saying, "First of all, Walter told you most of this, and Walter is full of shit. Second of all, Linda doesn't really like anybody. Third, if Sasha and Phyllis are lesbian lovers, I will eat my hat. I mean, don't you think if that were true, one of them would have confided in 'moi,' since I am the token queer of the group? So let's just put this aside for the time being, run the doggies, and let's not mention to anybody that we just came from Harish's office, where one of us made a fool of ourselves, shall we?"

Vivien said nothing as she popped open the doors and herded the dogs towards the picnic table while keeping Mooky's nose pointed away from the woods. She didn't feel foolish at all. Lenny was so sensitive and easily embarrassed sometimes. He was also the one who threatened to break Phyllis's neck because he wasn't invited to her holiday party.

Vivien scanned the cars in the parking lot and looked at her watch. Sasha's Subaru wagon, Linda's white Jeep Cherokee, Walter's ancient Volvo wagon. Perfect. She was getting better at identifying cars just by looking at makes and models on the road while she drove around. It made her feel useful, like she was in training for something.

"Are you feeling me, sister? Are you catching my drift and all?" said Lenny.

Vivien smiled, listening to him talking like a black girl. She wished she were funnier. Will liked to laugh. Who didn't, really?

"I hear you," she said. "You don't want me to embarrass you in front of your highfalutin pals."

"I don't want you to embarrass either of us, sweetie. Me or you." He put his arm around her shoulders. She leaned into him and they walked towards the picnic table. His embrace felt strong and powerful. He was certainly strong enough to strangle somebody. Phyllis's tender little neck would have been no match for him.

She looked at the table and took in the scene. Walter sat facing them, talking to Kevin, who was a semi-retired editor for *The Washington Post*. He owned a springer spaniel named Sadie. Linda stood away from the group tossing a ball towards her Great Dane. Sasha was at the opposite end of the picnic table from Walter, speaking to Chris, a radiologist who owned a bluetick hound named Lady. In between them sat Bill, a driver for an auto parts store who owned a Rottweiler named Snoopy. A diverse group of individuals brought together by the dogs that were running and jumping, scratching and barking around them. Was there a horrible secret hiding among them, or was Vivien just bored out of her mind? There was only one way to find out.

Vivien extricated herself from Lenny's embrace and made a beeline towards Sasha.

"Hey, everybody," she said as she weaved around people and animals, moving with what she considered to be cat-like grace. Her days of blundering were over, she told herself. It was time to get serious. Once again she verified that Phyllis was not at the picnic table and sidled up to Sasha. The regulars offered greetings in the forms of nods, "hellos," and "heys."

Vivien got into a position where she could overhear Sasha's conversation and she waited for a chance to join in. They were talking about a TV program that was on last night, a forensic investigation show that Vivien didn't watch. Being ex-law enforcement, she always found herself punching holes in the theories and procedures while not really enjoying the program. She pretended to stare off into the distance while eavesdropping as nonchalantly as possible.

In a few minutes, Lenny or somebody, but usually it was Lenny, would say the magic words, "Who's walking?" Then, the walkers—which she was one of—would begin their short hike through the woods with the dogs. Sasha was not a walker and was usually gone by the time the walkers got back from the hike.

Vivien thought the talk about the show would be a perfect segue to her own investigation, but at the same time she was trying to play it cool. She decided she needed to be more low-key in how she handled this. More diplomatic and sophisticated. As she considered her options, the conversation came to a natural stopping point.

"Sasha, does Phyllis have a sister in Connecticut?" asked Vivien.

There was a moment of dead silence as the question hung there in space, unanswered. As its effect gradually dwindled away in the warm air, not being addressed, Vivien felt that somehow another awkward moment was defining the rest of her life.

"What?" said Sasha. "What did you say?"

She was sitting at the table, peering up at Vivien. Her eyes were hidden behind her oversized sunglasses and Vivien though she could detect the gin smell again. Vivien imagined that the old woman's eyes were blinking in disbelief behind the dark lenses as she acted like she was taken aback at the question.

"I said, does Phyllis have a sister in Connecticut?" She spoke the words slowly and clearly, which made them come out with a slight edge. She was tired of the game playing. It was time to get the party started. She put a hand on her hip and looked down at Sasha. The sun was behind Vivien's shoulder so the older woman was looking into the light, clearly at the disadvantage.

"What does this have to do with what we were talking about?" said Sasha. "I swear, Vivien. I believe you're halfway 'round the bend on this thing. It's really none of your business."

The last sentence came out loud, and all the heads at the picnic table turned. Vivien had been outed and the smart play would have been to apologize, acknowledge her mistake, and move away from the whole thing. But she needed to know. Instead, she bent at the waist, feeling a slight pull of pain in her back, and brought her face close to Sasha's. Now she could really smell the gin.

"I was at Harish's office today, having my back checked," said Vivien. "I'm curious about where our friend Phyllis has gone, so I asked him why she hasn't been to the park." The words sounded almost accusatory coming out of her mouth. She was aware of how it sounded but she kept going. "I asked him if Phyllis had gone to India with him, like everybody seems to think, and you know what he said? He said that Phyllis is visiting her sister in Connecticut. So, can you do me the courtesy of telling me if Phyllis has a sister in Connecticut?"

The silence was gradually reduced by a few voices in the background asking, "Who are they talking about?" and "Who's missing?" Vivien ignored these comments since these semi-regulars were obviously out of the loop on the whole thing. Instead she continued to watch Sasha's face, wishing she could actually see her eyes behind the sunglasses to see where she was looking.

Sasha stood up, looking unsteady on her feet. Vivien considered the possibility that she was not going to get an answer. It was an outrage. She considered her options. She was being made a fool. Another blown opportunity. She felt sick to her stomach and hollow inside at the same time. She stood back a step to give Sasha enough room to leave. She had been stalemated again. Sasha brought her face close to Vivien's and lowered her voice. She looked uncomfortable being the center of attention. She suddenly seemed old and frail.

"No, Vivien. There is no sister in Connecticut, or anywhere else. No sister, no brother, no nothing. She's an only child. Now, will you please leave it be? Give it a rest, for God's sake."

Vivien turned her shoulder to let the woman walk by her while feeling a wave of relief wash over her. So there it was. A strong show of emotion and the first lie revealed. The next question was who was lying and why? Vivien put a hand on Sasha's shoulder as she moved past her.

"Thanks, Sasha," she said, while looking down at the ground.

She was aware that Sasha was making her way back towards her car. She could have followed her and pushed for more information, but she didn't want to press her luck. She congratulated herself on learning something useful and now this—she was actually playing it cool for once. Sasha wasn't going anywhere.

Vivien gathered her composure, pursed her lips, and looked up at the table. Everybody had gone back to doing what they were doing before the exchange—either that or they were doing a good job of pretending to be distracted.

Nobody was looking at her except Lenny, who had a look of barely concealed disbelief on his face. The look slowly morphed into a mask of consternation and a slight hand gesture that said, "What is the matter with you?" While still looking directly at her, Lenny said, "Who's walking?"

The words seemed louder than usual as Vivien looked for Mooky and moved towards a knot of people forming around Lenny. Mooky's ears perked up at the word "walking." The walkers began pulling themselves off the picnic table. "I'll go," said Walter. "I've been on the computer all day; I need to move."

Vivien was curious about that. Another example of unusual behavior from one of the dog park regulars.

"Come on Mooky, let's go," said Vivien. She looked at her dog, who was looking at her, her tail swooping back and forth in preparation for the highlight of the day. Their lives were so simple and easy—not complicated by the big brains of humans always hatching up evil and intrigue. Vivien watched Mooky's nose twitch. Her nostrils flared open for half a second and her head snapped towards the woods. She tried to imagine what the dog could be smelling.

Mooky looked at Vivien, then looked at the woods, and sprinted towards the trees. Vivien watched in disbelief as two of the other dogs, the bluetick and Walter's dog, Lucky, joined in the chase. They ran full speed towards the opening in the trees that led to where the bone was found. Some of the dogs were yapping and barking as they streaked across the road and plunged into the shadows. Just that fast, they were gone.

CHAPTER 31

The most magical smell in the world was back and Mooky was running towards it as fast as she could go. She'd been waiting a long time for the smell to come back and now it was here. She was aware that other dogs were behind her. The other dogs would want to possess the thing, play with it, roll around on it, pee on it, tear it into many pieces, bury it, pull on it, and take it back to the people. But whoever found it first would own it forever and Mooky was running well ahead of the dogs that followed her into the woods.

The conditions for finding the thing had never been quite right until now. The wind, the air pressure, the leash, the distractions, and the aroma level weren't right. Now was the time to find the thing. Now was the time of go. She felt the temperature change as she passed from field to woods, dodging small trees and bushes to get back to where she had been before. There were other smells competing for her attention, but one smell trumped them all.

She arrived at the spot where she'd found the magic bone and put her nose to the ground. It was definitely the spot and she could smell where people had been around the area, doing things. The smell called to her from deeper in the woods and she plunged in. The other dogs were behind her, their high-pitched barks indicating the extreme importance the smell held for all of them.

Mooky moved her head and twitched her nose, looking for the trail, and there it was, stronger now than before. She clawed against the soft dirt and ran across a small hill that hid a hollow in the earth. This place was not visible to her or anybody else, but the smells could not hide. She ran down the hill, her rear feet sliding a bit on piles of dead leaves.

Down she went and the smell was all around her. Down to a little flat spot on the ground, to a place overcome with smells. There were bits of clothing and shoes and rotting meat. There was moist earth and dust and flowers and musky aromas. There was much to choose from, and Mooky began working in a circle, moving around the site, nose to the ground, trying to decide where to start.

The other dogs were beside her now and her majestic tail swooped at their arrival. The dog pack went to work investigating the various parts and pieces of things in the area. The place was awash in smells and Mooky looked for something to own. Something that would define the space and something that would remain with her forever. She saw a shape on the ground that she recognized. It was round and the word "ball" sounded in her brain.

She'd found a ball! A beautiful hard ball that smelled like no other ball she had ever smelled. She began a game of Dig-Up-the-Thing. She growled a bit to tell the other dogs that she had found a thing and the thing belonged to her as soon as she got it out of the ground.

She dug around the ball and tried to move it with her paw. She tried to bite into it, hoping to sink her teeth in for a better grip, but it was hard like a stone. She worked around it and then one of her teeth slipped inside a hole in the ball. She lifted and pried until the ball began to move and eventually it slid out of the earth. It produced another outpouring of aroma. The ball was free and in her mouth and the other dogs had become interested in the ball.

There was much to explore in this place, but for now the ball belonged to Mooky, which made the other dogs want to have it. Mooky wanted to show her new ball to Vivien, who would praise her for finding such a wonderful thing. She waggled her head, growled, and began running back out towards the picnic table.

Everybody would soon want Mooky's ball, including the other dogs that hadn't followed her into the woods. The people would want the ball, too, but she would not give it to them. They would have to chase her for it and then play Pull-the-Thing. Maybe the ball could be torn into little pieces, which would greatly increase the amount of fun. She re-emerged into the field with the ball clamped in her jaws.

From here she could see Vivien and several other people. They were coming towards her, so they could find the new place and claim it for themselves, but Mooky had found it first and it all belonged to her, just like the ball. To lure everybody away from the site, Mooky ran towards the group, ears back, tail out, claws pulling her faster towards them.

"Mooky! Come here right now."

She recognized her name and "come." She was moving in that general direction anyway. Now the fun would really begin.

CHAPTER 32

As soon as Vivien saw Mooky coming towards her, she knew the dog had a human skull in her mouth. This time there wouldn't be any speculation from Walter or anybody else regarding the object in question. There would be no theories about deer bones. The jaw bone had fallen off the skull, but there was no denying that a dog, her dog, had unearthed the gory remains of somebody, right here in Rock Creek Park.

Vivien felt strangely calm and centered as she watched Mooky loping towards her with her prize. The other dogs were following behind her, occasionally nosing each other as they got closer. It looked like the bluetick had a scrap of clothing in his mouth. Vivien stood still in the field, her hands on her hips, and watched them approach. She was aware that Lenny had caught up to her and was now standing at her side.

"Is that? Oh, Jesus," he said and laid his hands on his face. His mouth hung open as he stood and stared at the approaching pack of dogs.

Vivien ignored him and said, "That's right, Mooky, come over here to me."

She reached her hand around her back, thought briefly about how the Sig Sauer 9 mm used to feel in her hand, and pulled the Safeway bag out of her back pocket. Walter approached Vivien, and out of the corner of her eye she saw him squinting into the sun towards the dogs, obviously trying to comprehend what he was seeing. "Holy fuck. Tell me that's not a human skull."

"Mmm-hmm," said Vivien. "Got a phone on you, Walter?"

"In the car," said Walter. He was blinking and exhaling like he was trying to whistle. Vivien wondered if he was going to be sick.

Finally a reaction from the great stone face—this is what it took.

"You mind calling the DC Police? Ask for Detective McCain or Detective Evans. Tell them more evidence has been unearthed from the site they've been investigating in Rock Creek Park—or were investigating, anyway. Tell them to send forensics and a coroner. I think this whole thing is about to blow up."

Walter continued to stand there looking at the pack of approaching dogs. One of them was his, but Lucky wasn't carrying anything. He just stood there and watched. For once, Walter had been rendered speechless.

"Walter?" said Vivien.

"Yeah?"

"Can you call them? I need to get this out of Mooky's mouth."

"Oh, yeah. Sure. I can call."

Vivien was aware that Walter had walked away but she never took her eye off Mooky. "Come on, girl, come right over here." The last thing she wanted was another tragicomic chase scene between her and her dog. She wanted this to be handled with as much dignity as humanly possible, as she dropped to her knee and said, "Come on, baby, come right over here. Let's see what you got."

Vivien could hear Walter warning the other regulars to stay away from the dogs and telling them that more bones had been found—maybe he wasn't completely useless after all. Out of the corner of her eye she saw Lenny trying to compose himself. He'd pulled a red bandana out of a pocket and wiped his mouth and his forehead.

"Oh Jesus, this is fucking gruesome. Are you okay? 'Cause I really can't do this. I just can't," said Lenny.

"It's okay," said Vivien. "I got it. She's going to come right over to me and drop that, aren't you, Mooky?" Vivien was a little surprised that Mooky did exactly that. She walked up, bowed her head, and dropped the skull, which landed with a solid thump. Vivien bent at the waist, again feeling a slight pain in her back, and used the Safeway bag to pick the skull up without putting any prints on it.

"Good girl," said Vivien. She ruffled the fur on the back of Mooky's neck. "Okay, you dogs, come on. Follow me." She ran a few steps to get the dogs excited. They quickly caught on to the new game and chased Vivien back towards the picnic table and said, "Okay, everybody leash up. We have a situation in the woods and the police are already on their way." She cradled the skull in her hand, the shape reminding her of a softball.

There were murmured questions around the picnic table as the regulars began getting up and herding their respective dogs back towards the cars. Vivien watched Linda begin to move like she was leaving. "Linda?"

"Mmm-mmm, I'm not doing this again," said Linda. "My dog wasn't in there. I didn't see anything, I don't know anything, I don't want to know anything. I'm going home."

"I'm not sure you can leave. I'm not sure any of us can leave. They may want to ask some questions," said Vivien. Some of the people were already walking towards the parking lot. Lenny was sitting on the picnic table with his head down, holding his dog by the collar. Walter stood slightly away from the group, staring into his phone, holding Lucky, and watching the exodus begin. Sasha had already disappeared.

Vivien realized as a private citizen she was powerless to stop any of them from leaving and after she thought about it a second, she figured it really didn't matter who was here and who wasn't. The important thing was more evidence had been unearthed, and she was sure there was a lot more.

"Lenny?"

He waved at her without looking, and said, "I'll stay. Just keep the you-know-what in the bag. I'll be okay."

"I'll stay," said Walter.

Vivien looked at him and said, "Good. Perfect. It will be interesting to see what else they pull from the site—if they let us hang out and watch."

Lenny coughed and said, "Oh, Christ. Stop, Viv. Just stop,

okay?"

Vivien stopped talking about it, put Mooky on the leash, and sat down to wait. It didn't take long. "Jesus, Walter who did you call?" asked Vivien as a fire truck, an ambulance, two squad cars, a black Suburban, and a beige Crown Victoria pulled into the parking lot. As the first responders got out of their trucks, milled around, and checked equipment, Vivien recognized Detective McCain, the large, deliberate investigator from the Natural Death Squad. He began walking towards the picnic table with a radio in his hand. His pace was measured; his face was a mask of calm. Vivien was actually looking forward to talking to him.

He stopped in front of the table and said, "So. Here we are again. Is that the, um, object in question?" He gestured towards the plastic bag sitting on the center of the picnic table and randomly patted the dogs. "Yes, Detective. Hi, I'm Vivien Szabo. We met before."

"I remember. Jimmy's presidential detail. Secret Service, retired. Right?"

Vivien felt like she was blushing and didn't know why. "That's right. You have a great memory. Anyway, the dogs came out of the woods from over there." She pointed towards the opening in the trees as she saw another car pulling in that looked like Will's. "Oh, is this Will?"

"Excuse me?" said McCain.

Vivien ignored the question for a few seconds and watched the car until she saw Will open the door, put on his hat, and begin walking purposely towards the picnic table.

"I mean, I think Detective Evans is here, too."

McCain turned his head towards Will but said nothing. After a few seconds of thick silence, Will stood at the table.

"Hello, Viv," said Will.

"Detective," said Vivien.

"You two know each other?" said McCain.

"Um," said Will, "yes, we do. I was here when they found the first bone."

"I'm aware of that, Detective, but you just called her, 'Viv.' What exactly are you doing here, Evans? Haven't you been reassigned?"

"Yes, sir. I was close by and heard the call on the radio—just thought I'd stop by and see if I could help." Vivien noticed that his tone was slightly subservient. He was such a good cop. Except now McCain knew that she and Will were . . . what were they, dating? Did it matter?

"I see," said McCain, "just in the neighborhood with the radio on."

"Correct, sir. Um, if I may, sir, I would like to ask Viv, I mean Ms. Szabo, a question."

"Would you, now? I have a few questions myself, but let's all just stand by for a second." McCain picked up the Safeway bag, looked inside, and had no reaction. There could have been a cantaloupe in there. "Nobody move," he said. He walked away from the table carrying the skull, moving at the same pace that carried him over.

Vivien watched him hand the bag to an EMT. Then McCain gathered some officers in front of him and pointed towards the break in the trees. After some quick instructions they began dispersing towards the woods. She looked at Will, who gave her a wink. She felt a stab of panic about McCain knowing that they were linked. Were they breaking some kind of rule? Wouldn't Will know if they were?

McCain came back to the table and said, "Okay, we're going to take another look over there, and they're bringing up the K-9 unit to find out if there's, um, more to be found. In the meantime that area of the park will be off-limits to dogs, dog walkers, and everybody else. Understood?" Lenny had now brought his head back up, Walter stood off to the side with a bored look on his face, and Vivien sat and nodded.

McCain said, "Okay, good. Now, where were we?"

"I just wanted to ask Ms. Szabo if she had a chance to talk to the English lady or the chiropractor," said Will.

"Excuse me?" said McCain.

"We believe, I mean there is some circumstantial evidence, that these bones, I mean remains, may have something to do with the disappearance of a woman from the dog park," said Will.

"I'm aware of that, Detective," said McCain. "Are we both working on the same case? Maybe you're getting in some practice for that job on Homicide you want so badly?"

Vivien watched Will drop his head and look at the ground. She suddenly felt sorry for him and defensive at the same time.

Just as quickly Will's head snapped back and he looked McCain in the eye. "There's just a lot of unexplained things going on around this event, Detective"

"I'm aware of that," said McCain. "Well, I'm no forensic pathologist, but I can tell you that skull these crazy dogs found has been in the ground for at least a year, probably longer. So I doubt very much that it has anything to do with the alleged disappearance of this . . . what's her name?"

"Phyllis," said Vivien.

"Right," said McCain. "Old Phyllis has probably split town with a boyfriend and doesn't want to be found. Now y'all can go home. I don't want to see anybody at this picnic table until further notice. The dog park is closed."

CHAPTER 33

This time, Vivien took the DC Metro Police at their word and stayed away from the park. The skull discovery made the papers and the TV news, but by the next day it died down and the world moved on. The upshot was that human remains had been found in Rock Creek Park by dogs playing in the area and the police were investigating.

In the meantime, Vivien took Mooky to Kandy Kane, a community recreation area farther down Beach Drive, which she used as her back-up dog park. There was a different group of people down there and a different group of dogs. There was no walking trail through the woods, but there was a pond and a small creek that ran through the area. But it wasn't the same vibe. She missed her normal routine and was frustrated she couldn't talk with the regulars about finding the skull. Calling them on the phone held no appeal; it somehow seemed too personal.

Will called her after the scene with Detective McCain and told her they needed to "cool it" for a while. Apparently his keen interest in the case as a friend of a witness and a professional law enforcement officer was muddying the waters. In the back of her mind, Vivien entertained the uncomfortable notion that maybe he was using the dog park mystery to advance his own career by getting onto the Homicide squad.

She didn't like to think about it too much and she tried to give him the benefit of the doubt, but at some point, assuming they ever saw each other again, they would have to talk about it.

Lenny didn't really like Kandy Kane, pronouncing the crowd that hung out there "standoffish." He refused to go. He and Vivien hatched a plan to return to Doggy Hill on the third day, which was today, and reclaim the area for the dogs and those who walked them.

With the regulars scattered, Vivien felt increasingly uneasy, like she was being stymied in her attempt to finish something of great importance. Now she was watching the clock and getting her things together for her triumphant return. To kill some time, she sat down at the computer to see what was on YouTube when the phone rang. Thinking it could only be Lenny, she picked up the handset and said, "Yes, Lenny?"

"Ms. Szabo, hello. It's not actually Lenny; this is Doctor Gopalakrishnad, you came in to see us last week?"

Vivien didn't recognize the name, but the voice sounded somewhat familiar.

"Doctor who?" she asked.

"Harish," said the voice. "Doctor Harish from the dog park. Phyllis's husband."

Vivien felt herself sit down as her mind began swimming. "Oh, sure," she said. Her voice sounded tinny and mechanical to her like she was a robot. "How can I help you, doctor?" It was an odd thing to say. How could she help him? Sometimes she really had no idea what would come out of her mouth at any given time.

"How's your back feeling today?" asked Harish. "Any problems?"

He was calling her to ask about her back? Maybe he was a nice man, a true care-giver. "Oh, no, it's fine. I haven't been walking as much, so I'm just kind of taking it easy," she said. She felt anxious because she had no idea what she was going to say next. She couldn't believe he had called to check on her back. "What's new with you?" she said. That's what came out.

"Actually, Vivien, I didn't call to discuss your back, but I'm glad you're not in any pain." His voice was very soothing with a trace of an accent. The "c" in call sounded kind of like a "g." The "p" in pain sounded almost like a "b." A picture of Deepak Chopra flashed in her mind. Harish also seemed like a very nice man—so calm and spiritual.

"I'm actually ashamed to tell you that I told you an untruth the other day when I said Phyllis was visiting her sister in Connecticut." Vivien held her breath and waited for him to continue. "The truth is, Vivien, I don't know where Phyllis is at the present time." "Time" sounded like "dime."

"Wow," she said. "Have you called the police?"

"The police. They have been here. Yes." He sounded like he was searching for words, obviously upset. "Perhaps you can help me, Vivien. Don't you have a background in law enforcement? Maybe you have some experience in these matters? Some calls you could make? As you may know, I was not born in this country and don't fully understand how these things work."

"Well, missing person cases can be quite complex, doctor. I'm sure you're aware of that." She liked the way that sounded. Like one professional talking to another.

"Yes. I know. Would it be possible to meet? I don't want to trouble you. Maybe meet at the dog park and we could talk about this? I'd be very grateful if you'd spend some time with me."

"Sure," said Vivien. She stood up, looking out the window towards the park. "I'm busy today, but any time after—"

"Tomorrow?" said Harish.

"Um, sure. Tomorrow is fine. What time?"

"Before it gets too crowded," said Harish, "I just don't want to answer a lot of questions. Maybe two o'clock? I can meet you at the picnic table?"

"Sure," said Vivien. "Thanks, doctor; that would be great."

"Tomorrow then," he said. "Also, one more thing, Vivien. I'm a very private person. This is very difficult for me. I appreciate your concern for my wife, but can you be discreet about our conversation? This one and also the one before? This is all very embarrassing for me, I'm afraid."

"Of course, doctor," said Vivien. "I totally understand. We can keep it just between us."

"Thank you very much, Ms. Vivien. Until tomorrow, then."

The line went dead before Vivien had a chance to say goodbye. She hung up, waited for the dial tone and then immediately dialed Lenny. She got voicemail but since she'd be seeing him in a couple of hours she didn't leave a message.

She toyed with the idea of working for Harish as a private detective to help him find Phyllis. It sounded appealing to her. She did an internet search to see how many detectives were listed and found pages and pages of them.

When she was on the force in Milwaukee she knew a guy who had retired and opened his own detective agency. He told her it was mostly spying on people cheating on their spouses and trying to catch them in the act. Not very glamorous, but he was making a living. A missing person case was certainly more interesting than adultery. She walked to the couch, lay down, and quickly drifted off thinking about it.

She took a quick nap on the couch and then began rounding up her supplies, which caught Mooky off guard, since they were at least forty minutes ahead of schedule. She herded the dog into the minivan and made the drive while thinking of nothing in particular—she was still a bit foggy from the nap. She pulled into her favorite spot and noticed right away that Sasha's car was in the lot. Perfect.

She hustled out of the van and walked purposely towards the picnic bench. Sasha was sitting by herself, flipping through a freebie newspaper. Polly the poodle came forward to greet them, the ball on her tail twitching back and forth.

"Hey," said Vivien.

"Hello, Viv," said Sasha.

Vivien made some small talk about the weather and wondered out loud if the park police would show up to shoo them away, purposely ignoring the last strained conversation they'd shared. "So Harish called me," said Vivien.

Sasha flipped a page and didn't say anything for what seemed like a long time. Vivien heard a crow cawing from the woods. She could smell fresh dog poop from somewhere and instinctively looked at her shoe, but it was clean.

"Harish? Whatever for?" said Sasha without looking up.

"He told me that he lied about Phyllis having a sister," said Vivien.

Sasha flipped a page, set her jaw, and said, "Well, bully for you, darling."

"He has a very nice office. I went there and had him check out my back," said Vivien.

Sasha flipped another page, impatience showing on her face. "He should have a nice office, considering what Phyllis was paying for it."

"Phyllis was . . . what?"

Sasha looked up at Vivien. She was wearing her oversized sunglasses as usual and her hair looked freshly coiffed. Vivien instinctively drew a breath in through her nose, sniffing for the gin, but she couldn't smell anything. Sasha laid a hand flat on the page and faced Vivien. "Her money," said Sasha. "That clinic has been a cash drain since they opened it. Why do you think they do those bloody awful commercials?"

"Really? But, Phyllis. I didn't know she even, I mean I've never seen her . . . "

"Work?" said Sasha. "She doesn't have to work, darling. She's rich for a living. You didn't know that?" She flipped another page. "Oh, I thought everyone in this little village knew. Her father was one of the founders of McDonnell Douglas, or was it General Dynamics? Grumman? Somebody like that. She sits on the board. They give away more money each month then we've all made in a lifetime. It's ridiculous, really. You Americans and your defense budgets." Sasha's head turned back to her paper and she flipped again.

"Phyllis? She's rich? Then, those parties . . . ?"

Sasha never looked up. "Routinely attended by those with more money than God, darling."

"But she never said . . ."

"No, Vivien. She never said a lot of things. Oh, hello, Leonard!" Sasha had turned her attention to somebody behind Vivien. For a second she couldn't imagine who Leonard was, until she turned around to see Lenny approaching, his dog's leash snapped around his waist. Buddy was trotting along at his side, until he peeled off to sniff noses with Mooky and Polly.

"Leonard?" said Vivien.

"Well, it is my name, snookums." He circled her with his arms, giving her a quick hug. "It's nice to be back, eh? Any signs of the police?"

"No, thank heavens," said Sasha. "And let's hope that they don't come back, so we can put all this behind us."

"Mmm-hmm. Have you heard about what they found? I hate watching the news," said Lenny.

"All I heard was that they found some remains and the investigation was ongoing," said Vivien.

"Really?" said Lenny. "That's it? What does Will say?"

"I haven't talked to him," said Vivien. She could hear the sadness in her own voice and immediately felt a little ashamed by it.

She felt Lenny's hand on her upper arm as he moved her shoulders to partially face him. He looked her in the eye and said, "What do you mean you haven't talked to him? He hasn't called?"

"No." Vivien looked at the patch of dirt under her feet to avoid eye contact with Lenny. "I think it has something to do with the investigation."

"Excuse me?" said Lenny. He put his hands on his hips showing or pretending to show mild outrage. "Child, he better be calling you now more than ever. Come on. We're walking." He became the black girl, one of Vivien's favorite characters, and she couldn't help but smile as he guided her towards the woods. Too bad he didn't like women. He was such a good friend.

They waved goodbye to Sasha, who said she might be there when they got back, but Vivien assumed she would be gone. They headed towards the regular entry point into the woods, which was on the other side of the road from the path where the dogs had found the skull. Even from here, Vivien could see the yellow tape still stretched across the opening. When they were out of earshot of the picnic table, Lenny said, "So?" Why hasn't the lug called?"

"I don't know. I think he kind of got in trouble because we've been doing . . . whatever we've been doing. We met because of an investigation, and now the investigation is back on and I'm wondering if he wasn't just hanging out with me because he thought it would help him get transferred to the Homicide Squad."

They walked a few steps in silence as the words hung there in the air. "Wow," said Lenny. "That's a lot."

They walked a few more steps, their feet slicing through the tall grass of the field. Traffic noise from Military Road hissed in the background as the dogs trotted in front of them. "And what sucks is I think I really like him. I mean, this is the first guy I've met in a long time that, you know . . ."

"I know, sweetie. And I think he likes you, too. He doesn't seem like the all-about-career type."

She felt his arm sling across her shoulders and for a second she felt like she was going to cry. "Plus, Harish called me."

Lenny stopped dead in his tracks, looked her in the eye and said, "What?"

She looked back at him and then at the dogs to make sure they were heading in the right direction. "Yeah. He called me right before I came here. First he started asking me about my back, and then tells me he lied about Phyllis and how he wants me to help him find her or something. I'm supposed to meet him here tomorrow."

"Meet him here? You? You and him?" said Lenny, who was obviously struggling with the concept.

"Pretty crazy, huh?" said Vivien. "I'm thinking of opening my own private detective agency. What do you think? Vivien Szabo, P.I.?" She made a gesture like it was a TV show title appearing on a screen, and for a second she was proud of herself—she'd made a joke . . . kind of.

"Ummmm, I think something smells fishy about the whole thing, for starters." The arm came back across her shoulders and they turned towards the woods. "What do you think he wants?"

"He just wants help," said Vivien. "He sounded kind of upset."

"And he calls you instead of the police? I mean, it doesn't make sense."

"The police have talked to him, Lenny. They aren't getting anywhere—it happens all the time. That's why they have private detectives."

"Mmm-hmm," said Lenny. He brought a finger to his lips as they slid into the shade of the tall trees that separated the field from the woods. "I think you need to be careful, Vivien. Very careful."

CHAPTER 34

Mooky lay in the pool of sunshine by the front door, keeping an eye out for squirrels, people walking by on the sidewalk, and the cat who lived up the street. It was warm in the spot and she felt her eyes starting to close. It was the perfect time for a nap before it was time to enter the world of "go" and head to the dog park. The smells coming to her in this spot were mostly uninteresting—a bit of dust, newspapers, and the remnants of yesterday's supper, which was now in the trash can.

She could easily knock over the trashcan, which would put the contents on the floor, making them easy to get to, but if she did it while Vivien was home she would be a bad dog and possibly not get to go. So she ignored this smell and laid her head between her paws until a sound jarred her awake. Vivien was moving things around in the closet.

Vivien kept her things in the closet—fabrics and leather, lots of shoes—but it was a small, dark space and Mooky didn't like to stay in there for very long. It was a good place for a few quick sniffs—that was about it. From the sounds, Mooky knew that Vivien was playing her own game of "Find-the-Thing." She didn't pay a lot of attention because it was Vivien's thing. And the thing would probably be clothing.

Nevertheless, her tail thumped a few beats as she thought about what the thing might be. Maybe it wouldn't be clothing. Maybe Vivien would come out of the room with a ball or a stick. It could happen. Instead, Vivien came out with a box, which she carried into the dining room and put on the table.

Mooky raised her head and watched closely as Vivien used a piece of metal to open the box. She pulled the thing out and Mooky knew what it was. She hadn't seen this thing in a while, but she remembered it as she watched Vivien pick it up and look at it. Vivien pointed the thing at the wall and the floor, looking it over. This was not a stick or a ball. This was a hard, heavy metal thing that always smelled like smoke, fire, and oil.

The man who had been coming to visit had one of these things. When Vivien played with this thing it created cracking, snapping noises that made Mooky anxious. One piece of the thing would snap into another and it would make a sound. The thing was alive as Mooky watched parts of it sliding around in Vivien's hand, making the sounds.

Mooky dropped her ears and thumped her tail softly, waiting for the thing to go away. She watched Vivien stand up and hide the thing under her clothes. If she were to play Find-the-Thing, Mooky knew right where it was and this made her tail thump quicker. She watched Vivien move around the house, finding the things that meant it was time to go.

Finally she heard the magic words. "Come on, let's go." Now was the time of go. She stood up, stretched, wagged her tail, and pushed Vivien's legs with her nose. It was very exciting to go and she moved from the back door to Vivien and back again, very anxious to get into the car. Then they were outside in the van, moving towards the park. Mooky smelled the dust in the car and traces of herself, then the road smells of cars and oil, followed by the scents of trees and flowers rushing by. She stuck her head outside the window. It was good to go.

Now they were here. She got out and ran to the picnic table, but there was nobody else here yet. There were smells of other dogs everywhere. Mooky went to work, claiming the area for herself. Soon the other dogs would be here and the games could start. They would run in the woods, smell for new things, and then maybe play Pull-the-Thing. The most amazing smells that ever came from the woods came from the other side of the road, but they appeared to be gone. She raised her nose, breathed in, and flared her nostrils, looking for a trace. But there was nothing.

She moved in widening circles around the picnic table, expanding her territory and looking for anything that could be used to start a game. She found a sad old tennis ball, but it smelled of wet mud, so she ignored it. She heard a car door slam, and turned. Her tail stopped as she looked to the car to see who it was. It was a man, a man with a stick. She didn't recognize this man, and the stick had a funny shape. Her beautiful tail swooped a few times as she watched the man with the funny stick approach the table.

She watched Vivien watching the man and saw her reach behind herself where she had hidden the heavy metal snapping thing. Mooky dropped her ears and began panting while walking towards the man. She needed to give him a sniff, and she wanted a closer look at the funny stick. From here it looked like an excellent stick for playing Pull-the-Thing.

As she got closer, she could smell the man. He smelled like flowers, oil, and sweat. He moved uncertainly, like he was nervous about something, and this caused Mooky to stop, raise her ears, close her mouth, and watch him closely. He came to the table and shook hands with Vivien, which identified him as a friend. Mooky approached them cautiously, curious about the man and the funny stick. She smelled his leg and felt his hand come down on top of her head, which made her jump a little.

The pats on her head that he gave her were short and uncertain, and Mooky decided that she would claim the man as her own. She brushed her coat against his leg, transferring her scent to him. Now he belonged to her. She raised her head, looked at the man, and began softly panting, feeling very good about her new prize.

Soon he would start playing with her. She looked for a stick that he could throw. The curious stick was on top of the table, and she moved around to the other side to get a better look at it. The man and Vivien were talking as Mooky got into position to make her move.

CHAPTER 35

Vivien sat at the table with Harish sitting next to her. She thought that was odd. What was he doing over on this side? The "massage cane" he'd brought her as a gift lay on the table in front of them. Such a lovely gesture. The cane was made of plastic and could be used to apply pressure to certain problem areas of the back. It looked like one of those things shepherds carried in Bible pictures.

Harish gave her a quick lesson in how to hold the cane so the knobby end could be used to exert pressure on cramped muscles. Vivien noticed that Mooky seemed very interested in the cane. Harish was really a sweet man and obviously upset by his wife's disappearance. She decided she had nothing to worry about and she now felt a little stupid about carrying her weapon to the park. What was she going to do, shoot a chiropractor?

Lenny had gotten her so spooked the day before, and she was so wrapped up in this private detective thing, that she'd gone completely paranoid. She had stuffed the gun into the back of her pants and jammed her cell phone in her pocket, causing her to feel fat and lumpy.

Harish began the conversation by telling her how he and Phyllis had met when they were in college and how his parents had objected to the relationship since she was American. Of course they got through all that, but now this—a total disappearance.

"We'd had a fight the night before I left for India. She told me she wasn't going to go," said Harish. "I thought it was over and settled, but when I got home from work the next day, she was gone. Poof!" He made his hand do a gesture for "poof" and Vivien looked at his hands. He had long brown fingers, with nice nails and tracts of dark hair along the knuckles. Attractive hands. The hands of a healer. Vivien could see how some women would find him attractive.

"And so you haven't heard from her or seen her since?" said Vivien. She wished she had a little memo pad to take notes and she made a mental note to shop for one on the way home.

"Not a peep," said Harish.

This sounded funny to Vivien. Peep was a funny word and she stifled a laugh. "What?" said Harish.

"I'm sorry. Peep is a funny word. I always think of those candy Peeps they sell around Easter time."

"Oh. Peep is funny?" said Harish.

"Kind of," said Vivien. "Peep is kind of funny."

"Peep then," said Harish. "Peep. Peep. Peep." And then he started chuckling and smiling at Vivien.

Vivien laughed out loud and thought Harish was a very strange man. Strange but funny, as she laughed with him. She felt his shoulder nudge against hers, a nice feeling that made her nervous and excited at the same time.

"It's such a nice day; may we take a walk in the woods, Vivien? Maybe you can show me where your dog likes to run."

"Well, she really likes to go where she's not allowed—which is over there where the yellow tape is. But we usually walk to the point by using the path over there. But Phyllis never liked to walk." She clamped her mouth shut as soon as she said it, realizing she had spoken of her in the past tense.

She didn't want to be rude or crush any of Harish's hopes. He seemed awfully relaxed, considering his situation. She looked at his face, searching for an emotional clue.

"It's okay, Vivien. This is all going to work out the way it's supposed to. Come. Walk with me, won't you?"

They pulled themselves off the picnic table benches and began strolling towards the woods. She had never seen the park so empty. It was just her and Harish. The regular crew of dog park regulars showed up every day around five but she'd heard that there was a separate group that came earlier—a day shift of dog people. She and Harish were in a time slot in between the day people and the afternooners. Like a dead zone. This made her think of her cell phone, and she patted her pocket to make sure she still had it.

She didn't like to carry the cell phone and usually left it in the car. Lenny always had one on him and at some point she'd pretty much stopped carrying hers. The path to the woods took them by the parking lot and Vivien decided to drop the phone off back in her car.

"I'll be right back," said Vivien.

"But, where are you going?" asked Harish. He sounded concerned by her sudden change of course.

"I just want to put my phone in my car; I'm always afraid I'm going to lose it." She began fishing the phone out of her pocket and stole a glance at Harish's car, a late model Audi that looked freshly washed. The windows were partially down and Vivien half-turned to tell Harish, in case he didn't want to leave the windows open. She stopped, thinking she saw somebody sitting in Harish's car. The way the shadows fell across the windshield made it hard to tell, but as she got closer she could definitely make out the shape of a person sitting in the passenger seat.

She passed closer, curious and a little concerned that somebody had broken into the car, but as she got closer the face looked up at her and she instantly knew who it was. Mina. The girl from Harish's office and the TV commercial. Pretty Mina was sitting in the front seat with a cell phone pressed against her ear and a blank expression on her face. She didn't smile or speak, and after a second she broke off her eye contact with Vivien and stared off into the distance.

Vivien's hand stopped on the front of her shorts, giving up its mission to extract the cell phone. Vivien walked to her van, popped open the door, looked inside for a second, and then closed it again. What the hell was Mina doing here and why was she waiting in the car? Vivien pulled her hand through her hair and rubbed the back of her neck.

She put her finger on the bulge in her pocket where the phone was, then reached behind her and touched the pistol with her finger. She took note of how she was walking and squared her shoulders. She didn't look back at the car and instead watched the ground in front of her. She glanced up at Harish standing there with the massage cane in his hand. Why was he bringing that? So nobody would steal it? A few more steps and she was close to him again. He was looking around at the sky like he'd just noticed where he was.

"It's beautiful here, isn't it, Vivien?" said Harish.

"It is," said Vivien as they fell in stride with each other and moved towards the shadows of the tall trees.

She waited for him to say something about the girl in his car, but instead he said, "So what do your police friends tell you about what they found over there in the other part of the woods?"

They passed under the canopy of the giant oaks and were now picking their way down the little incline that would dump them off into a dried creek bed. From there, the path went back up for a bit and then across the top of a long, rounded hill. Vivien knew every tree and rock along the way.

"Actually, my police friends haven't told me much. All I know is what I've seen on the news." Vivien was aware that Harish was baiting her for some reason. Probing to find out what she knew. She imagined an ice cube in her head. She needed to be icy here—just this once.

"And what was that?" said Harish. He almost sounded angry when he said it. Like he was in a hurry. Now he had an edge, where before he was funny and kind. She looked at how he was carrying the cane. He wasn't carrying it like a cane, but more like how you'd carry a rifle, with his hand in the middle to balance the weight.

She checked the position of her dog. Mooky was ahead of them, nose to the ground, looking for whatever it was that she looked for. Vivien glanced at Harish, taking note of how he was dressed. Light-colored, open-collar linen or silk shirt, navy blue slacks, loafers, black socks. He wasn't prepared for a walk in the woods, but maybe he hadn't thought it all the way through before he cooked this little scheme up.

"They just say some remains were found, but I already knew that—I mean, I was here." She decided to test him. She slowed her pace. She was a little ways ahead of him and she waited for him to catch up. There was a wide spot in the path and they walked abreast. "But what they found that day couldn't have been Phyllis. That skull had been in the ground for at least a year."

She watched his face for a reaction but there was nothing. No grimace or frown, no upraised eyebrows. He was the one that was icy. She figured she'd take another shot at him. "Why do you ask, Harish? Do you think what they found has anything to do with Phyllis's disappearance? I mean, Phyllis never even walked in the woods. She always sat at the table with Boopsie. Which reminds me, is the dog gone, too?"

"Hmmm? Oh, yes. The dog is also missing," he said.

Vivien felt her heart sink as she pondered what could have happened to Boopsie the bichon. Granted, she wasn't her favorite dog in the park, but she was still a dog, who was now god knows where.

Harish stopped walking and Vivien considered that this was where he would break down and show some emotion. She felt herself growing upset. "So this is where you walk every day?" he said.

"Pretty much," said Vivien. "Sometimes we take the shortcut if it's too muddy."

"And the dogs who found the remains . . . they were over on the other side?"

"Yeah," said Vivien. "The smell must have made them run across the road. You know the more disgusting a thing is, the more a dog wants it. They just can't help themselves." Vivien turned her head to see that Mooky had gotten several yards ahead of them. She could barely see her tail sticking out of a patch of ferns.

"And you talked to the police, Vivien? That day?"

"Oh, yeah, we all talked to them."

"And you've talked to them since—about me?"

"About you? Umm . . . what do you mean?" It was an odd question, and she looked at him, cocking her head trying to figure out what he meant. He was standing near her with the cane in his hand, looking at her with a blank expression on his face. She couldn't see Mooky at all now, but could hear sticks cracking and leaves crunching in the distance.

He took a step towards her and said, "I asked you not to talk about this. Did you respect my wishes?"

Another odd question. Respect his wishes? He was now standing very close to her and she was feeling more uncomfortable. She moved to take a step back and her foot hit a root. She was suddenly on her back and he was standing over her holding the cane. She couldn't read the look on his face. She was embarrassed by the fall and as she lay there her cell phone went off. "Shit," she said. Everything seemed to stop and she reached into her pocket, pulled it out and hit "talk." She held up a finger to Harish, who was now bending over and reaching for her. She could scream help into the phone or quickly hang up and hit 9-1-1.

She was surprised but happy to hear Will's voice. "Viv, I've been trying to call to you. Why don't you answer your cell phone? Listen. I just got a look at the forensics from the site. There were two sets of remains. One old, one more recent. One could be—"

And the connection went dead. "Who was that? Your police friend?" asked Harish. The cane was still in his hand, still gripped like a weapon, and Vivien became aware that she was lying on her gun because it was digging its way into the tender flesh of her lower back.

Before she could reach for it, out of the corner of her eye, Vivien saw a flash of movement. Harish's arm jumped like somebody had tied a string to him and gave it a good jerk. Vivien instinctively flinched and saw a dark shape appear from out of the greenery. She heard a growling noise and saw Harish's body being pulled around in a half circle, away from her. Now, between his legs, she saw Mooky, her jaws clamped on the cane, her feet digging into the dirt as she pulled Harish and the cane away from her.

She rose to her feet, reached around, put her hand on the gun

handle, and said, "Mooky! Stop! . . . She just wants to play, doctor."
Harish had obviously never been on one end of a massage cane with a
hundred pounds of black Lab on the other. It looked suddenly comical as
Vivien ran through a decision-making process in her head. Did Harish
mean to do her harm? Was the cane a weapon? Why was Mina waiting in
the car? Should she draw her weapon and fire? From this distance she
could take him out with one shot. She considered what was behind him
in case she missed. Any houses over there?

"Mooky! Drop it! Just let go of it, doctor."

Mooky didn't listen, but Harish did, and he let go of the cane.
Mooky growled in a satisfied way and then dropped the cane where she
stood, looked at Vivien, and began panting.

Vivien brushed a hand through her hair and mentally checked her back to
make sure she wasn't injured from the fall. She took her hand off the butt
of the gun and said, "Actually, that was my police friend, doctor. I think
we all should be heading back now. I'm sure your friend in the car is
getting hot."

CHAPTER 36

"Are you saying he attacked you? With a massage cane? And Mooky saved your life?" asked Lenny. "It sounds like an episode of Lassie, for God's sake." They were sitting in Vivien's kitchen. Lenny had insisted they have a glass of wine and found a bottle of Manischewitz in Vivien's refrigerator. She had bought it for a Hanukkah party that she had never gotten around to having.

Lenny took a sip, then made a face like he had tasted something horrible. "Wait. Before you tell me more about what happened, promise me you'll never buy any more of this. This is bad wine, sweetie. I don't think the Jews really like it or actually drink it. Now. Speak to me."

He put the glass back on the table, hunched over a bit with his elbows on the table, and looked into her eyes. Vivien actually didn't mind the taste of the wine. It was sweet and kind of bubbly. She thought it was kind of exciting to be drinking before dinner, and wondered if Lenny actually ever went to his office. She had called him when she got back to her house, still a little shaken by the turn of events. He'd actually answered the phone for a change and came right over with Buddy, who was now out in the yard with Mooky.

"I'm not sure what he was doing. He was acting very strange. First he was funny, and then he seemed mean. But he's definitely interested in whatever the police know about the remains."

"Which takes me to my next question," said Lenny, "Will called you and said what?"

"I called him back before you got here. He said they found two sets of remains in the area. One set was there for at least a year—that was the skull the dogs brought up. The other set was in a different site a few yards away, and belonged to a middle-aged, Caucasian female. She's only been dead for a couple of weeks."

"Jesus fucking Christ," said Lenny. "So it actually could be Phyllis. The newer one, I mean."

"Will's looking at the forensic report later today. He's working till nine, but coming over here later."

"Well. That's a good thing." Lenny patted her knee. "I mean, he's calling again, right?"

"Yeah, but I still have the suspicion that he's more interested in cracking the case to get transferred to Homicide than he is in me. I mean I had sex with him on the first date, for God's sake."

"Well, that's water under the bridge at this point, sweetie. The point is he's still in play and, more importantly, this theory of yours could actually be real. It's un-fucking-believable, really."

Vivien watched him drain his wine glass, make a face, and pour himself another one. She couldn't remember Lenny ever cursing so much. She studied the wine stain on his thin lips.

If he was a murderer, he'd want to stay close to the investigation and he'd be emotionally involved, which would explain his swearing like a sailor. No. That was crazy. Lenny wouldn't hurt a fly. He was clearly freaked out when the skull came out of the woods in Mooky's mouth.

"So what is your plan?" asked Lenny.

"About what?" said Vivien.

Lenny pinched the bridge of his nose like he had a headache and said, "What are you going to tell Will about the Harish incident, Viv?"

"The truth, of course. What else would I say?"

"And the truth is what?"

"The truth is he was acting strange, he had what's-her-name in the car with him, and she didn't get out or even acknowledge me. It's very suspicious, Lenny. It's usually the spouse in these cases, you know? That's always who they question first. He's the prime suspect."

"The prime suspect." Lenny didn't say it like a question, it was more like a statement of fact, and the words hung in the air between them for a while. Vivien watched him drain the wine glass again.

CHAPTER 37

Vivien and Lenny went to the dog park as usual after the debriefing in her kitchen. Compared to the scene with Harish, the second visit was uneventful, which was good because she wanted to be in a calm state when Will showed up later that night. He was working an afternoon shift but expected to be off early. He pulled a double the day before and he told her to expect him around nine. Already, their relationship or whatever they were having had changed. His time of arrival was now "around" a time instead of "at" a time. He was coming from work and wasn't sure what time he could get out—but Vivien still felt like something had already shifted between them.

She almost married a cop once-upon-a-time, a handsome piece of work named Mike who had a killer smile and a chiseled chest that Vivien still thought about when she needed a shot of libido. Physically, Mike was built similarly to Will, but his moods skewed towards dark and moody. He was a nice guy when sober but also a secretive, stone-cold alcoholic who hid bottles in her apartment. He lived with her for two years until she ran out of patience with the lies and blackouts.

For a while she thought she could change him. He went to the meetings, would do fine for a couple of months, and then would believe he was cured. One beer would lead to a bottle of cheap liquor and the next step was passing out on the floor. After he kicked Mooky in a drunken rage, Vivien gave him the boot. She hated herself for a while, assuming she was being overly judgmental. He ended up living with another female officer, until he was caught passed out in his squad car in a puddle of his own making. He left the force soon after that and she never heard from him again.

She didn't date for a long time after that, but she'd had a few flings when the opportunities arose. Will was the first guy since Mike that made her think about a serious relationship with a man. A man who was now late. At 9:47 she heard a car door slam. She walked to the window to see the stocky form of Will Evans trotting across the street. He was wearing a grey suit and adjusting his hat as he jogged—such a cop.

She tugged at the front of her shorts and opened the door, abandoning any try at nonchalance. She was looking forward to seeing him in more ways than one. She stood in the doorway as he opened the storm door, greeted Mooky with pats on the head and said, "Hey, you crazy, bone-finding dog."

"Detective," said Vivien.

"Ma'am," said Will, as they played the game of talking to each other like the day they first met.

He took his hat off, entered the room, and immediately seemed to fill it up. Vivien wasn't used to seeing people in her space, especially since removing piles of stuff from the house, and the sight was a little unnerving—it was like she was seeing herself in somebody else's house that looked similar to hers, except neater.

"How was work today?" she said. He didn't try to kiss her on the way in and she wondered if they would ever get to the point where they would kiss hello and goodbye on a consistent basis.

"Long," he said. "Have any beer?"

"Sure, let me get you one." She had prepared for this by going to one of the wine stores in Chevy Chase and buying a sample pack of microbrews. She didn't know what his favorite brand was.

"Do you like Brooklyn Lager?" she called out from the kitchen.

"Anything," he called back, "as long as it's cold."

She popped the bottle open, poured most of it into a special beer glass that she'd bought for an Oktoberfest party that had never happened, walked back into the dining room and handed it to him.

She watched him take a sip as he looked at her over the glass. As he wiped away a beer moustache she said, "Do you drink a lot, Will?"

"Every time I get a chance," he said with a smile.

"No, seriously. You don't think you're an alcoholic, do you?"

"Hell, no. Alcoholics have to go to meetings." He dropped his hat on the end table and took off his jacket.

"I'm serious," she said. "I dated a guy pretty seriously for a while who was a drunk and it ruined everything."

"I'm not a drunk, ma'am. But I am a tired cowboy. We had four stiffs this week. It's always worse when the weather gets hot. People are dying all over the place." He plopped himself on the couch and she felt good that he could be so comfortable so fast in her house.

He patted the couch next to him and said, "Come sit down and tell me what's going on with you."

She ignored the offer, folded her arms, and said, "No way. You need to tell me what's going on with the bones in the dog park."

"Oh, right. Okay, so like I told you on the phone. Two sites, the second one further down the hill. Two sets, one at least a year old, the second, more recent. Caucasian woman, fifties, maybe sixties. We're just waiting on dental records to confirm her identity. There's a good chance victim number two is your missing Phyllis."

Vivien felt a rush of heat rise to her face as she considered the possibility that she had been right about this all along. But at this point she was still a bit concerned with Will's motives in the whole thing.

"And you helped the investigation through your dealings with me," said Vivien.

His face went blank as he slowly raised a hand to the top of his head and began to rub the bristles of his crew cut. He reminded her of a gorilla. A puzzled gorilla. "Well, actually, Vivien, I didn't have anything to do with it. Your dog found the bones both times. I've just been trying to help you figure it out." He looked at her with squinted eyes. "What's this about, anyway?"

"I heard the way you were asking me questions in front of McCain. I don't mind you trying to look good, but I don't think you should be giving people the wrong idea so you can get transferred to Homicide."

"Who said that?"

"I'm saying that."

"Wait a second," he said and threw his hands up like he was saying "whoa" to a runaway horse. "I do want to get transferred to Homicide. Everybody knows that, including McCain." He stopped for a second like he was trying to figure something out and said, "Maybe I was a little over-the-top, but I'm getting caught up in the drama, Viv. Just like you. I'm a cop. Of course I'm going to try and crack the case. It's what I do, for crying out loud."

"I realize that. I just want to make sure you're not just spending time with me because you want to be involved with what may become a homicide case."

"What?" he said.

For the first time, Vivien heard what could be considered anger in his voice. It frightened and irritated her at the same time. She really didn't know him all that well, even with what they had been through.

He set his beer on the end table and drew himself off the couch like he had aged five years since he sat down. He came close to her and she could hear him breathing hard through his nose like he was trying to keep from losing his temper. "Look, Vivien, I was attracted to you as soon as I saw you at the picnic table. Your involvement in whatever this turns out to be was an excuse for me to keep in touch with you, I'll admit to that. If this does turn into a homicide investigation and I can stay involved with it somehow—it could help my career. But that's not why I'm here. I'm here because of you. Does that make sense?"

Vivien was standing with her arms crossed. She remembered from a course on reading body language that she was in a defensive position. Sub-consciously she must be feeling threatened. She could feel the fabric on his shirt just grazing the fine blonde hairs on her wrist. She could smell the beer on his breath and feel his body heat radiating off him. It was humid outside. Genuine summer weather had moved into D.C. She heard a bus go by outside, groaning around the corner. She considered his question. He was looking at her with a blank expression that she couldn't read. He was waiting for some kind of an answer.

"Tell me the part about the picnic table again," she said.

A smile stretched across his face and he said, "You're a little devil, ma'am."

He moved closer to her and laid his fingertips on her forearms and the grin came back to his face. He really wasn't anything like Mike the drunk and Vivien could see this scene quickly turning into another sloppy romp on the couch.

She wanted to throw herself on top of him right then as she looked at him, standing there running a finger around the rim of his beer glass. She imagined his fingers on her, tracing the curve of her breast as she reached for the button on her top to see if it had magically started to unbutton itself. "Will?"

"Viv?"

"Come with me, Detective."

She took him by the hand and guided him to the steps. She kept Mooky outside the bedroom door and closed it behind them. She came to him as he wrapped his arms around her, pulled her close, and kissed her softly on the lips. She reached for the knot in his tie, sliding it down, feeling the fabric sliding through her fingers. "No quickies on the couch this time," she said. She felt his hands on her breasts. Now the buttons were popping for real as his mouth went to the side of her neck. She felt her top sliding down her arms as she reached for his belt buckle, shivering as his tongue tickled her earlobe. She helped him with the hooks on her bra as she cradled his head to her breast.

She felt herself being lifted, his hands under her hips. He set her down on the edge of the bed and pulled his shirt off. She unsnapped her own jeans, pulled down the zipper and lifted her hips as he tugged them down. Her panties went next. He giggled like a mischievous child as he as threw them across the room. She laughed with him, slowly opened her legs and watched him struggle out of his trousers. The light in the room was dim but she could see that he was already partially aroused.

He settled himself between her legs and kissed her lips. She felt him rubbing between her thighs as he began working himself inside her. She helped guide him and threw her arm around his round shoulders, moaning as they began moving as one. She was a good girl who deserved to be a little bad. She owed herself this. She was finally probably right about something and she deserved some happiness. She told herself that, pushed away feelings of self-doubt, and allowed herself to be in the moment. One with Will.

It was a lively session. At first Vivien worried about breaking the bed, but eventually gave in and hoped that it would break. During the lull, the day's events came stealing back into her thoughts and she said, "Will, I have to tell you about what happened at the park today with Harish."

They were both lying on their backs as she looked at the ceiling. She could see the shape of him next to her, his naked body covered by just a sheet. Her voice sounded calm and restrained as she described the events to him. Will listened closely, occasionally asking questions to clarify certain key elements. "Did he touch you at any point? Because if he was threatening and physically touched you, that's assault right there," he said.

"No, No. No. It wasn't really like that. I mean he did seem agitated when he was asking about what I had told the police, and I'm not sure why he needed to bring that cane with him. Now that I've had time to process it, I don't think he was actually trying to attack me. But I do think it's curious that he had what's-her-name waiting for him in the car."

"She's a younger, attractive woman?" said Will.

"I guess you could say she's attractive," said Vivien. "She's in his TV commercial. She's definitely younger than he is."

"Mmm-hmm. That's an easy one. He's fucking her. Or trying to.

Excuse my French, ma'am."

"What?" Vivien couldn't believe the way that men's minds worked sometimes. "Oh, come on. That's not nice, Will. His wife is missing and presumed dead, for God's sake."

"Right. And he doesn't seem that upset, does he?"

"Oh my god. There's another thing. I also just found out that Phyllis was wealthy. Sasha told me that her father started one of the big defense contractors in town."

"Bingo," said Will. "He gets rid of the wife, gets the dough, lives happily ever after with little Miss Cutey Pie, game over. But then you show up at his office asking a bunch of questions. He knows you're ex-law enforcement, he thinks you're suspicious; naturally he's going to want to find out what you know and who you've told. And I'm sure his young squeeze is very interested in the money and the outcome. That's why she was in the car—to make sure he didn't screw it up." He stopped, shifted in the bed, and laid a hand on her hip. "He probably wasn't planning on killing you, but if the opportunity arose . . . You're walking through the woods, he gets behind you with this cane—he's a doctor with medical training; he knows how to choke somebody out."

"Oh my God," said Vivien. "Do you really think that's what's going on?"

"I've worked on stranger cases. This one seems pretty cut and dry. Once we get positive ID on the remains—if it's her, I'd recommend they bring Dr. Harish in for some DNA samples. If he was at the crime scene, they'll know pretty quick after that.

Vivien ran her hand across the material of the sheet, feeling the fine threads of the fabric and experiencing a disconnected feeling from the conversation she was having. It was like she was watching one of those forensic shows on TV and she was the special guest star. She was also aware that she was enjoying the interplay, the theorizing, and the deductions.

She was feeling very close to Will right now. He seemed protective and interested, plus he was taking her seriously, which made her feel needed and important as she felt herself drifting towards the black peace of sleep.

CHAPTER 38

The man spent the night. Mooky knew this because of the noise and smells seeping out from under the door in the bedroom. The smells were warm and earthy and Mooky very much wanted to come into the bedroom to get a better sniff. Unfortunately she was locked out. She scratched at the door a few times with her paw, but soon only the sounds of sleeping people greeted her. She retreated to the hallway and lay down with her back against the wall. From this position, nothing would be able to sneak up behind her while she dozed, and if anything came out of the bedroom, she would wake up.

The man was up early the next day when the light inside the house was still gray. He carried his shoes and his metal snapping thing quietly about the house, putting things on and adjusting other things. He made coffee, which made Mooky's beautiful tail thump on the floor as she anticipated entering the time of go. The man drank some of the coffee and fed her small bits of a cookie, which she thoroughly enjoyed. She was hoping to go into the yard with the man, as this was an excellent time to see the morning animals. The cat that lived down the street usually made his rounds about this time.

When the man was finished with his coffee and cookie, he patted Mooky on the head and slipped quietly out the door. Mooky climbed the stairs and returned to the bedroom. To take full advantage of the smells, she hopped onto the bed with Vivien. She sniffed around a bit, but most of the smells had lost their strong appeal. They were weaker now, slowly fading into the textures of the fabrics. Mooky turned around once to gather her legs beneath her, tucked her tail where it would keep her warm, and plopped down, settling her back against Vivien's legs.

When the light became brighter, Vivien woke up, let Mooky outside, and then fed her breakfast. Vivien seemed happy today. She made whistling noises and moved about the house with a bouncy energy. This caused Mooky to pay attention, her tail thumping occasionally, her ears up and alert. Something was about to happen. The time of go felt very close. "What do you think, Mook—want to go for a little ride this morning?" said Vivien.

Mooky didn't know many of these words but she did know "go" and "ride," so her tail thumped louder against the floor as she cocked her head, anticipating the move to the car.

"Mommy needs stamps, so we can drive to the post office before it gets too hot. What do you say? Do you want to go?"

"Go" was the best word of all. Mooky rose and barked a positive response. She stretched her back and went to Vivien's knee, pushing against it with her wet nose to tell her that yes, she did want to go.

"Okay, okay . . ." said Vivien. "Just let me find my keys and we'll go."

The best word of all caused her to spin in circles and bark a few more times. It was unexpected to go at this time of day and very exciting. She ran in tight circles around Vivien, leaving her scent on her so she wouldn't be able to get away without Mooky smelling where she had gone. They left the house and Mooky ran across the back yard to the building where the car lived. She stood and barked at the door, until Vivien let her in and she leaped into the car.

Mooky had a few favorite spots in the car. She liked to lie across the back seat when she was tired after a run at the dog park. If she was very tired or looking for a cool place, sometimes she would go to the very back, where it was flat and smelled like oil. She had thrown up back there once when she was a puppy, and if she smelled hard enough she could find the exact spot. There were still traces of the old woman's smell in the car, but they were very faint. Mostly the car smelled of dust, old fabric, Vivien, and herself.

The next favorite spot in the car was the front seat next to Vivien. It was hard to balance on this seat sometimes, but when the window was down, this was the best seat. Mooky could put her head outside and feel the wind on her face. Smells would come at her, one after another. It was hard to take them all in as they rushed by.

Today she took this seat as the car backed out of the building. Mooky put her nose on the glass, hoping it would go down. "Want some air?" said Vivien.

Mooky didn't know any of these words so she just looked at Vivien until the sound of the window going down caused her to swivel her head and poke her nose outside. As the car started to move the smells began coming to her faster and faster. Smells of flowers and cut grass, food cooking, animals, car exhaust, dead things, and dust, all rushing towards her so fast she couldn't enjoy them all. The car stopped and started at various places, which gave Mooky a chance to look for animals and other dogs going for their walks or riding in cars.

They came to a stopping place as another car pulled up next to them. Mooky looked out and saw a dog she recognized. Her tail tried to wag but she was sitting on it, so she stood up on the seat and whined because she knew this dog and the person in the car. It was the old lady from the dog park who usually smelled like sweet, sweet flowers. Mooky looked for Polly in the car but she didn't see her. Instead, she saw the small white dog that used to stay under the table.

This was an old dog that didn't move around much, and Mooky knew the dog and her smell. The windows were up in the other car, so Mooky couldn't smell her, but she knew this dog on sight. She barked to attract the other dog's attention. Perhaps they were all going to the park now. Perhaps this was the time of go and Mooky barked again, standing up on the seat, barking at the car until she saw the old woman turn her head and the car drove away. Mooky continued barking after the car hoping they would come back and they could all go to the park.

"Holy shit," said Vivien, "it's Boopsie!"

Mooky didn't know what these words meant as she stood on the seat, panting now, excited about seeing the little white dog and hoping they were still going to go.

CHAPTER 39

Vivien put her hand to her forehead like she was checking herself for a fever. "What the hell is going on here?" she said. She said it out loud and she could still see Sasha's car, now three blocks ahead of her. She could still make out the Union Jack bumper sticker that positively identified the green Subaru wagon. She rubbed her eyes, looked up to see that the light had changed, and made the left turn, wondering if she had seen what she thought she saw. Boopsie. Phyllis's dog. Riding in Sasha's car. And Sasha obviously avoiding eye contact with her.

Vivien reached for her cell phone. Since the incident in the park with Harish she now kept it handy. She dialed Lenny's number, but while it was ringing, another call came in from somebody at the DC Metro Police. It had to be Will, probably calling to talk about the good time he had the night before. He was so sweet. She abandoned her call to Lenny and hit "talk."

"Hel-lo," she said with a smile in her voice.

"Hi, sweetie."

It was Will. "Listen, I can't talk long, but I just wanted to tell you we got a match on the bones in the dog park. They found an ID or something in the clothing. Apparently, the more recent set does belongs to a Phyllis with a long, hyphenated Indian name. Which I'm assuming is your Phyllis. She's only been dead two to three weeks. The coroner says it was probably blunt force trauma—a blow to the head with a baseball bat, a rock, something like that. We're actually on our way to pick up the chiropractor to question him and take some DNA samples. It looks like you were right about this all along. You and that crazy dog of yours."

Vivien heard the words and felt the earth pause in its rotation. There was no sound, no movement, just a sensation of stillness. She was right. She was correct. All the self-doubt and uncertainty were brushed aside by the words coming through the cell phone. A flower of pride pushed out from deep inside her. It was beautiful for the few seconds it lasted, but it was quickly followed by a wave of horror, then concern.

"Wow," she said.

"Yeah. Wow is right. Listen, the other thing is, I can't talk long, but I did want to tell you I had a great time last night. I'm sorry I couldn't stick around this morning."

"Oh," she said, "that's okay, Will, don't worry about it." What a great guy. Why did she ever doubt him? She liked the sound of her calling him by name and quickly moved onto the morning's breaking news. "You're not going to believe this, but I think I just saw Phyllis's dog, Boopsie, in the car with Sasha."

"Who's Boopsie?" said Will. "Oh, shit. Listen, I gotta go. I'll talk to you later." And the line clicked dead.

So Will was on his way to visit the prime suspect in the case, Dr. Harish and his massage cane. Could that have been the murder weapon? Vivien bit her lip and tried to pay attention to her driving while theories began growing in her mind. She tried to imagine a massage cane swung by a powerful man, the blow directed at his wife's skull. No. It didn't sound right. It wasn't heavy enough.

Her mind quickly switched gears back to the most intriguing development of the day, Boopsie in Sasha's car. Before she could completely understand her body's movements, she took the next available right, which caused the numbskull behind her to lay on his horn—presumably because she hadn't used her turn signal. Vivien fought back the urge to flip him off as she half-stopped through an intersection and made a beeline for Sasha's house. She hadn't really decided what she would do when she got there, other than get a closer look at that little white dog.

Vivien and Sasha both lived in Chevy Chase, a suburban oasis that straddled the line between Montgomery County and the District.

Neither of them resided in the really expensive section, but they were both proud of their neighborhood. Vivien had been to Sasha's house only once, for a garden party. The festivities had left her bored out of her mind and she was actually grateful she'd never been invited back. She remembered the street that Sasha lived on, but wasn't completely sure which house it was.

If she could catch up with that green Subaru, she could park on the street unobserved and watch them entering the house. Boopsie was an old dog with arthritis and hip dysplasia, which gave her a distinctive half-hopping gait that Vivien was sure she could recognize. She took a shortcut, made a left, then a quick right, and she was on the street. She slowed down and swiveled her head from one side of the street to the other, looking for the car or something she would recognize.

She rolled by one, two, three blocks and could see the street terminating into the next cross street. Shit. She must have gone right by it. She was sure this was the right street and then . . . there it was. The green Subaru was parked outside the garage. With her window down, Vivien could hear the engine still ticking as it cooled off.

There was a half-crumpled bag of plant food in the yard and a pair of garden shears on the front porch. Bingo. This had to be the place. Vivien sped up a little and drove by the house, just in case Sasha might be watching out a window. What could Sasha have possibly been thinking? That Vivien hadn't seen her? At that stop light, Mooky had been close enough to lick Sasha's window.

She turned the minivan around in the T-intersection, doubled back, and parked on the opposite side of the street, where she had a good vantage point. Mooky had her head out the opposite side window and was sniffing the air like she was onto a scent.

"Smell Boopsie?" asked Vivien, and for a second she wished her nose was as sensitive as her dog's. There wasn't anything to see and Vivien started making calculations in her head. How long could she park here without being noticed? Probably all day, but the temperature was already heating up and even with the windows down the van would quickly become uninhabitable.

Sasha's garden was in the back yard. From what Vivien could remember, it was fenced-in, laid out on multi-levels with fruit trees, grasses, and perennials. The old woman grew tropical plants on the back porch, which had been partially closed in. The party that Vivien had attended last fall was in celebration of some kind of plant that bloomed once a season—at night. Whoopee ding-dong, a bunch of people sitting around drinking snooty wine while staring at a plant. Vivien didn't get it, but she figured if she was going to get another look at the presumed missing Boopsie, it would be in that back yard.

She considered going to the next block over and sneaking through the neighbor's yard, but immediately decided that would be dangerous. Too easy to be seen. For once, she was going to play it cool, go home, make a plan, and stick to it. Her instincts had been right, she told herself. It was time to pay closer attention to her own inner wisdom. That thought sounded so soulful and mystical to her that she flashed briefly onto Deepak Chopra and Dr. Harish.

Vivien spent the rest of the day biding her time at home and putting an actual plan together. She kept the phone nearby in case Will called to update her on the Harish situation. She resisted the urge to call him, and prepared to go to the park early. She would go during the in-between time, arriving before the regulars were there so she could confront Sasha about how and why she had come to acquire Phyllis's dog and why nobody had seen Boopsie since then. That was the odd part—what was she hiding?

She purposely avoided the computer. YouTube would have to wait. She didn't need to shop for anything. She didn't need to read anything, clean anything, or run any errands. She just needed to get this one thing right. She assembled her belongings, loaded the dog into the minivan without fanfare, and made the short drive to the park.

She parked in her regular spot, which was easy, because she was the only one there. She herded Mooky towards the picnic table and sat down on top of the table in a position where she could watch the parking lot. She rubbed on some sunscreen, adjusted her sunglasses, took a sip of water, and waited. Mooky sensed they were not going anywhere for a while and settled into the shade under the table with her head resting on her paws. It didn't take long.

Vivien pulled a sheen of sweat off her forehead with the back of her hand and reached for a bandana in the pocket of her jean shorts as she spied the green Subaru wagon making its way into the park. She briefly considered what she would do if Sasha got out of the car with Boopsie. That would actually make things easier, but Vivien was fairly certain this was not going to happen. The car traveled at a reasonable speed as it curled around the road and then seemed to slow down as it approached the parking lot. Maybe because Sasha recognized Vivien's car and didn't want to confront her? Maybe.

The Subaru paused for half a second, turned into the parking lot, and pulled right next to Vivien's minivan. The old woman had gumption if nothing else. Vivien took a sip of water and watched as Mooky reacted to the slam of the door, rose from her spot under the table, wagged her tail, and woofed a greeting. "Go ahead, Mooky. Go say hi. In fact, go over there and tell me if you can smell Boopsie in that car."

If the black Lab could develop the power of speech that would put an end to this little charade in a hurry. Vivien watched Sasha make her way to the back of the car to pop the hatchback, and Polly the poodle came bouncing out. Mooky barked and began trotting towards the parking lot with her tail wagging.

Vivien watched Sasha collect a dog leash and a newspaper from the front seat and then she started making her way towards the table. Vivien studied her gait, looking for a clue about what was going through the old lady's mind. Sasha was walking towards her, the newspaper under her arm, sunglasses on. Occasionally she made gestures to Polly, who was stopping to sniff and pee as they made their way to the table. The dogs met nose-to-nose about half way and Vivien could hear Sasha talking to them. She didn't seem to be in a hurry to arrive at her destination, but Vivien couldn't say that Sasha was actually walking slowly to avoid the meeting.

Vivien was wearing sunglasses and an old Minnesota Twins baseball cap with the visor pulled down low over her eyes. Nobody would be able to tell who or what she was looking at—which at the moment was Sasha, taking her sweet time approaching the table. She had to have seen Vivien at the stoplight unless her peripheral vision was completely gone.

Vivien resisted the urge to approach Sasha and blurt something out. It was what she really wanted to do, but she fought it back. She sat on the table, poker-faced, waiting and watching. Eventually she could hear Sasha's footfalls and she felt Polly the poodle's nose touch her wrist. "Well, hello, Polly. What are you doing, baby?" said Vivien, still ignoring Sasha. Vivien rubbed the dog's curly-haired head and gently pinched those secret spots behind her ears. The silence between the two women was driving Vivien nuts, but she held true to course and said nothing. Finally it happened.

"Scrumptious day, isn't it, dear?" said Sasha.

Vivien stopped her scratching and said nothing, letting the words hang there unanswered. Something in her shifted and she now embraced the tension. The longer she said nothing, the better she felt. She was in control of the conversation. She had a plan and knew what she wanted to know. For the first time in a long time she had the upper hand in whatever this was turning out to be.

"It is," said Vivien. "Not too hot yet, but it's coming." That was it. That was all she said, which was really nothing. Playing it cool, staying neutral.

The silence rejoined them. Vivien pretended to flick a piece of lint off her shorts but it was all an act. There was nothing there. The whoosh of traffic noise from Military Road was low and subdued but still present. The press of rush hour was still an hour ahead of them. Vivien pretended to look off into the woods.

"You're here early today, aren't you, darling?" That's what came out of Sasha. It was a true statement. Yes. She was here early. Vivien continued staring into the woods where the bones came from. It was coming down to this. A little chess match at the table in the dog park. It was her move.

"I am." And then back to the silence. Was Sasha squirming a little? Vivien zeroed in on her body language. She was scratching her head and looking towards the woods. Looking for what? Vivien looked at the bottle of water on the table but didn't take a drink. She just sat, waiting.

"Is Leonard coming today?" asked Sasha.

Leonard. That killed her. She was really grasping at straws. Time to bait the trap. Vivien half turned her body towards Sasha so she could look at her straight on.

"Yeah, I think he's going to be here later, you know, at his regular time. I was just bored at the house, so I decided to come early. Might as well enjoy the weather while we can, right? Does it ever get hot and miserable in Britain?" Vivien liked the way this sounded. She wanted to sound normal, put her subject at ease, and then bounce the conversation ball into a place where the old woman would enjoy going.

"It gets hot and miserable at some point everywhere, darling," said Sasha.

She was back to being her condescending self. Perfect. "Mm-hmm, I'm sure you're right. It must be wonderful to have traveled the world and lived in so many places."

Sasha sniffed and said, "Well, I do miss seeing different sites, but travel these days has turned into such an ordeal. I'd rather not be bothered."

"Sure," said Vivien. Mooky was standing in front of her and she reached out and ran her hand down the lab's back. "Does the heat bother Polly?"

Sasha's head pivoted towards her dog, who was sniffing around a ripped-up baseball lying a few yards away. "No. That's the good thing about poodles; you just give them a haircut when it gets hot."

"Mmm-hmm. You're lucky that way. And her hips don't bother her either, right? I mean I'm kind of worried about that with Mooky, so I've been giving her glucosamine. You don't have to do that with Polly, do you?"

"Oh, heavens no, she's as fit as fiddle, this one. Aren't you, pretty Polly?"

"Mm-hmm. How about Boopsie? She's on glucosamine, isn't she?"

"Boopsie. Oh, God, it's five pills, three times a day," said Sasha. She ended the sentence abruptly because she knew what she had just done and so did Vivien. Vivien watched her through her sunglasses. The older woman's face was frozen for a second. Then she looked at her feet and said, "Bloody hell." She said it softly and almost to herself. Vivien let it hang there. She let Sasha hang there as well. Hanging in the air by a rope of her own design.

Vivien heard a car door slam and turned to see Lenny herding Buddy out of the back of his VW station wagon. Perfect timing, really. His arrival would only add to a sense of urgency. A desire to finish this once and for all so they all could move on and get back to normal life in the dog park.

"Is there something you want to tell me, Sasha?" Vivien sniffed the air for the smell of gin.

Vivien stroked the hair on Mooky's back, watched Sasha and waited. Out of the corner of her eye she could see Lenny walking towards them. From this angle he looked like he was moving in slow motion. Sasha pursed her lips and continued looking at the ground. Vivien said nothing and waited for a while longer. Lenny was getting closer. "Sasha?"

"You couldn't let it go, could you, Viv? Just couldn't do it. Like a dog with a bone."

"Do you want to talk about it, Sasha? You might feel better."

Sasha glanced towards Lenny like she was measuring the distance and calculating how much time she had left to respond before she would have to explain things to two of them. She drew herself up and faced Vivien head on.

"Certainly, darling. Why don't you come by for a cocktail after dinner, say seven-ish? You do remember where I live, don't you?"

"I do," said Vivien, "and I'll be there. With bloody bells on." She smiled as she said this last part. She may be getting the hang of this joke-telling thing. "But, um, do me a favor, darling? Let's keep this just between us, shall we?" said Sasha.

"Why, certainly," said Vivien, and she winked behind her sunglasses.

CHAPTER 40

Vivien showed up at Sasha's door at precisely 7:00. She'd considered bringing her weapon but decided against it. Sasha had to be at least 70 years old and, although she could be described as spry, Vivien didn't consider her to be a physical threat. She pushed the doorbell and heard chimes—a sound from another time that still worked here in the world of Sasha. It reminded her of that old commercial, "Avon calling!"

Vivien could hear movement inside the house and briefly reconsidered the decision to show up unarmed, till she felt a wash of relief from the sounds of Polly the poodle barking a greeting. The presence of dogs had a way of normalizing things and returning her to a place where everything made perfect sense. Vivien had one hand in her pocket holding the cell phone that she now took with her everywhere—just in case.

She had called Will earlier to find out what happened with Harish, but had gotten his voicemail. The sound of the doorknob turning and Polly's barking redirected her attention back to the here and now. The door opened and there was Sasha telling Polly to be quiet and beckoning Vivien inside.

"Oh shush, Polly. Come in, darling. She'll settle once you're inside." From behind Polly and the old woman, Vivien could see Boopsie the bichon nervously sniffing the air and walking back and forth in her half-hopping way of moving. Vivien felt a tear forming in the corner of her eye and fought back the urge to cry over Boopsie coming to the door hoping to see her owner and being disappointed—forever. "Oh God. Hello, Boopsie. Maybe I should have brought Mooky; they probably would have enjoyed seeing each other," said Vivien.

"Oh no, it's fine. Two dogs are almost too many; three would have been horribly distracting. Come in, darling, come in."

Sasha led Vivien into the living room. Vivien instinctively scanned the corners of the room looking for anything that didn't seem right. She kept her hand inside her pocket, holding the cell phone like a weapon.

"Shall we talk in the kitchen, darling? I have a bottle of wine already open," said Sasha.

"Sure, that's fine," said Vivien. "Where I come from, everybody always hangs out in the kitchen anyway."

Sasha led the way, walking delicately like she'd already had a few. The small kitchen was in the back of the house and Vivien took a seat at the table, noticing pill bottles of dog medicine grouped on the countertop, along with the leftovers of a frozen dinner and the wrappings from the top of the wine bottle. "Is red okay with you?" said Sasha, already pouring her a glass.

"Oh sure. Red. White. Pink. Whatever," said Vivien as she pulled the cell phone out of her pocket and laid it between them on the table along with her keys. Her eyes fell to the floor and she noticed the two sets of dog bowls. One set was stainless steel and sat on a little rug— obviously these belonged to Polly. The other set rested on the floor on the other side of the room. There was a chipped salad bowl and a plastic container that Vivien recognized as the ones the Chinese place on Connecticut Ave used for their carry-out. Apparently Boopsie's arrival wasn't planned and Sasha was making do with what she had.

Vivien watched Sasha pouring the wine. She picked up the glass and said, "A toast?"

Sasha hesitated for a second and said, "To departed friends."

The ladies nodded at each other and Vivien took a sip, anticipating making a face by assuming the wine would be warm and tart. It was warm, but she actually liked the taste and said, "Mmm, tasty."

"Yes, a pinot from your West Coast," said Sasha. "So. Shall we get down to it, then?"

"Of course," said Vivien, as she watched herself touching the cell phone and looking at the top of the table.

"How did you come to end up with Boopsie, Sasha?" Vivien noticed that the small bichon had curled into a ball at Sasha's feet and her ears didn't even move at the sound of her name. She fought back the urge to cry.

"Well. I was the logical choice, wasn't I?" said Sasha.

"That's not what I meant, Sasha."

"I know what you meant, Vivien. Phyllis and I were very close." She closed her eyes and bowed her head like she was going to start praying. Vivien looked at Sasha's hands and considered laying her own hand on top of them.

"I understand. When was the last time you saw her?"

The room went silent and Vivien waited, looking at the décor of the kitchen. It was like going to your grandma's house—if your grandma had spent a good part of her earlier life traveling the world. There was a mahogany desk in the corner with brass accents. Vivien could see little scale models of the Taj Mahal and a pyramid placed just so. There were snapshots of a younger Sasha adorning the walls. Most of them showed Sasha shaking hands with men in suits or gathered in a group of ladies in formal wear. "I saw her the day she died, Vivien. I was with her."

"My god," said Vivien and now she rested her hand on top of Sasha's. The skin felt soft and thin. "What happened?"

Sasha studied her as Vivien fought the urge to squirm in her seat. Finally, Sasha said, "Well, perhaps I'll feel better if I tell somebody. He was going to leave her. Harish." She spat the name out like a foul taste.

"But why?" said Vivien.

Sasha shifted in her seat and said, "It doesn't matter, really. I thought it was good news. Especially considering how close we had become. She was even thinking about moving in here. Would have livened the place up a bit, don't you think?" Sasha looked around her house like she was considering a makeover and sniffed.

Vivien watched her and reconsidered the possibility that Walter had been telling the truth the whole time about the two women. Apparently they were much more than dog park friends. "So what happened?" asked Vivien. "I mean, how did it happen?'

Sasha looked at her like she had just appeared in front of her and was somewhat surprised by the discovery.

"You really are a nosey woman, aren't you, Vivien? So bored with your own life you feel the need to get involved in everybody else's?"

Vivien felt the sting of truth but was tired of the fencing. "For Christ's sake, Sasha, your best friend was found dead rotting in the goddamn woods. Don't you think somebody should do something about that?"

Sasha's lips clamped shut and Vivien thought she saw them actually tremble for half a second. "It wasn't supposed to happen the way it did," said Sasha. Silence slipped into the space as Vivien felt the thump of her own heartbeat. It seemed to go on forever but she waited, watching Sasha's face till she spoke. "Something in the woods. Those bones no doubt attracted the dogs. Polly took off and Boopsie followed right behind her, and Boopsie never goes into the woods. We thought they'd come right back, but they both disappeared down that damned path."

"It was just you and Phyllis?" said Vivien.

Sasha took a healthy swig from the wine glass and said, "Yes. We were meeting early. She was breaking it off and telling Harish that she wouldn't agree to a divorce. Something about how the pre-nuptial agreement was worded or something—I don't know. She didn't want him to have her money."

"It was about the money?"

"More than the money. He told her he was in love with some young thing at work. An Indian tart that he'd taken up with."

"Mina?" said Vivien as her mind flashed back to the scene in the park.

"I don't know her name," said Sasha, "I'm sure she sees a

payday in the whole thing, too."

"Mmm. Sure," said Vivien. She needed to keep her talking. She was so close to the truth. "I think I've met her; she's the receptionist at the clinic. She's quite a bit younger."

"Yes. Well, she's also not a blonde American, is she?"

"No. She's definitely not a blonde," Vivien said. "So Harish was having an affair and wanted out of the marriage, but Phyllis wouldn't agree to it, and you two . . . you and Phyllis were also . . . you were, um . . ."

"We were very close, Vivien. Let's just leave it at that, shall we?" Sasha saved Vivien from herself, helping her out of the awkward corner the conversation had turned into. Vivien really wanted to know, but she let it go. First things first.

"So the dogs ran into the woods and you two followed them in?"

Sasha had been looking away towards the window, the question brought her back. "Yes. Well. It was clear they weren't coming back. Onto the scent, I imagine, and so we picked our way down. We found our way to that awful spot. The dogs were digging and pulling at things. We were quarreling. It was horrible. . . . And then . . . she fell."

"Phyllis fell?" said Vivien. "While you were quarreling?"

Vivien covered her mouth with her hand as she watched Sasha's eyes well up. "The dogs were underfoot," said Sasha. "Barking. I reached out for her. She leaned back. She went down in an awkward angle. Her head hit a rock. I think I actually heard her skull crack."

"And that caused her to die? I mean, she was unconscious at that point?"

Sasha squared her posture in the chair and said, "Not exactly. She was injured but quite conscious. Conscious enough to blame me for pushing her and then this outpouring of blame and insults. She accused me of latching onto her, sucking her dry like all the rest, and then told me she never loved me. I was just another one of her playthings. A plaything with a charming British accent. A slightly exotic keepsake to be trotted out at the parties and then set back up on the shelf, at the dog park."

Sasha fell silent and then slowly twirled the wine glass around by the stem.

"That's horrible, Sasha. She really did have a mean streak."

"Yes, well. I bloody well lost my temper after that. I wanted her out of my sight and, for the moment anyway, out of my life completely. I grabbed Polly by the collar, picked up Boopsie and walked away from her. I made my way back to the table without ever turning around and sat there waiting for her to follow me out." Sasha took another large sip from the wine glass, swallowed, and wiped her lips on a paper napkin as Vivien waited for the rest.

"And so I waited at that table, like a fool. An hour went by, then two. It was getting close to the time when everybody would be arriving. My concern began to outweigh my pride and so I retraced my steps. I went back to the spot. But she was gone."

"Gone? What do you mean, gone?"

"Gone as in she was no longer in the spot. There was blood on the ground. But she was just gone. I thought maybe she came out a different way, so I took the dogs, came back here for a while, and then returned at the regular time, half expecting to see her. But nothing. She never came back."

Vivien's cell phone lay between them on the table, the green "power" light staring at them like an accusing eye. "But why didn't you tell somebody, Sasha? You could have called the Park Police, the Fire Department, somebody . . ."

Sasha held up a hand to stop the questioning. "Initially, I thought she was purposely hiding from me. Plus, I was angry about the turn of events, Vivien—angry and scared. You can understand that, can't you? We were going to travel and do things. The whole thing just . . . it got out of hand. Days went by and it started to seem like maybe it never happened." Sasha drained the wine glass, looked at Vivien and said, "So there you have it. Now it's over and I have to live with it."

"Over?" said Vivien. "Not quite, missy. Not by a long shot. You just confessed to leaving an injured friend in the woods to die. You might be guilty of manslaughter or something. Not only that, the police think Harish did it. They were on their way over there today to pick him up for questioning."

"Good," said Sasha. "He's a horrible little man. And as for the confession, I'll deny it all. It'll be your word against mine. Doesn't that count for something?"

Hardly," said Vivien, "and besides that I'm not the only one who heard what you just said—at least I don't think I am." Vivien picked up the cell phone, put it to her ear, and said, "Lenny? Did you hear that?"

"Un-fucking believable," said Lenny. "I heard every word."

Sasha's eyebrows shot up as she connected the dots. "You mean he was listening? Leonard was listening in? The whole time? What is it you want from me, Vivien? What do you intend to do?"

"I'm going to do the right thing, Sasha. Which is what you should have done in the first place." She was already pushing herself away from the table, anxious to get out of the space and clear her head.

"Oh fine, Vivien. Go ahead. Ruin what's left of my life if it will make yourself feel better. See where that gets you."

CHAPTER 41

Vivien began doing the right thing by exiting Sasha's house as gracefully and quickly as possible, leaving the woman at the table, the wine bottle on its way to a slow death, just like Phyllis. She checked in briefly with Lenny over the phone, then hung up and called Will. She got voicemail and left a message that Sasha had basically confessed to helping the sad demise of Phyllis by not helping.

She tossed and turned that night with the covers up to her chin, with the evening's events churning over and over in her head. As usual, Mooky curled into a large ball of fur at her feet and softly snored through the night. While Vivien was having coffee the next day, Will called to tell her that Harish had made a confession of his own—that he was having an affair with Mina and therefore wasn't all that disappointed when his wife went missing. The lack of any traces of his DNA at the crime scene added weight to his claims that he had nothing to do with it.

"What do you think is going to happen to Sasha?" said Vivien. Will was in a bad cell zone and he sounded like he was talking to her from the bottom of a tin can.

"Sounds like accidental death. I'm not sure she can be charged with anything, other than being a lousy excuse for a human being—so probably nothing," he said. "That's assuming that she's telling the truth and didn't actually bash her friend's head in with a rock or push her down. But even if she did, there are no witnesses. Old Phyllis probably had a concussion, wandered around, got confused, maybe died from an internal brain hemorrhage. Happens all the time."

Will assured Vivien that he would pass the information on to the right people and that she and Lenny would have to come in and make a formal statement about what they'd heard. She hung up and fell into her normal routine of the day, feeling strange and disconnected. She searched for the peace of mind offered by the ritual trip to the park, but she really wasn't looking forward to going. In her head, she wrestled with telling people and what she would reveal, if anything.

She pondered how she would she deal with Sasha, if in fact she showed up. She wasn't sure what was going to happen next or how quickly things would move. She also tried to guess what Sasha would do now that her secret had been uncovered. Vivien brushed aside the idea that she might try to harm herself. She just didn't seem the type for anything that dramatic.

Strangely enough, Lenny hadn't called to review the events of the previous night. Maybe he was actually seeing patients today. She checked her email and kept herself busy by puttering around the house and watching the clock. She still felt uneasy when it was finally time to pack up the dog and hit the trail. She would go to the dog park early today, and planned on getting back home as quickly as possible.

She was the first to arrive and felt a bit relieved there weren't any other cars in the parking lot. She released the dog, slumped over to the picnic table, and sat down. Linda pulled in a few minutes later and set Zena the Great Dane free. Vivien watched Linda moving towards her in no great hurry, casually carrying a Kong toy for the dog. "Hey," said Vivien. "You're here early."

"Off today," said Linda. "Catering business is slow in the summer time."

"Yeah, I guess that makes sense."

Vivien remained silent as Linda threw the toy a few times, watching the huge dog bound up the hill and lope back down. "You all right?" said Linda. "You seem kind of down."

Vivien stared off towards the woods and said, "Last night, Sasha told me that she left Phyllis in the woods after she fell and hit her head on a rock. The second set of bones they found were hers."

"What? Left her in the woods? Why? She's really dead? Sasha told you that?"

"Yep, and Lenny heard it, too."

"No shit. So what happened?"

Vivien took in a large breath and said, "Turns out Sasha and Phyllis were, um, together."

"Together-together, as in like, girl-girl together?"

"Yup," said Vivien, "Girl-girl together."

"Get out of here. And what, they got into a fight or something?"

"Yeah. Harish wanted a divorce. Sasha thought she and Phyllis were going to be together. The dogs ran into the woods, just like ours did. The two women went in after them, and got into some kind of fight. Phyllis fell and hit her head on a rock, then said some horrible things to Sasha, who left her there. She went to look for her later and said she was gone. Phyllis probably walked deeper into the woods, got confused, and then died in a more remote spot. Can you believe that?"

Linda gave the Kong another mighty heave and said, "I can believe anything around here. But that is some sick shit. This place must be a magnet for crazies," she said. "Hey, were you here when that bitch Estelle squirted me with Mace?"

"No. But I heard about it."

"She's totally psycho. Anywho. So what's going to happen to Sasha? Is she in jail or what?"

"I don't know," said Vivien. "I'm curious to see if she shows up here today."

"Yeah, well, if she's not in jail she'll show up. She's like clockwork."

Linda looked out towards the hill to check on what her dog was up to, called to her once, and then went silent, looking out towards the woods where the whole thing started. Vivien watched Linda and tried to guess what she was thinking or what she'd say next. After a few more seconds of silence Linda turned towards her and said, "Hey, did you see 'NCIS' last night?"

"The TV show? No, I don't watch it."

"Ah, man, you gotta watch it. It's a great show. It kind of reminded me of this place."

Linda seemed genuinely excited about whatever happened on the show and began to explain the whole plot to Vivien, who quickly tuned out the conversation. Somehow she thought there would be more discussion about Phyllis's death, the Sasha situation, and how Vivien had cracked the case wide open. She sniffed the air and pivoted her head to see who else was arriving. The couple with the English bulldog showed up, then the old lady with the basset hound, but no Sasha.

Vivien felt a slight wave of relief when she saw Walter's beat-up minivan pull into the lot. She watched him haul his lardy ass out of the vehicle and release Lucky Dog. He took his time strolling to the table and when he was close enough, she drifted away from Linda and said, "Hey, Walter."

It came out sounding more cheerful than she meant but she didn't care. She needed to get some feedback from somebody. He offered a lazy wave and moved like he was angling for a seat at the picnic table until Vivien stepped in front of him and touched his upper arm. She leaned in close to his face and said, "Did you hear what happened?"

He stopped his movements, looked mildly perturbed, and said, "No, Vivien. What happened?"

"The second set of bones did belong to Phyllis. She and Sasha were arguing in the woods, Phyllis fell, hit her head on a rock, and never came out."

Walter's face showed nothing for a full beat, and then he said, "No shit. I told you they were fucking."

Now it was Vivien who was momentarily dumbstruck. "How do you get that from...? Oh never mind, Walter."

She turned away from him and pinched the bridge of her nose.

What the hell was wrong with these people? A woman was dead, for God's sake, and Linda wanted to talk about TV shows and Walter wanted to talk about sex. It just didn't make any sense. Had the world gone crazy? She looked again towards the parking lot, hoping to see Sasha's green Subaru pulling in. Hoping that all this was just a bad dream and she would wake up in her bed with Mooky curled up in a ball at her feet. Had she really done the right thing?

But there was no Subaru. Instead she saw Lenny's car making its way into the parking lot. She looked at her watch. Was it that late already? Thank God Lenny was here. The voice of reason. Maybe. She leaned a hip onto the tabletop and briefly tuned into a conversation about a movie that nobody had actually seen. She tried to look nonchalant as she squirmed and stole glances at Lenny making his way towards the table. Would he know something? She bit her lip and watched him approach. "Hello all and good afternoon," he said in an overly formal tone.

She felt herself smiling already. He could be so funny without even trying. She was so lucky to have him as a friend. A few disjointed "hellos" and "heys" came out of the group as Lenny approached her in no hurry, opened his arms, and gave her a mock serious hug. "And how is Ms. Vivien, today?"

"Swell," said Vivien. "Can I talk to you a second?" She didn't wait for an answer and pulled him away from the group by tugging his arm.

"Well of course you can, darling," he said. He threw his arm around her shoulders as they walked slowly into the field where the pack of dogs was running and chasing.

"Have you heard anything from Sasha?" she said. "She's not here and I'm kind of worried if I did the right thing. I mean, you don't think she'd, I mean she wouldn't . . .?"

"No, she would not," said Lenny. "I talked to her majesty earlier today and I believe she'll be just fine. She's meeting with her attorney this afternoon and he's already told her that since it was an accident, she's in very little danger of being charged with anything. Assuming of course that she's telling the truth—and especially since she tried to tell everybody that the remains belonged to Phyllis when the first bone was discovered. Nobody believed her; remember that part?"

"Wow," said Vivien. "I totally forgot about that. Everybody just thought she was a hysterical old lady."

"True that," said Lenny. "Including me."

They were now a few yards away from the table and Vivien found herself checking on the whereabouts of Mooky, who was working the edge of the field, sniffing and peeing. She felt Lenny turn her around as they started strolling back towards the picnic table. Before they got too close, she said, "And these people. You know? I told Linda and Walter about what happened and they're just like . . . They don't get it, you know? Walter wants to talk about how Sasha and Phyllis were lovers and Linda wants to talk about TV shows and the time she got sprayed with Mace."

"I know, sweetie," said Lenny. "Everybody is wrapped up in their own shit. They're not here to listen to you or me. They're here for them—the dogs on the hill." And then he spun her gently around as she looked at the gentle roll of the hill. The traffic of Washington hissed just beyond the trees, the sun was slowly making its way down towards the horizon. And there on the hill was a Weimaraner chasing a yellow Lab, a man throwing a tennis ball to a springer spaniel, and a Dalmatian lying on his back scratching himself into the warm, green grass of summer.

A cicada buzzed somewhere off in the woods, and Vivien became aware that the air was starting to feel thick. She looked at clumps of dog owners chatting and waving away insects. Dogs panting and scratching, sniffing, chasing sticks and balls. Despite the recent events, everything felt perfectly normal in the field by the hill. Summer had returned to Washington.

Lenny turned her back towards the picnic table and bellowed out, "All right, who's walking?" And then it was all gone. The thrill and the intrigue were wiped away. It was just another day at the dog park.

Vivien brushed away a tear and pulled a hand through her hair. "Come on, Mooky, let's go for a walk."

CHAPTER 42

Mooky rose that morning as she did every morning, by yawning and stretching herself until her belly almost touched the floor. She followed Vivien down to the front door as her beautiful tail swooped back and forth, anticipating the pure joy of being let out into the world. The door opened and the outside smells rushed forward to greet her. There were smells of cut grass, cars, some rotting garbage from the cans out back, and flowers in the side yard.

And then, there it was. She detected one of the best smells ever, and it was close. She pivoted her head and flared her nostrils to get a direction. Her body reacted and she immediately began trotting towards the hedges with her head down, ears up, totally focused until she saw it. The cat that lived down the street was peeing under the hedges. She had seen this cat many times. She knew what the cat looked like and what it smelled like. She had chased the cat many times and never caught it. But the cat had never been this close before.

Because the cat was preoccupied, Mooky was able to come up behind it without being seen. She lowered her body to a stalking position and moved in silently. Her instincts told her that she should grab the cat by the back of the neck and give it a good shake. She also remembered a scene with a cat when she was a puppy. She remembered the cat had sharp claws that scratched her nose and make her yelp. The cat was not to be underestimated even when it looked defenseless.

She stopped moving just outside of scratching range and stood absolutely motionless, just watching the cat. She tensed her body, preparing to spring into the hedges and surprise the cat. But then she heard the front door open. "Come on, Mooky," Vivien said. "Let's get something to eat." She knew the word "eat." This was a good word.

The noise startled the cat, which turned its head and now for the first time noticed that Mooky was very close.

The cat made a terrible hissing noise—like a ball being bitten—as Mooky dived under the hedge. Mooky could feel the cat's soft fur on her nose as her jaws opened, looking for that soft spot behind the neck, but she could tell that the cat was already moving away from her.

There was a scratching noise. Mooky felt the fur move away from her mouth. Just that fast, it had turned into a fast moving game of "Catch-the-Thing." She clamped her jaws shut but there was nothing there. The cat had somehow vanished. She barked and plunged deeper into the hedges, caught a whiff of the cat, and looked up. The cat had jumped straight up in the air and landed on the porch railing. It was now running across it.

Mooky pulled herself out of the hedges, the branches sticking to her coat and trying to pull her back in. She barked angrily at the cat for getting away and she chased it around the porch. The cat took two leaps and seemed to fly to the other side of fence. Mooky ran to the fence and barked at the cat, which now turned around to look at her.

She wanted the cat to come back, so she barked at it and put her paws on top of the fence. The cat just looked at her and licked its paw until it got bored, then turned and walked away. Mooky could hear Vivien calling her to eat, but she wanted to make sure that cat wasn't going to change its mind and come back to play "Catch-the-Thing." It didn't, and now Vivien was standing in the yard. "Come on Mooky, leave the cat alone; it's time to eat."

She pulled herself off the fence and followed Vivien into the house to eat. After eating, it would be time to take a nap, or several naps, until it was time to go—and that was the best time of all. After the go was over there would be more eating and napping and then it would start all over again. Mooky followed Vivien into the house and sat on the kitchen floor with her beautiful tail twitching beneath her as she watched Vivien put the food in her bowl. She looked up and smiled at what was happening and couldn't wait till it was time to go.

#